Secrets
at
Deep Lake

a Kate Tyler novel

Secrets

at
Deep Lake

a Kate Tyler novel

Nancy Wakeley

 Torchflame Books

Copyright © 2023 by Nancy Wakeley
Secrets at Deep Lake
Nancy Wakeley
nancywakeley2@gmail.com
www.nancywakeley.com

Published 2023, by Torchflame Books
www.torchflamebooks.com

Paperback ISBN: 978-1-61153-582-2
E-book ISBN: 978-1-61153-583-9
Library of Congress Control Number: 2023919379
-

To the millions of men and women
who open their hearts and lives
to children who need a family
and to the children
who seek to know their roots.

1

"DO YOU KNOW WHO YOUR FATHER IS?"

Dr. Bartlett eyed Kate Tyler kindly over the thin metal rim of his glasses but his gaze still pierced her. She flinched at his words. "I don't mean to be harsh, but it's a question of necessity."

The truth was that Kate did not know who her biological father was. She knew she was adopted, but she didn't know the actual circumstances of her birth until three years earlier when she found her real birth certificate.

It was then that she discovered she was one of triplets. Born August 16, 1990. Two girls. One boy. Her mother's name was Jenny Howard, age seventeen. The father was also seventeen. But the space on the certificate which should have revealed his name was blank.

The triplets were not placed together in the same homes. Kate and her sister Becky were adopted by Clarence and Maggie Tyler, a couple from Virginia, who traveled extensively for Clarence's job. Her brother, Billy, was adopted by a local couple, Calvin and Mimi Zink, who raised him in the small town of Eden Springs, North Carolina.

The two sisters never knew of Billy's existence until Kate discovered the original birth certificate. She found it hidden in the bottom of an old trunk at Howard's Walk, the large estate in Eden Springs she had inherited from her sister Becky three years ago. On first reading the document, Kate thought it was simply a coincidence that the birth day, month, and year happened to be the same as hers and Becky's. But she and Becky were twins, not part of triplets and while it was puzzling, it meant nothing to her at the time.

It did trouble her, though, to see that the father's name for the triplets was missing. She thought it created the most fragile of attachments between a parent and child. But that problem was for someone else's life, and while sad, was not personal to her.

Not long after that, she made the life-changing discovery that she and Becky were indeed part of those triplets, that Billy Zink was their brother, and that Jenny Howard was their birth mother. Then that blank spot where a father's name should have been screamed, "*I do not want you.*"

It quickly became personal.

Kate was sure she would never want to know that man. He was a nobody. Anyway, he could never be a replacement for what she had known her entire life; a home with a loving mother who cherished both of her daughters and a father who indulged her sense of adventure, cheering her on in whatever she attempted. To search for them would be a betrayal of her adoptive parents and the love and family life that they gave her. No. Her biological father was simply an empty spot on a piece of paper. She decided that under no circumstances would she ever need to know who he was. And her biological mother Jenny? Kate didn't know where she was or if she was even still alive.

"Kate?"

A small air conditioner, wet and rusty at the corners from age and condensation, rattled, coughed at the curtains, and then grew quiet again. The air in Dr. Bartlett's office was stuffy, smelling of antiseptic, and Kate found it hard to breathe. She blinked twice and pushed away the unsettling memories about the origins of her birth that had crept into her thoughts. Her attention came back to the man sitting behind a large, cluttered desk.

Kate pulled her backpack up onto her lap, creating a bulky barrier between her and the news the doctor was about to share. He had called her into his office to review her brother Billy's medical report. She knew it was bad news and tried to focus. She gripped the strap on the backpack, pressing the buckle into her skin.

"Yes, Dr. Bartlett. You were saying?"

The elderly physician ran his hand over a round head of thinning hair, wiping away beads of sweat. A patient's file lay open on the desk in front of him. He lifted his kind, hooded eyes, and folded his hands.

"The reason I'm asking is that Billy's blood and urine tests are positive for several things which concern me," he said.

He tapped the thick stack of papers that comprised thirty-two years of Billy's medical history. "His blood pressure is elevated, and he has swelling in his legs. And, as you know, he told me he has lower back pain."

The doctor's words hung in the space between them as if waiting for Kate to absorb and make sense of what he was saying. Her heart skipped a beat. She held her breath for a moment, then exhaled as she explained. "He's never been one to complain much so it's hard to tell when he's not feeling well. But we could tell something was wrong."

Billy was not in the room to hear the doctor's report and he wouldn't be told of his diagnosis unless it became necessary. Even then, it would have to be done with extreme care. He was the last of Jenny Howard's triplets to come into the world. Now he was a loving and gentle man who saw the world in a simpler way than those around him. Dr. Bartlett had already told Kate the likely reasons why her brother was the way he was. He had said that a lack of oxygen to Billy's brain before birth could account for developmental delays, learning disabilities, delayed speech, and a low IQ score, all of which had been observed in him from a very young age. Billy would need help from others for the rest of his life.

Kate had tortured herself wondering if she and her sister were somehow to blame. Did they crowd him out, cutting off oxygen and nutrients? Did they take something vital from him that he needed? She consoled herself by saying, "*I never knew.*" Of course, she couldn't have known. But the thought still gave her pangs of guilt.

As his physician, Dr. Bartlett probably knew Billy better than anyone but there was one glaring gap in her brother's medical records, just as there was for Kate. The blank space on the birth certificate where a father's name should be meant that there was no medical information on him at all.

"Do you have any knowledge at all of your biological parent's medical histories?" Dr. Bartlett said. When Kate didn't answer he pressed on. "Even if there's nothing of significance, it would be important for me to know that, too. Now, I know about Jenny when she was younger, and I cared for her parents over the years, and I don't see anything of note there, at least not related to Billy's current problem." He settled his glasses on his nose and flipped through Billy's chart. "But your father is another matter. I'm assuming you still don't know who he is."

"No, and I've never tried to find out," Kate said firmly, without feeling a need to apologize. She assumed her birth father wished to remain anonymous and wanted nothing to do with his children's lives. That's what a blank spot on a birth certificate proclaimed to the world, at least in her eyes. Kate had nothing more to say about it. She sat up straighter in her chair and changed the subject.

"Dr. Bartlett, you just said were Jenny Howard's doctor. And I know maybe you can't say much because of confidentiality, but is there anything you could tell me?"

"You're right, I can't share any medical information about my patients. But I can tell you I didn't treat her during her pregnancy. I didn't even know she was pregnant at the time. And I didn't know the connection to the three of you until you discovered it." He leaned back in his chair. "I don't have any information on what happened to her. Bessie and Enoch never spoke of Jenny except to say that she had gone off to another high school during her senior year and was doing very well. As they were her parents, I had no reason to question them about it. And of course, I never treated her after she left Eden Springs."

"What about her medical records?" Kate persisted. "Maybe they were requested by another doctor or hospital?"

"No, not that I'm aware of. But I wouldn't be able to divulge the name of the requester if that had happened. You need to know that Billy most likely has Berger's Disease. Simply put, it's a disease where an antibody builds up in the kidneys and causes inflammation, making it harder for the kidneys to filter waste from the blood. Now, the only way to definitively diagnosis it would be with a kidney biopsy but in Billy's case, I want to avoid that. But all of his symptoms point to Berger's disease."

Kate nodded her head in agreement. She knew it would be challenging to have Billy undergo any type of procedure, no matter how minor.

Dr. Bartlett continued. "Your parents' medical history is important because if they are otherwise healthy, they could be a potential match for a kidney transplant if, and that's a big if, Billy would ever need it. Of course, in Billy's case, we first need to determine if he would even be a viable candidate to receive a transplant."

Billy's disease now had a name. *As if he doesn't have enough problems,* Kate thought. A friend of hers had undergone a liver transplant a few years ago and Kate knew the risks that came with a procedure like that. Kate pushed back against Dr. Bartlett's words.

"But there might not be anything to find out," she said, hoping there was some way out of what he was asking her to do. "I mean, there's no one left here in the family except me and Billy. And he doesn't know anything. Neither does Mimi." She moved to the edge of her seat. "There's no trail for either of my birth parents. And for my father, I don't even have a name to start with. There has to be another way. I'll take the test to see if I'm a donor match, and I'm sure Ben will, too. Or we can find another match if it comes to that, right? It doesn't have to be a blood relative, right?" Kate didn't hesitate to volunteer her boyfriend, Ben Evans, to take a donor test, too, but she heard the desperation in her voice as she said words that all sounded callous and defeated and frightened.

Dr. Bartlett sighed. He removed his glasses and laid them on the desk. "Kate, I realize this is very difficult for you. I know the situation with Billy is complicated with his mother convalescing in the rehabilitation center. The stroke has taken its toll on her. She'll need a lot of care herself when she goes home. You took on the job of being responsible for Billy until she came home. And I applaud you for it. But his health needs are part of the responsibility you have now. Yes, there are other ways to find donor matches and we will certainly use them if and when we need to. But I think it's not just in Billy's best interest, but yours also, to find out what you can about your parent's medical history and current health status. It's that simple."

It wasn't simple for Kate at all. Locating her mother was one thing, but she had never contemplated a search for her father. She had convinced herself that it was best not to know anything about him. But deep down, she knew Dr. Bartlett was right. Now Billy's health and future could be at risk. And that changed everything.

Kate's phone sounded a text message alert, and she glanced down at it.

Took Billy for a walk.
Meet u outside when u r done.

The text was from Ben. She tucked the phone inside her back pocket and lifted her backpack onto her shoulder.

"I understand what you're saying. This is something I've never had to think about before. But now, I guess I know what I have to do." Even while saying the words, Kate began to think of ways she could avoid doing exactly that.

"Good." Dr. Bartlett reached over the desk to shake Kate's hand. "In the meantime, we'll take care of Billy. Nothing much to worry about right now but my recommendation is that you do not delay your search. You can pick up his prescriptions at the pharmacy in town. The nurse will have information on how to control his symptoms and some simple lifestyle changes which will help him. She'll be at the desk out front, and you can pick them up on your way out. Just let me know if you find anything, okay?"

Kate nodded, bracing herself for the decisions she would need to make in the days ahead.

2

KATE STEPPED OUTSIDE into an oppressive wave of heat. The blistering temperatures of August had marched on into September. The leaves on the shade trees surrounding the pink and white Victorian home where Dr. Bartlett had his office hung limply from days without rain. The flowers in Mrs. Bartlett's prize gardens along the walkway were drooping and dusty.

Kate sank into a cushioned swing on the wraparound porch, her legs suddenly weak and shaking. The nurse had printed out Billy's instructions and Kate folded the sheets in half, creased the edge, and fanned herself until she was able to take a deep breath.

She closed her eyes, wishing she could go back to a time before the tragic accident that took her sister Becky's life. Becky had always been her rock and her guiding star. Kate felt the huge void left by her death every day.

It wasn't until her sister's will was read that Kate learned about Howard's Walk, a house named after the Howard family who built it over seventy-five years ago. Becky had bought it just before her accident and she had left everything to Kate, whose first instinct was to sell since she had no desire to be tied down to such a monstrosity. Her career as a travel journalist kept her unencumbered. The freedom to travel where and when she chose was all she had ever wanted. But then the discovery that Jenny Howard was their biological mother also meant that Howard's Walk and the public gardens her grandparents created there were her legacy. It made her take a different look at her life, and she found that Howard's Walk was exactly where she wanted and needed to be.

She wished her adoptive parents were there for advice and counsel, too, but ten years had passed since they died. She had Becky to lean on during that terrible time. But now, her only remaining blood relative was Billy. Now, she was the older sister and even though his adoptive mother was still alive, Kate had, as Dr. Bartlett pointed out, taken much of the responsibility for him on her shoulders.

The screen door slammed next to her, and the sound shook her out of her thoughts. Kate looked down the street towards the town park where she was sure Ben had walked with Billy. But they were nowhere in sight. She hoped they had stayed out of the sun although Billy would have wanted to be near the town pond where there was little shade. Her brother hadn't been doing well in the North Carolina heat that summer and, knowing his diagnosis, Kate now understood why. He loved being outdoors but now ... she pushed away the thoughts about how each of their lives would be changing.

Billy's widowed mother, Mimi, had suffered several strokes and a second fractured hip in recent weeks and Kate had insisted he come live with her at Howard's Walk until Mimi was able to care for him again. Kate had promised her she would always do whatever she could to help her brother and it was a promise she wouldn't break. But she had spoken the truth to Dr. Bartlett. She had no idea where to start the search for her parents and there was no one to ask.

Kate had lived in Eden Springs for three years and not one person had ever hinted about her mother's relationships or boyfriends. Jenny's parents, Enoch and Bessie Howard, had died years before Kate came to live at Howard's Walk. There might have been rumors at the time about the young girl from a nice local family who had to leave town, but if anyone did know, the secret was tightly held, and the trail of her whereabouts grew further out of reach with each passing year. But it was her father, a nameless, faceless entity, who had given her and her siblings half of his DNA, whom she also had to find. She shook her head at the enormity of the task ahead of her and the absolute aversion she had to even start the search.

Kate looked up and saw Ben and Billy in the distance and waved at them. Billy waved back eagerly, swinging his hat in the air. He soon lumbered up the sidewalk towards her, breathing heavily, with Ben in tow.

"Hey, Kate! We went to the park and saw the ducks!" Billy exclaimed between breaths. Ben handed him a bottle of water as Kate stepped off the porch to meet them. She took Billy's hat and placed it on his head. An unruly mop of straw-blond hair stuck out stubbornly from beneath the brim. She straightened the straps on his bib overalls which always seemed to slip down off his broad shoulders and thought back to the first day they met.

Billy appeared at Howard's Walk shortly after Kate moved in. She had been pulling weeds in the old gardens when he approached and she was astonished, and a bit intimidated, by his size: six foot two inches and two hundred twenty-five pounds at his last physical. He claimed that he could help her *'move stuff'* and he appeared to be well up to the task. His mother Mimi arrived soon after, apologized for the interruption, and introduced herself. She explained that they lived on a farm on the other side of the woods, not far from Howard's Walk, and that she thought Kate might need some help in her gardens. Kate, unaware of Billy's real connection to her, decided to accept their offer of help and from that day forward, he became a fixture at Howard's Walk whenever he was allowed.

If only life could have remained that uncomplicated. Her lower lip trembled but she smiled at Billy, and he grinned in return, wiping his mouth with his sleeve after another gulp of water.

"That's great Billy. You didn't scare them this time, did you?"

"No, Kate. I was very quiet. I didn't mean to scare the ducks, I didn't." His eyes grew sad. Every emotion Billy felt could be seen on his face: happiness in a broad grin or sadness in the slump of his shoulders. She reached for his large, calloused hand and managed to hold on to two of his sausage-sized fingers. She looked directly at him so he would focus on what she was saying.

"It's okay, Billy. I know you didn't mean to." His eyes brightened at her reassurances. "How would you like to go visit your mama now?"

"Yes, let's go now!"

Kate took Billy to the rehab facility to see his mother as often as possible during her convalescence but today she had another reason to visit. Mimi was the first to notice a gradual decline in Billy's activities and general health and had alerted Dr. Bartlett that there might be a problem. After weeks of tests, it had come down to the diagnosis which Kate needed to share with her.

They reached Ben's truck and Billy clambered into his designated spot, riding shotgun in the front seat. Ben opened the back door for Kate but put his hand on her shoulder before she got in.

"Everything okay?" Kate felt a dampness in her eyes and willed a smile to her face to hold back the tears. She nodded. He linked his fingers through hers and pushed his sunglasses back on his head so there was no barrier between them. Ben's blue eyes were like a beacon to her, seeing her as she was with all of her faults, cares, and heartaches. She knew he had burdens, too, but at times like this, when she was at her lowest, she felt his love the strongest. They didn't need words between them to know that now was not the time for whatever news she had to share.

"Let's go, Ben!" Billy called from the front seat.

"In a minute, Billy," Ben said. He turned his attention back to Kate. "We'll talk later?"

"Later."

As they drove, Billy pointed out each store and landmark along Main Street in Eden Springs. Routines like this were important to him, as were many of his daily patterns. While it was a challenge for him to remember many things, the town that he grew up in and the people he knew all of his life were a comfort to him. He waved at familiar faces through the open truck window and called out their names and they waved back.

Ben pulled into the parking lot of the Eden Springs Rehabilitation Center and they went inside. The lobby was decorated with fresh floral arrangements in reds and yellows. Banners hung across the archway to the dining room to celebrate the coming of autumn.

A woman in a nurse's uniform at the front desk hurried to hug Billy when she saw him.

"Billy! Good to see you, dear!"

"Hey there Miss Jeannie!" Billy beamed. "I'm here to see my mama."

"Well, you go on then, I know she's waiting for you," Jeannie said with a smile and returned to her spot behind the counter while Kate signed the visitor's log.

Billy was greeted with high-fives and fist bumps from staff and residents alike as they made their way to his mother's room. It seemed his cheerful presence chased away the grim realities of life in the place. Kate and Ben simply followed in his wake.

As always, Kate entered Mimi's room first.

"Mimi, are you awake?" she whispered when she saw the woman lying in the hospital bed with her eyes closed.

Mimi's eyes fluttered open. Her gray hair, usually in a tight bun, was braided and lay over her shoulder. Her face was lined with age, showing that the worries about Billy had taken their toll. But she managed a brief smile.

"Just resting my eyes a bit. It's so good to see you, dear. Did Billy come with you?"

Kate sat on the edge of the bed and took Mimi's hand. "Oh, yes, he's here and anxious to see you. How are you doing today? Did you have physical therapy this morning?"

"Yes, it's going very well. I can't wait to get out of here, you know. So, I'm doing my best."

"Good. Let me get Billy, and we'll talk afterward, okay?"

Mimi nodded and Kate went out into the hallway to let Billy know he could go in to see his mother.

"I guess you're wondering what Dr. Bartlett told me," Kate said when she and Ben were alone. She explained the medical issues that Billy was facing.

"I'm so sorry," Ben said, pushing a tendril of Kate's auburn curls behind her ear. "I was hoping it was nothing serious. So, what do we do now?"

"I have some instructions for his diet, things like that, and the prescriptions. But," she said with a sigh, "Dr. Bartlett said it's important to learn more about our birth parents' medical histories."

Ben's eyes narrowed. "Why's that?"

"In case Billy ever needed a kidney transplant, his blood relatives would be the best chance for a good match."

"But you could be tested, right?"

"Sure, I will be. But he was pretty insistent about finding the information. We could go through a donor registry but that could take years. So, if I find my parents, but especially my father at least, it might shorten the waiting time."

"So you have to search for them."

Kate nodded and swiped at her eyes.

"Everything in me is fighting this. I lost mom and dad and I dealt with that. I lost Becky and I dealt with that. I never,

ever, wanted to be put in the position of being hurt by my birth parents, so I vowed I would never look for them. And I never needed to. But now, I guess I have to put my fears aside for Billy's sake. I have to look for them. At least I know Jenny Howard was our mother, so I have her name to start with. But I don't have any idea who our father is. And Dr. Bartlett seemed to think it was important." She leaned against Ben's chest, and he put his arms around her. "I don't know where to begin. But I don't know what I'd do if I lost Billy, too."

"We'll get through this, Kate. It sounds like there are things we can do for Billy right now to help him. So we'll just take one step at a time." He tipped her face up and wiped away a tear with his thumb. He smiled. "It's going to be fine, I promise." Kate snuggled back into his arms.

A few minutes later, Kate and Ben went into Mimi's room to retrieve Billy.

"Come on, Billy," Ben said. "Let's wait out in the hall for Kate, okay?"

Billy nodded and waved goodbye to his mother.

Kate sat down in a chair beside the hospital bed. Mimi was small and appeared frail against the white sheets. She and her husband Calvin had worked on their farm all of their married life and adopting a child with Billy's disabilities in her forties had no doubt aged her, but Kate knew her to be tough and loving, and accepting of whatever life threw at her. She knew that Mimi needed to be part of the decisions about Billy's treatment plan. And she knew she needed to tell her about Dr. Bartlett's request to search for their biological parents. But she felt sure that Mimi would want everything possible to be done to help her son.

Kate gently wrapped Mimi's thin, blue-veined hands in hers.

"Thank you so much for bringing Billy," Mimi began. "He said you were at the doctor's today. What did Doc Bartlett have to say?"

Kate relayed everything he had told her. "I'll make copies of the paperwork he gave me, so you'll have it."

"Thank you, dear. I wish I could have been the one to take him, but I'm glad you were able to." She squeezed Kate's hand gently. "From what you've told me, you need to look for your parents, don't you?"

Kate nodded. Mimi's deep brown eyes teared up.

"Well, I know how hard that will be for you, but I can't lie. I want everything that can be done for Billy to be done. And if I could help, or do it myself, I would." She turned her head towards the window and sighed. "You know your grandmother Bessie never confided in me about the trouble Jenny was in. I don't know why Bessie thought she couldn't talk to me about it. We were such good friends and neighbors. But the fact is that she didn't. She held it all inside." She looked back at Kate. "So I think this is up to you, dear."

"Yes, I know."

"But there is one thing I can do for you." Mimi smiled and pushed herself up higher on her pillow.

"What's that?"

"My doctor will be stopping by today and I'm going to make him see that I need to go home so Billy can come back home, too. You don't know where this journey will lead you and I don't want you and Ben to be worried about him, too."

"But, Mimi, if you're not ready, you shouldn't push it."

"No, I've made up my mind. If there's a way that I can go home, with help of course, then I'll do it. Don't you worry. I'll work things out and let you know what the doctor says."

"I think that would be good for both of you," she agreed. She leaned in and kissed Mimi on her papery cheek. "I'll let Billy come in to say goodbye. Then we need to get him home."

Mimi took Kate's hand and squeezed it gently. "Thank you, dear, for bringing him by so much. It does my heart good to see him and you and Ben. You can do this. I know you can."

Kate went to the door and motioned for Billy to come in to say goodbye to his mother.

"How did it go?" Ben asked when they were alone.

"Pretty well, actually. And Mimi is anxious to have Billy at home with her as soon as possible."

"That's great news, right?" Ben asked.

"It will free us up to take the next steps." She put on a brave smile. "So yes, that's a good thing."

3

A THIN FILM OF SUN CREPT UP behind the peak of Howard's Walk, steadily lighting the blackness of the woods that lay beyond. It filtered through the gauze curtains of the bedroom, nudging Kate out of her dreams. She blinked and decided, along with the sun, that it was morning.

Sleep had come to her slowly, the troubles of the previous day colliding with solutions that were discarded one by one until she felt she had nothing to go forward with.

She slipped out of bed as Ben continued to snore, a soft whistling sound. Billy's snoring could be heard from his bedroom down the hall; low, rumbling sounds in what was no doubt a deep dreaming state. She slipped her feet into a pair of yellow clogs, took a light robe from the end of the bed, and wrapped herself in the silkiness of it as she padded down the wide curved staircase to the first floor.

Howard's Walk had been neglected for over fifteen years before Kate moved in. There had been remnants of life here and there on her first visit; a table in the foyer underneath a cobwebbed chandelier and the trunk in the upstairs bedroom. The house was her sister Becky's dream, not hers. The renovations that were needed to bring it back to its former state overwhelmed her initially. But the house finally drew her in, and Kate was able to see past the brokenness to the beauty of what it could be, and she tackled it head-on. Instead of an abandoned shell, it became a home, hers and Ben's. And, someday, it would be Billy's, too.

Now the expansive foyer gleamed with hardwood floors from the front entrance back to the kitchen. Kate had reset circles of marble around six columns spaced out along the walls and replaced cracked panes of glass in the French doors with the help of local artisans. Once she had committed to refurbishing the house, she was as hands-on as possible.

A large vase of fresh flowers picked from the gardens the day before sat on a marble-topped table in the center of the foyer. Kate stopped to rearrange the flowers and pinch off blossoms that were past their prime. She tossed them into a bin outside, then went back into the house.

In the vintage-style kitchen, Kate turned on a light over the stove and fixed a mug of coffee. She changed from her robe to a sweatshirt hanging by the back door and stepped out onto the stone patio. The sound of squirrels in the treetops drew her eyes up the trunk of a nearby magnolia. It was the majestic centerpiece of the Gardens at Howard's Walk which were now reopened to the public. The tree was ancient, a living anchor for the replanted gardens, and she imagined its roots spiraling deep into the earth, an unshakable monument to the passing of time. A few well-placed blossoms, large and cream-colored, still clung to the tips of the branches among the jade green leaves.

The squirrels shot down the tree trunk, tumbling through the underbrush and finally out of sight. Kate took a deep breath, inhaling the scent coming from Rebecca's Rose Garden, one of the first to be refurbished at Howard's Walk. She followed the flagstone walk to it, feeling the cool morning air on her face. But the day was predicted to grow unseasonably hot once again.

Kate longed for the first clear, crisp autumn day to arrive at Howard's Walk, when the sun held itself back from rising in the morning and left earlier in the evening. She closed her eyes and recalled images of the brilliant reds, oranges, and yellows painting the landscapes in the north, the sound of leaves crunching underfoot, and cozy blanket-wrapped evenings around a crackling fire. But as much as she loved the thought of the quintessential autumn of the northeast, she was more than content in her corner of the world and had no urge to leave. And right now, that was not an option anyway. She had a long to-do list that would take priority over anything else.

The local tree service was scheduled to come at nine o'clock to clear out a few dead trees around the side of the house and she walked there to make sure the trees were tagged correctly. She would have to meet the workers when they arrived. A load of gravel was coming that afternoon which Ben would handle. Her email inbox was piling up with requests for tours of the gardens and of the public parts of the house. And a busload of third graders was scheduled to arrive at two-thirty to learn how to plant seedlings in the greenhouse. Then a tour group from Winston-Salem would be there at three-thirty to tour the public gardens. It was a typical day at The Gardens at Howard's Walk.

Kate hadn't been away from home in several months. Sometimes she missed the excitement of her previous life as a freelance travel journalist, but she had chosen instead to travel closer to home when she could and still keep up with her online blog, *The Wayfarer*. Even that was becoming harder to do because of her responsibilities with the house and gardens and now with Billy. She couldn't see a way for her to stop all of that to search for her parents, but she knew it had to be done, and soon.

Her phone buzzed and brought her out of her thoughts. She answered it when she saw it was Mimi, who apologized for the early hour but said she had good news. She had arranged for a physical therapist to come to the house and a caretaker to stay with her and Billy at least for the near future. Kate was happy to hear the news since Mimi would finally have her son home with her. But it was also one less impediment to beginning her search.

Kate paused at the sound of voices coming from the house. She finished the last of her coffee and set the mug on the stone patio railing. A glance at her phone told her it was only seven o'clock and yet there was singing coming from the kitchen of Howard's Walk. Her morning quiet time was over.

Billy's deep off-key voice against Ben's nice tenor floated to her and made her smile as they belted out the old folk song, "She'll Be Coming Round the Mountain." They would be making pancakes, she guessed, which were now Billy's specialty and the only cooking he was allowed to attempt. It would mean a big cleanup job, but she welcomed it since it showed one of the tasks that Billy was able to do.

Ben and Billy connected on a level that met Billy where he was: happy with the simple things in life, content with hard work, and an eagerness to help. Billy had a curiosity about everything even though he might not remember or understand what he was told. Kate often felt inadequate in her role as sister and quasi-mother figure. But this was where Ben met Billy every single day, filling the gap of a male influence in Billy's life which had been missing since his father passed away.

She stopped at the kitchen door and assessed the situation. Billy was dressed in his dinosaur pajamas and red and green chef's cap and apron, a Christmas present from their friend Rosie at the local diner. Ben wore cut-off sweatpants and a bright green Howard's Walk tee shirt. In a few short minutes, the kitchen had been transformed from one of order and cleanliness to chaos with bowls spread out on the table, spoons dripping with batter, and pans of all sizes scattered over the stovetop. But laughter erupted as they worked, and Kate's heart lurched. This was what made each day special, seeing the two of them together, making a special connection. No matter how her search for their biological parents ended, she knew in her heart that every day could be a good one with Billy and Ben.

She put on a big smile and strode into the kitchen. "What's so funny?"

"Kate! We made—"

Ben put a hand on Billy's shoulder. "Wait, Billy. What did we say we were going to do this morning?"

"Oh, right, it's a surprise. I forgot."

"Right. So, what do we do next?"

Billy thought for a moment, then opened the door of the kitchen leading into the foyer and, following Ben's motions, bowed and invited Kate to follow him. Kate did and was amazed to see a small table set with her favorite heirloom tablecloth, a bud vase of daisies, a juice glass, and three floral-patterned plates, silverware, and napkins.

"How did you do this? When ...?"

"Sit, Kate!" Billy said and again, followed Ben's prompting to hold out her chair. After she was seated, Ben whispered, "Wait here," then motioned for Billy to come back into the kitchen.

They soon returned with a steaming plate of pancakes, some burnt around the edges, some oozing batter from inside, and Billy set them on the table in front of Kate.

"Good morning, Kate," Billy said, a serious look on his face as if trying to remember his lines. "We hope you like your breakfast. We have to eat in the kitchen but that's okay."

"No, Billy," Ben quickly corrected him. "We don't have to eat in the kitchen. What I said was that since Kate was outside," he said glancing at her with a grin, "we had to set the table up inside. And, if the lady of the house would like us to join her?"

"The lady of the house would insist that you join her."

Billy fist-pumped the air and hurried back to the kitchen to get more pancakes on the griddle. Ben brought two more chairs to the table, leaned down, and kissed Kate. "Good morning."

"Good morning to you. Whose idea was this?"

"Well, a bit of Billy's and a bit of mine. You can probably guess which was which."

"Yes, I can. But it was very thoughtful of you both. What's the occasion?"

Ben sat down across from her and tipped back in his chair. "No occasion, just a beautiful morning with my two favorite people."

"This makes you happy, doesn't it?" Kate asked, pouring syrup over her pancakes.

"Of course it does. Doesn't it make you happy?"

Kate cut a wedge with her fork.

"It absolutely does. But ...."

"But what?" Ben tipped his head. "I know what you're thinking. You're thinking that things are about to change, you don't know where this search will lead or what Billy's diagnosis will mean for all of us. There are a lot of unknowns that we'll have to deal with. But in the meantime, I say we have this beautiful morning to eat pancakes and sing and decide to be happy and thankful for every day we have together."

Kate fought back tears. She could tell Ben had just gotten up and hurried to fix this nice breakfast for her while she was still outside. He hadn't combed his hair, maybe ran his fingers through it, so it stuck up on one side. He had slept in that tee shirt and shorts. He needed a shave. But those intense blue eyes and that quirky smile ... she couldn't look away. He showed her tenderness she didn't deserve. He was right. She needed to be thankful for the morning, and the songs, and the pancakes.

"But we're so busy here right now," she said. "We had big plans for the gardens this fall. And the Christmas open house? We have to start planning for it now."

Always the practical one, Ben reached out and took her hand.

"We'll figure it out, okay? Take whatever time you need to do your research. I can help with that if you want me to. I can spend more time here instead of at the garden center. And Sam and Martin can help plan the open house. You know they'd love to help."

Kate met their friends Sam Bingham and Martin McDonough soon after she moved into Howard's Walk. They had arrived at her lowest point, before she had begun to fight her way out of the grief of losing her sister. They were Becky's friends whom she had hired before her accident to help restore the gardens. Kate had to break the devastating news to them that her sister had died. Eventually, they were the ones who encouraged her to work in the gardens, no matter what her final decision was about staying or leaving. It would do her good, they had said. And they were right.

The two men had also taken over management of Ben's business, Eden Springs Nursery, as partners after Ben moved in with Kate. She knew they would be more than happy to help her in any way they could. But she still had her doubts about the rest.

"That all sounds great," she said, "but the research? No, that has to be me. And anyway, I've been thinking, Ben. I should start with my father first. It might take longer to find him so I should start now. And if I find him, I'll ask him about his health history. Then, depending on what he says, I'll convince him to be tested to see if he would be a match for Billy if he ever needed a kidney transplant." She quickly ran through her thoughts as she pushed the pancake pieces around on her plate. "If he is a match, I could just stay in touch if it ever happened that Billy needed it, and he can keep his distance and we can keep ours. I mean that's obviously what he wants, right? Billy doesn't need to know anything about him, and I don't care to stay in touch or anything, only if I need to for Billy's sake. And if he's not a match then the same thing, things go back to the way they were and ...." Her words trailed off and she took a sip of her orange juice.

"And what, Kate?"

She shrugged, her eyes blinking away tears. "And we can forget we ever found him," she said softly.

"Would you really be able to do that?" Ben asked. He reached across the table and covered her hand in his. "If that door is opened, I'm not sure it would be right for you to be the one that closed it. Especially if he were to agree to be a donor."

Kate stabbed at a remnant of her breakfast. "Maybe that's what he would like, too. Did you ever think of that?"

"I suppose."

"Well, then it's not your problem, is it?" Her tone was harsh. Ben sat back in his chair and crossed his arms. Kate could hear his foot tapping on the floor. She had hurt him when he didn't deserve it. She couldn't look up to meet his gaze.

"I'm not going to argue with you about this," he said. "You need to do it your way. But don't shut me out, Kate. I want to help. You're not alone in this."

"Ben!" Billy shouted from the kitchen. "Pancakes!"

"I guess that's my signal." He stood to go into the kitchen, but Kate grabbed his hand as he walked past her. He stopped and pulled her to her feet. She wrapped her arms around him.

"I'm sorry," she whispered in his ear. She took his face in her hands. "I love you, Ben. I need to do this by myself. But I promise I won't shut you out."

"Ben, hurry!"

Ben untangled himself from Kate's arms. "Got to go!" He kissed her quickly and headed into the kitchen.

Kate scolded herself for lashing out at him. She knew he was always there for her but somehow, she felt alone on this journey. No one, not even Ben, could understand what she was feeling. She had tried to conjure a vague idea of who her biological father might be, what he was like, and what his excuses were for abandoning his children. Yes, she knew he was only seventeen at the time according to the birth certificate but still ... She forced the thought out of her mind. He just didn't seem real. She couldn't envision his facial features, or his build, or the color of his eyes. Did he have a natural smile? Was he a big man with blond hair like Billy? At least she had some idea of what her mother might look like since she had seen pictures of her. But those pictures were over thirty years old. What she looked like now was a mystery. She could have passed either one of them on the street without the slightest hint that they were her flesh and blood. She shivered at the thought.

Ben and Billy returned with a fresh plate of pancakes. Kate brightened at their enthusiasm, and she pushed aside her worries.

Kate said, "I have some good news for you Billy. I talked to your mama this morning. You're going to be able to go home pretty soon."

Billy clapped his hands. "Really, Kate? I can go home?" His face dropped. "But Mama's in the hospital."

"They're going to let her go home and a friend of yours, Miss Sara, is coming to take care of you both. Will that be okay?"

"Sure, Kate. If Mama will be okay, then I'll be okay, too. And I'll help Miss Sara. She's a nice lady. Can I go now, Kate? Is she home now?"

"No, not yet. Probably in a few days. So we'll have time to get your things ready, okay?"

"Okay. I'll go home soon."

Kate looked across the table at Ben.

"And while you're home with Mimi, Ben and Sam and Martin will help me with some things here. Right, Ben?"

He smiled. "We're ready whenever you are, Kate."

4

AFTER MEETING WITH THE MEN from Cooper's Tree Service, Kate circled the house calling for Ben and Billy, but there was no answer. She reached the front driveway and saw that Ben's truck was gone; the two men had probably gone to the garden center for supplies.

Since there was nothing to stop her from starting the search for her birth parents, Kate went back into the house to a large room off the foyer and slid open the pocket doors. The room had once been used as a place to store Becky's household and personal items after Kate cleared out her apartment in Winston-Salem. Most of the furniture had since been sold, donated, or used throughout other rooms in the house. But Kate remembered she still had a white antique writing desk tucked away in this room. It always reminded her of Becky, and even though she could never decide what to do with it, parting with it was never an option. She found it pushed into a corner next to a large fireplace.

She cleared some of the stacks of books and papers off the desk and inched it over to face one of the floor-to-ceiling windows on the other side of the room. Heavy brocade drapes which appeared to be original to the house covered the windows. Kate tugged on them until they opened, scattering dust motes into the room. She wiped away a layer of grime on the windowpanes and realized that once cleaned, she would have a pleasant view of her private gardens from that vantage point. It was a shame she hadn't discovered the potential of this room sooner. She made a mental note to do a thorough cleaning and redecorating. She filed that undertaking into the back of her mind and got to work.

Kate dusted the desk, emptied the drawers of miscellaneous items, and set up pen and pencil holders. After retrieving her laptop from the bedroom and setting up a small printer, she was ready.

As she sat down at the desk, she noticed from her new view out of the window that the private area on this side of the house looked overgrown. She caught herself standing up to go outside to work on it and sat back down. She didn't want to start the process she was faced with, and realized she would rather do anything else. But the laptop screen came to life, reminding her of what she had come to do, and she quickly created two new files, naming them 'The Search' and 'Billy.'

Kate had just told Ben that her first focus would be to locate her father. But, to get it out of the way, she did something she had never done before. She googled the name *Jenny Howard*. There were many hits and she scanned through them quickly, but none seemed to match. She tried *Jennifer Howard* with the same results. There was no middle name that she knew of that would further filter the search results. She assumed it would have been on the birth certificate if Jenny had a middle name, but it was blank on the document. She hadn't seen anything other than *Jenny* on anything she found in the house. She made a few notes, left the website, and refocused on finding her father, which she expected would be a much more daunting task.

After an hour of looking at online websites and taking notes about ways adoptees can begin searching for their biological parents, Kate closed all the sites and opened her email app.

Her cousins, Quinn and Orson Corbyn, now living in London, were nephews of Kate's grandmother, Bessie Corbyn Howard. Bessie had been born and raised in England and had moved to Eden Springs with her new American husband, Enoch Howard, after World War II. They built Howard's Walk together, creating stunning gardens that reminded Bessie of her native country. But after Enoch died, Bessie returned to England to be with her family. Howard's Walk remained empty, and the gardens slowly declined from neglect and stayed that way until Kate arrived.

The Corbyn men and their wives had visited Kate and Billy for the grand reopening of The Gardens at Howard's Walk, and she knew they would be interested to know how Billy was doing. But she wondered, too, if there was anything Bessie had ever told them, or left them, which might give a clue as to the identity of her and Billy's biological father.

She typed an email to let them know about Billy's diagnosis and her need to find out whatever she could about her parent's medical history. She added that she hoped they could help her learn who her father was.

She hit send. It was a long shot, but she had to try everything she could. Kate knew firsthand that following a string of seemingly unrelated clues could lead to the answers she needed. It was how she first discovered who her biological family was after inheriting Howard's Walk, and it was how she doggedly followed random historical facts on a recent trip to England to uncover the truth about a mysterious legend. She was able to do it before and decided to trust that she could do it again.

Kate picked up a stack of folders that had been sitting on the desk untouched for months and began to sort through them. Everything related to her adoption was in these folders and Billy's medical information and adoption papers were in another. Legal papers relating to Becky and the estate were in a third folder. Kate set these aside.

She knew she wasn't up to the task of probing through the legalities of her search without some help. Her first thought was of Wesley Carroll, the same attorney who had advised her when she first moved to Eden Springs. She put the folders for her and Billy in her backpack and headed into town.

Thirty minutes later, she pulled into a parking spot in front of the attorney's office in Eden Springs. She stepped inside the cool outer office where Wesley greeted her.

"Kate!" he said as he laid a folder in his assistant's inbox. "What a nice surprise!"

Wesley was a tall, distinguished-looking man with salt and pepper hair and a trim goatee. He was, as always, dressed in a three-piece suit. Kate couldn't picture him in anything remotely casual. She and Ben had become close friends with Wesley when his romantic relationship with Ben's divorced mother, Elizabeth Evans, began to blossom. Kate had put her trust in him on many occasions and was sure he would be able to give her the answers she needed.

"I don't have an appointment," Kate apologized, "but I wondered if you have a minute?"

"Of course."

She followed him into his office. He sat behind his desk.

"What can I do for you, Kate? Is everything okay with Billy?"

"Yes, well, that's kind of the reason I came to see you." She sat in a comfortable chair across from Wesley and shared the information Dr. Bartlett had given her.

"So, you need to find out your family medical history."

She nodded.

"Well, you have a challenging task ahead of you. I'll do anything I can to help, of course."

"I guess I need some advice." She pulled out the original birth certificate for the triplets that she had found at the house.

"As you know, this is where it all started," she said as Wesley reviewed the certificate. "According to that, Jenny Howard gave birth to triplets on August 16, 1990." She handed him three more certificates. "Now two of these show that Becky and I were born as twins on that date; there's one for each of us. The last one is the copy of Billy's birth certificate that I got from Mimi that says he was born as a single birth on the same date. We've already proven that we're triplets through the DNA tests we took. That isn't the issue anymore. But as you can see, the original birth certificate copy doesn't list a father."

"I'm familiar with all of these documents. If I recall correctly, you said you had found this original certificate in an old trunk at Howard's Walk?"

"Yes, it was in an envelope with a note on it written by Becky that said, 'show Kate.' But she never mentioned it to me."

Wesley pondered this for a moment. "Normally, the original birth certificates are under seal with the state and can only be released with a court order. Do you suppose Becky, as an attorney, began a search for information about your parents at some point and requested the court release it to her?"

"I suppose it's possible. Honestly, though, I never thought about how it came to be in the trunk. But she never had the chance to tell me she bought the house before her accident either. So she wasn't telling me everything back then. Maybe she found out information about our birth parents and meant to tell me about that, too. But I don't even know if she knew that Billy was our brother. Honestly, I wasn't available to her like I should have been back then. I guess I wouldn't be having all these questions now if I'd stayed in touch more."

"There's nothing you can change about that now. It was a tragic accident that took Becky's life. We can only go forward."

Kate nodded.

"Now, having this original birth certificate was key in learning that you were Jenny's children, obviously. Have you searched for her yet? If you found her, she could tell you who the father was, if she chose to. It's always possible she would know where he is or what might have happened to him." When Kate didn't respond, he continued. "Were there any other legal documents in the house when you found this birth certificate? Or in Becky's papers?"

"No, just that. I've been through everything." Kate didn't mention it to Wesley, but the three baby blankets she had also found in the trunk had spoken more to her than any legal document. Someone had cared enough about the triplets to create something for them that would last. She assumed it was her grandmother, Bessie Howard. But that caring was not enough to stop their adoption to two different homes. She shook off the feelings that threatened to lead her down a dark path.

"Meanwhile," Wesley said, "I would suggest you continue to do online searches, find out whatever you can through social media, and keep me apprised of whatever you find." He stroked his goatee. "Have you thought to contact Bessie's relatives in England?"

"Yes, I just sent an email." She stood. "Thank you, Wesley. You've been a big help."

"Of course. I'm sorry to hear about Billy's problems. He's special to us, too. Elizabeth and I are happy to help in any way we can."

Kate mentally checked off another task on her list.

5

KATE SET ASIDE HER SEARCH EFFORTS to focus on preparations for the busy Labor Day weekend at The Gardens at Howard's Walk. After the weekend came and went, they found that the number of visitors was double last year's. It was a good sign of future success at the gardens, and they celebrated by taking the next day off to relax. But on Wednesday, they were back in business with another tour group scheduled for late morning.

As Kate was preparing for the tour group, she heard a knock on the front door and opened it in time to wave to a Fed Ex delivery man hopping into his truck. He had left a large package on the porch and Kate saw that it was from her cousins in England. They had already responded to her email and apologized for not thinking to look through Bessie's things before this to see if there was something Kate might have wanted. But since she mentioned needing more information in her email, they had pulled boxes from storage and looked through them, enjoying memories of their Aunt Bessie and talking about Howard's Walk. But now they felt it was time to turn them over to her; at least this first box was a start.

Kate dragged the box to her office and closed the door. She could have asked Billy to carry it in for her, but he would have been too curious about its contents, and she wanted to be the first one to look at what her cousins had sent.

She found a box cutter and slid it across the packing tape. As she opened it, and laid the contents out on a card table, the aroma of the past filled the air. Like the old trunk Kate found when she first moved into the house, everything in the box spoke of history and memories and lives fully lived.

There were several photo albums from the fifties and sixties. In a faded manila envelope, she found yellowed newspaper and magazine articles that Bessie had written about horticulture, both in the States and England. Kate unwrapped a set of four dessert plates decorated with a colorful botanical design. A note was attached to them saying there was more to the set if she would like to have them. She pulled out a batch of letters, tied with a faded blue ribbon, from Bessie and Enoch to each other during the war. And, in the bottom of the box, she found three Eden Springs High School yearbooks from the years 1987, 1988, and 1989. A sticky note was attached letting her know that Bessie hadn't kept any other yearbooks that they were aware of.

Kate methodically organized the items on the table, trying to absorb the treasure in front of her.

She heard Ben calling her name as the pocket door slid open. He came in and closed it behind him.

"Where's Billy?" Kate asked.

"He's with Sam in the garden. They're doing some cleanup after last night's storm." He approached the table and let out a low whistle. "What's all this?"

"A box came from my cousins in England. This," she spread her arms over the table, "is more of my family history. And apparently, there's more where that came from."

"Do you think this will help?"

"I'm hoping it will. Especially those." She pointed at the yearbooks. "But I'm afraid to open them." She crossed her arms. "I just can't get my head around this yet. I've seen pictures of Jenny, but this is where I might find clues about who my father is."

"What if we look at everything else first?" He picked up the faded newspaper articles. "Looks like Bessie was still writing about horticulture even after she returned to England. We could display these in the visitor's center, right?"

"That's a great idea. And these plates, too. But these letters are from the nineteen forties. I think they're probably personal so I might not display them, but I do want to read them." She carefully pulled one out of a water-stained envelope and unfolded the yellowed stationery. It was clear that the letter had been read many times; the paper was coming apart along the folds. After a deep breath, she began to read it aloud.

> May 8, 1945.
>
> My dearest Bessie, What a celebration here in Paris! The war is finally over! I am counting the days before I can see you again. I will leave Paris soon and arrive in London by train. I will find you!
>
> All my love,
>
> Enoch.

Kate leaned into Ben, and he put his arm around her. "There was so much love between them. I can see it in the photographs from when they came to Eden Springs, too. What a heartbreak it must have been for them to know they had grandchildren who were lost to them. And I can't even imagine how hard it must have been for Bessie and Enoch to know that their friends Mimi and Calvin were raising Jenny's son right here in Eden Springs and not be able to say anything to them about it."

She opened one of the photo albums to pictures of Bessie, Enoch, and Jenny that she had never seen before. There were photos of the Howard family at the beach and in the mountains, probably all in North Carolina. When the photographs transitioned from black and white to color, there was a collection of plant and flower photos that Bessie had labeled with names and dates.

Ben's phone buzzed and he checked his texts. He was needed outside.

"The bus is here. Do you want to help, or would you rather stay here?"

She smiled, relieved she could take a break from all of the memories. "I'll be there in a minute."

Kate refolded the letter and slid it back into the envelope. The letter was touching. It spoke of love and commitment in their relationship, and she could see that in what they had built at Howard's Walk. As she mentioned to Ben, there must have been heartbreak in their decision to handle Jenny's pregnancy the way they did. But, if she were being honest with herself, Kate discovered that she also had a wound, and with every step she took in the search for her biological parents, it was being ripped open, one bit at a time. Kate wondered if it could ever be healed.

∽✕∾

After the tour from the senior center was over, Ben stood at the steps of the bus, lending a hand to the ladies and even to some of the men to reach the first step. They all left with a packet of flower seeds to remind them of their trip to the Gardens at Howard's Walk. Several couples said they had visited the gardens many years ago as children and remembered Enoch and Bessie Howard, and said what a shame it was that she had moved to England and let the gardens go. But as one woman declared, "That's life. We have to know when it's time to do what we need to do. And what a blessing that young man Billy is," she said. "Bless you all for letting him take part in this." Ben could only nod in agreement.

The bus started up and pulled slowly down the driveway, passengers waving at Ben from the windows. He scanned across the property for Kate and Billy but didn't see them. There was more work to be done that day and he went into the house to change into his work clothes.

He found a clean tee shirt in the dresser and as he unfolded it, a small blue velvet box dropped to the floor. He grabbed it and threw it back into the drawer. He looked around the room, out the window, and then went to the balcony that gave a view of the foyer. Kate was nowhere in sight. He called her name but there was no answer.

Back in the bedroom, he pulled the box out again and opened it up. Nestled in the velvet interior was a brilliant square-cut diamond with a platinum band. He pulled it out and turned it against the light, so it sparkled. He couldn't remember the number of times he had wanted to get down on one knee and propose to Kate. He was at fault for a lot of the missed opportunities. Others were simply bad timing, like last week, before Billy had his final appointment with the doctor. He had everything arranged. Sam and Martin were going to take Billy into town for ice cream. Ben was going to prepare a nice meal for Kate. They would eat on the patio in the waning light of the day. He would get down on one knee, and .... He shook the thought away. It had turned out to be rainy and windy. Billy hadn't felt well, and Kate didn't want him to get sicker from eating ice cream. So everyone stayed home. And the proposal was put off for another time.

Ben had fallen hard for Kate the moment they met. She had walked unannounced into an Eden Springs town meeting three years ago. No one knew her at the time since she had just arrived to work through her sister's estate with Wesley Carroll and the realtor. She had a sad look about her, but her emerald eyes assessed him, and he already felt inadequate. He had walked her back to her room at the Park Inn in town and from that moment on, he knew this was a woman he could spend the rest of his life with.

As the months passed, he realized that she felt the same. He was confident that he loved Kate. He had known couples who were happy together in their marriage. But his parents' marriage was not a good example. His father was a domineering man, a liar, and a cheat, and his mother had only stayed with him for Ben's sake as he was growing up. She finally had enough and divorced Max soon after Kate had moved to Eden Springs.

Ben had a few serious relationships, but they had all ended badly. Kate was different, but their relationship was still complicated. Some days he knew it would work and on one of those days, he bought the ring. On other days, he doubted, because there was a part of her that she kept hidden. She claimed that she wasn't shutting him out but no matter what he did to try to convince her that he was always there for her, she kept a wall around her heart.

Ben knew she was under a lot of pressure, but he only wanted to help her. Most of all he wanted her to be happy. He didn't have any siblings so he could only guess how he would act if he were in her shoes. He might react exactly as she had. The thought had crossed his mind that Kate might have to make Billy a priority in the future. He understood it. But where would that leave him?

"*You idiot,*" he said to himself. Billy was very important to him, too, and he knew that the male bonding they had developed had helped Billy tremendously. There was no way he could back out on him now. So far, the three of them had worked out pretty well together and Billy would soon be going back to live with his mother. Maybe that would be a better time to propose. Yes, that would be much better.

He wrapped the ring box in an old sweatshirt and pushed it to the back of the bottom drawer of the dresser where Kate would never find it. He changed his clothes and went back downstairs.

6

BALANCING A TUMBLER of ice water, an apple, and a bagel in one arm, Kate unlocked the pocket door to her makeshift office with her free hand, then closed it behind her.

The room still held the aroma from the contents of the box which were now spread out across the card table. *Memories have their own fragrance,* she thought. *Especially when they've been hidden away for years.*

She set down her lunch that was hours late, tore off a piece of the bagel, and pulled a chair up to the table.

The first Eden Springs High School yearbook she chose was the 1987 Sentinel. Ben had explained to her that the history of using the figure of a sentinel for the school started after the First World War. Many young local men were sent to fight in Europe and tragically never came home. Their deaths devastated the small farming community, and a statue of a soldier standing watch had been erected in the town park in memory of those men. The image of the sentinel was used on the school football uniforms, the school newspaper, and on the cover of each yearbook. A life-sized mascot dressed in the sentinel's uniform was always on hand at the football games to rev up the crowds. Ben confessed that he had even donned the uniform a few times in his junior year.

Kate leafed through the first pages of faculty and administration photos, candid shots of the students, and posed photos of the band, chorus, and Future Farmers of America. It was a year of big hair on the girls and mullets on the boys.

She skipped over the elementary class pictures and found the high school freshman class. Small square black and white photos, twenty to a page, comprised what would become the Class of 1990. There were about sixty pictures in all, but that small number was not unusual for a rural high school like Eden Springs High.

Kate scanned the pages of pictures and finally found a familiar face. J. Howard, top row, third from the left. Kate had seen pictures of Jenny before in the albums that had been left in the house, so the young girl was easily recognizable. She was pretty but had the features of her father, Enoch, a strong jaw and a determined look in her eyes. Kate couldn't remember that Jenny had been smiling in any of the pictures she had seen of her. Surely, her life couldn't have been that unhappy. Kate suddenly sat back in her chair. What if this young teenager felt trapped in Eden Springs? What if she had dreams of wandering the world and felt stifled in the rural setting? What if Kate's wanderlust was part of the DNA passed down from her mother? What if their personalities were ... similar? Kate shook off the thoughts. There was no confirmation of this. She was interpreting the photographs that captured one brief moment in time too deeply. Her adoptive parents, Clarence and Maggie Tyler, traveled extensively, too. They were stationed all over the world for her father's career. No, that's where she got her love of travel from. Things like that weren't passed down in DNA. Were they?

Kate turned her attention back to the yearbook and found a few more candid and posed photos of Jenny with the cheerleading team. She flipped to the front and back inside covers but they were empty of any autographs, best wishes, or silly comments from girlfriends. She scanned through the entire yearbook and found no notes at all. Kate was never that interested in getting people to sign her yearbooks, but Becky's were filled with autographs from friends and even teachers, so the lack of them in these yearbooks puzzled Kate. Jenny seemed like a popular girl, involved in extracurricular activities, but there could be many reasons why her classmates hadn't signed her yearbook. It probably didn't mean anything, and Kate closed the yearbook and moved on to the next one.

Jenny was fifteen in her sophomore year and Kate saw a noticeable difference in her appearance from the previous year. She had blossomed over the summer from a shy girl to a young woman. She was still involved in school activities and there were candid photos of her with small groups of girls. Some had even captured a shy smile. In this yearbook, Kate found several handwritten notes addressed to Jenny.

Have a great summer!

Love Susan

Will miss you –see you next year!

Millie

Inside the back cover was an anonymous note, in the typical looping handwriting of a teenage girl, that said "*Have fun with you-know-who this summer!*" Kate went back through the yearbook thoroughly but there were no other clues as to who this 'you-know-who' might have been. She closed it and opened the yearbook for 1989.

This was the yearbook for Jenny's junior year in high school. It appeared that the only activity she was in that year was cheerleading for the football team. So Kate was a bit surprised when she saw the junior prom photos where Jenny had been crowned prom queen. A handsome young man was by her side. Kate wondered if this was the guy that she might have had a great summer with. But she couldn't be sure. There were no autographs from boys in any of the yearbooks so far, so she didn't know if Jenny had been dating at that age or not, although it seemed logical that she might be.

Kate went through the yearbook again, looking carefully at each picture. She knew that any one of the young men in Eden Springs High School at that time could be hers and Billy's father. She could have walked past them on the streets of Eden Springs or taken them on a tour of the gardens. Of course, it could have been someone from another town, too. But what would be the chances of that? Eden Springs was a small town; kids dated each other, probably ones that their parents knew and trusted. But someone had broken that trust, whether it was a local boy or not.

Kate realized that this was the last yearbook available for Jenny according to the note from her cousins. She guessed it made sense since Jenny probably got pregnant in January 1990 and had the triplets prematurely in August of that year. She probably would have left school in the middle of her senior year and the yearbook, for obvious reasons, was never purchased by the Howards.

Kate felt that she was no further along in her search than when she started. She had thought that the clues she was looking for were here in these books, but her first look through them had not yielded anything interesting. Then a thought came to her. Instead of looking for Jenny's potential boyfriends, she needed to look for Jenny's girlfriends, ones she might have confided in, ones that might still be around. By Jenny's junior year, there were only about fifty teenagers in what would have been her graduating class, and about half of them were boys.

In casual conversations with women she had become acquainted with in Eden Springs, she learned that they didn't know Jenny well at all. The Howards would have been upper middle class during those years and many of the women still in the range of Jenny's age were part of the farming community. The others had married and moved away.

But Kate still felt it might be worth looking at the names more closely. She first looked for the girls who had signed the yearbooks. The names under the class photos were first initials and then the last name, so Kate was at a loss to match a first name with just an initial. She looked through the class picture from Jenny's junior year again and looked at each of the last names, running her finger along the list.

"Davidson, Duvall, Franklin, Gerrity, Green, Hoover, Howard," she said out loud.

She stopped and went back to one of the names, C. Duvall. The name was familiar, from recently even. She could have heard or seen it anywhere. But the person in the matching photo was undeniably familiar: a square face, thin lips, serious piercing eyes, and a chin raised in defiance. Kate knew this woman from somewhere, there was no doubt in her mind. From what she recalled, the face hadn't changed that much over the past thirty years.

She searched her memory. She was sure that she had talked to C. Duvall in the past few years, not here in Eden Springs but where? Suddenly the name came to her. Celeste Duvall.

The woman must have kept her maiden name since Kate remembered interviewing her for an article she wrote as a freelance journalist. Ms. Duvall lived in Winston-Salem and had hosted an outdoor exhibit of Parisian artists at her home a few years ago. With her fondness for Paris, Kate enjoyed interviewing her and taking a tour through the exhibits and gardens. Ms. Duvall might have mentioned that she was from Eden Springs originally, but it would not have meant anything to Kate at that time since it was before she came to Howard's Walk. She searched the yearbook again for any clue that Celeste and Jenny might have been friends or at least might have known each other in their junior year of high school. But there was nothing that offered that as a possibility.

Kate opened her laptop and began a search for the name Celeste Duvall in Winston-Salem, North Carolina. There was really nothing new to learn. She was married to

Gregory Benedict, a well-known financier and banker in both Winston-Salem and Charlotte, North Carolina. In their photos together she appeared much younger than Benedict, but with her strong features and his no-nonsense facial expressions in all of the photos, they appeared well-suited for each other. A true Southern power couple. Kate recalled that their Winston-Salem home was one of three. They also owned a condo near Grandfather Mountain and a beach house on Nags Head. She searched further for more recent information but there was nothing there that she didn't already know from her previous interview. The article that Kate had written about the art exhibit had appeared in Southern Living magazine and the full piece popped up as a link. She opened and read it with a critical eye, noting ways she would have written it differently now. All in all, she thought it was a good piece.

Kate knew that at one time she had a contact number for Celeste's assistant and planned to find it later. But for now, she had to think of a logical reason for her to visit this woman again. She continued to search through online social media and news articles about the couple and discovered that Ms. Duvall was hosting a new art exhibit in October, this time featuring women artists.

Kate munched on her apple and took a long drink of iced water. Maybe it was time for her to do an article for *The Wayfarer* about things to do in Winston-Salem this fall and include the art event. If it worked once, it might work again.

Before closing the yearbooks, Kate flipped through the pages one more time and became aware of a new feeling. She had seen photographs of Jenny before, although very few. These yearbooks put her in a different context, that of a typical teenage girl.

Kate thought back to her own high school years. For her, it wasn't the best time of her life, if she were to be honest. Long-term friendships were not part of the picture in those days because her family moved so often. She was too awkward for the cool girls' crowd and too independent for boyfriends. Her mother once said that Kate always wanted to be somewhere other than where she was, which turned out to be true. Still, high school was a rite of passage for her, as it was for all teenagers, as it must have been for Jenny.

But Jenny had lived a small-town high school experience in Eden Springs. She probably had lifelong friends up to that point. She was pretty, she was a cheerleader, and she must have had crushes and the heartbreaks that went along with them. She probably had hopes and dreams just as Kate and Becky had. But Kate was sure that never had her dreams included being pregnant at seventeen and giving birth to triplets and making the difficult decision to give them up for adoption.

Life is simply a series of unexpected events and choices. No one knew that better than Kate. No matter how much and how carefully people plan out their lives, they can be blindsided by the unforeseen. It was that way for her and Becky. And she was beginning to understand that it must have been that way for Jenny as well.

Kate scrolled through the contacts on her phone and found the name of Celeste Duvall's assistant, David Snow. She dialed the number hoping he was still connected to Ms. Duvall, but it had been five years and she realized he might have moved on.

"David Snow." The deep male voice that answered caught her by surprise.

"David. Hi. This is Kate Tyler. I don't know if you remember me. How are you?" There was a moment of silence.

"Well, well, well. Kate Tyler. Where have you been hiding? What's it been, five, six years?"

Kate breathed a sigh of relief. At least he remembered her.

"Five years since I met you at Ms. Duvall's home. For the art exhibit, remember?"

"Sure I remember. That was a crazy couple of days for us. But then it's like you fell off the face of the earth. I was always hoping we could get together socially after that."

Kate had forgotten but it came flooding back to her. A late-night interview with Ms. Duvall after a successful event, a celebration, one too many glasses of champagne, and a very forward David Snow almost ended in an embarrassing confrontation. Why hadn't she remembered that before calling to ask him for a favor? It was too late, though. She pressed on.

"I've been really busy, traveling, you know."

"So, what can I do for you today?"

Kate asked if he was still working for Celeste Duvall.

"I am, but not as her assistant. I'm doing her event planning now. It's freelance work but gives me time for my hobbies."

"Well, that's great! Listen, I saw that she was holding another art exhibit soon and I'd love to do another piece on it. I was hoping you could hook me up?"

He sighed. "Well, I get a lot of requests like that and have to hand them off to her new assistant. She's a stickler for protecting Celeste's time. Not many people get through to her anymore. But, for you, Kate? Sure, I'll give it a try."

"Thank you, David. I appreciate it."

"How's the rest of this week look for you?"

"I'm open. I'm living in Eden Springs now, so I'm not far."

"Eden Springs? That's not where I pictured you at all. You should be in a condo here in Winston-Salem or Charlotte, not out in the middle of a tobacco field somewhere."

Kate laughed. If he only knew that she was the owner of The Gardens at Howard's Walk in addition to her work with *The Wayfarer.* She decided not to share too much, at least not yet.

"You'd be surprised how stimulating country life can be, David. Anyway, I appreciate this. You've got my number so let me know when it works for me to meet with Ms. Duvall."

"Will do." And he ended the call.

David texted Kate later that evening.

```
David: Tomorrow--Thursday, 9
AM, at Bedford House. One hour
with Celeste.
Confirm.

Kate: Confirmed.
Thanks.
```

She was one step closer to finding another clue.

7

IT HAD RAINED OVERNIGHT, a welcomed change from several weeks of hot dry weather. When Kate came downstairs the next morning, the French doors had been left ajar and a puddle had formed on the hardwood floor. She grabbed a towel from the kitchen and mopped it up before stepping outside onto the dampened flagstones. Remnants of the night rain dripped from the trees onto the ground below. A light mist curled into the corners of the garden, floating unhurriedly as if searching for a home. A squirrel, which Billy had named Mr. Chipmunk, sprinted towards her, braking hard a few feet away as if wondering who this interloper was in his garden. Kate told him, "Good morning." He darted up a nearby pine tree.

She walked to the end of the greenhouse and breathed in the bouquet of dampened soil, flowers, and moist air. The setting in front of her took her back to her first days at Howard's Walk. It seemed a lifetime ago although it had only been three years. It was supposed to be a temporary stay, just until she could get her sister's affairs taken care of and make plans to sell the old house and gardens. But life had other plans for her, and she was still there, thriving, happy, and content. Howard's Walk was her home now; hers and Ben's, and one day, Billy's, too.

Ben had moved in with her two years ago. It was the longest relationship she had ever been in and although there had been some rough patches, they had always worked things out. She couldn't imagine a life without him, and she thought he felt the same.

The subject of marriage had never come up. But he had always told her that he would never leave her—whatever that meant in terms of marriage. Kate had no problems with marriage; in fact, she thought that marrying Ben would be the most wonderful thing in the world. But she was worried that Ben might think differently, mostly because his parent's marriage was such a sham and had ended in a bitter divorce. And so, she had never hinted at it, nor had he. She believed he was committed to her and the running of Howard's Walk and the gardens. And she could not think of a better big brother for Billy. She shivered at the thought of what life would be for Billy if Ben were not in it.

It had not occurred to her before this moment what an impact it would have on Billy if her and Ben's relationship didn't work out. Kate knew that living with his mother would make Billy very happy, but the life that she and Ben were building for him here was helping him grow to the best of his abilities, to have a daily purpose, a routine, and fun. Sometimes she forgot that she and Billy were the same age. Ben was only two years older than Kate and Billy, so they were all more like friends even though they had to parent him, too.

Billy didn't know that Kate was his biological sister. And she doubted that she could ever tell him in a way that he would understand. And now with his diagnosis, and her decision to search for their biological parents, any plans with Ben might have to be put on hold, all because of this one, unexpected circumstance with Billy's health.

Kate walked back into the house through the kitchen and heard Ben and Billy talking upstairs. She slipped into her office and closed the doors to prepare herself for her meeting with Celeste Duvall.

Two hours later, Kate parked her car on a tree-lined street one block away from Celeste Duvall's home, Bedford House. It was a well-known historic home in a quiet neighborhood just outside of Winston-Salem. Celeste renovated the entire estate twenty years earlier after she and her husband bought the 1915 Colonial Revival. Her dinner parties were exclusive and the art and music events on the Bedford House's back lawn were legendary. Celeste and her husband were passionate supporters of the arts, and this upcoming art show *She Paints* was advertised as the celebration of female artists from around the world.

Kate planned on doing a real interview with Celeste as a feature in *The Wayfarer* because she truly was interested in the art event. But somehow, she had to get the conversation turned around to Celeste's relationship with Jenny Howard. She still had no idea how she would do that but trusted her instincts to find the right time.

A minute before nine o'clock, Kate started her car again and made the turn onto the circular drive of Bedford House. She checked herself in the rearview mirror, gathered her tote bag, and made her way to the front steps.

She rang the doorbell, and a few moments later the door opened and she found herself face to face with David Snow. She was startled when she saw him, expecting Ms. Duvall herself or her assistant to greet her. But there he was.

David wasn't tall, like Ben, but she always remembered his erect posture and bearing. He was leaner than she remembered, too, probably had been working out and had lost some weight. He wore a three-piece suit, as he always had, a neatly trimmed beard and mustache that showed a hint of gray already. He could have been a banker or a lawyer; at least that was how he liked to present himself, but those were also the circles he was in now on the coattails of the Duvall-Benedicts.

"Kate, good to see you again." He smiled as he leaned in to give a quick hug. She kept it brief.

"Good to see you, too, David."

"Come on in. Celeste asked me to bring you out to the patio."

She followed him down a long center hall lined with antiques and tasteful artwork to a brick patio at the back of the house. A fan turned slowly over a wrought iron table and chairs, creating a gentle breeze. David backed away and closed the patio doors behind him. Celeste rose to greet her.

"Kate, welcome to Bedford House again," she said, reaching out to shake Kate's hand. Celeste had not changed since their last meeting. She was still stylishly dressed, this time in camel-colored slacks and a white shirt, tailored to fit, gold jewelry, and wore the same skeptical expression on her face that contradicted a friendly tone. Kate hadn't found her to be overtly two-faced during their last interaction together, but the look in her eyes told her to be careful.

"It's nice to see you again, Ms. Duvall."

"Please, it's Celeste." She motioned for Kate to have a seat.

"Thank you, Celeste. I appreciate your meeting with me."

"Of course. I was extremely pleased with the write-up you did last time. I'm glad you reached out. I hope to see the same for this event."

"I'll do my best. I'm doing my own blog now." She handed Celeste her business card with the name *The Wayfarer* prominently displayed. "My reach locally in the Carolinas and Virginia now is over five thousand subscribers and even more than that across the US, so it will find a large audience."

"Excellent. Exactly what we need. Tea?"

Kate nodded and Celeste poured two glasses of sweet tea over ice from a cut glass pitcher.

After gathering information about the *She Paints* event for Kate's articles, Celeste said, "Now tell me what you've been doing since we last collaborated."

"I've been busy traveling and launching my blog, of course. I had a wonderful trip to England last year." Kate saw her opening and forced a smile to hide her nervousness. "But I'm living in Eden Springs now. At a place called Howard's Walk."

Celeste's eyes showed a hint of surprise and she set her glass on the table. She dabbed at her lips with an embroidered cloth napkin. "I see. With your family of course?"

"Well, I inherited it from my sister, Becky Tyler, three years ago. She had bought it just before … before a tragic accident that took her life."

"I'm very sorry to hear that," Celeste said with a concerned look. "Rebecca Tyler? That name is familiar. She was an attorney here in Winston-Salem, correct?"

"Yes, she was."

"So, you've settled there?"

"Yes. I've opened the public gardens again. There's a lot more work to be done, but it's coming together."

"I must come and take a tour."

"Yes, please, anytime." There was a lull in the conversation, but Kate let it play out.

Celeste pushed back her chair and walked to the edge of the patio. "I grew up in Eden Springs," she said over her shoulder.

"Oh? I didn't know that." Kate was glad that Celeste's back was turned to her. She took a sip of tea, noticed that her hand was shaking, and set the glass down, reminding herself not to give away too much.

"Nice little town, but I was eager to get away."

"It was an adjustment for me, too, but I've grown to love it there. And I still get to travel when I want to."

Celeste walked back to the table and sat down. "Did you know the Howards that used to live there?"

Kate decided to tread carefully. Celeste either didn't know or wasn't revealing that she knew of Kate's relationship with the Howards. But it was easy enough to stick to the truth in that regard.

"I never met them. I learned that Ms. Howard had left many years before my sister bought the house."

"Ah, yes, Bessie Howard. Her daughter Jenny and I were classmates growing up."

"Interesting." Kate plunged ahead. "I came across some photos that were left in the house. Some of her and her parents; at least that's how they were labeled. Actually, I have some old yearbooks from her high school years, too."

Celeste laughed. "Well, those should probably be burned! I wasn't the homecoming queen type that Jenny was. She was a very pretty girl. Very popular."

"I'm curious though. There was no yearbook from her senior year. I wondered why ... but I guess maybe it was just misplaced," Kate said as nonchalantly as she could. She wasn't ready to be completely upfront with Celeste; there could be any number of secrets kept by a close friend of her mother's that might be embarrassing for her to talk about.

"Well, perhaps." Celeste hesitated as if debating what to say. "But there is one possible explanation. Jenny did leave rather abruptly in the middle of our senior year and never came back. I don't think I ever saw her again after that. Rumor was that she went to another high school or boarding school to graduate." She tapped a manicured nail casually against the glass tabletop. "There were other rumors, too. But I shouldn't gossip. All I know is that she should have been part of the debutante ball in her senior year with the rest of us, but she left before that happened. She was talking about going to Peace or Meredith College in Raleigh. And, of course, she would have married well. But then, perhaps she did."

Kate absorbed this and risked more questions, trying to keep the conversation light even though her heart was beating double-time.

"So, dating opportunities were not great in Eden Springs, I guess?"

"That's true. Lots of farm boys there, of course. Nice enough fellows but nothing that I, nor Jenny, was interested in. We were more intrigued with the boys from Winston-Salem Prep back then."

"Oh?" Kate had not given much thought to the idea that Jenny might have dated boys from other schools. "I guess that makes sense."

"Yes. She did socialize with a young man named Davis from there. I remember because I always thought the name Davis was 'cool.'" Celeste curved her fingers in air quotes. "Our school football teams had a fierce rivalry. They always won, but all the girls still wanted to date guys from WSP, so it wasn't only Jenny."

"Were they serious?"

Celeste tipped her head, her eyes narrowing. After a moment she said, "Her and Davis? No, I don't think so. But that's the last boy I knew her to date before she left town." Celeste suddenly pushed a button on the side of the table and Kate heard a faint buzzing from somewhere in the house. "Is there anything else I can help you with for your article then?"

Kate began to gather her things. "No, I think I have everything I need. Thank you so much," she said, following Celeste's lead, and stood.

"I'll make sure you have tickets for the art show. You'll be able to pick them up at the door. I'm looking forward to reading your blog."

"That's very kind, Celeste. I can't wait for your event."

Celeste followed her to the front door. Kate turned. "Celeste, you don't happen to remember Davis's last name, do you?"

The woman hesitated as if she remembered but was reluctant to share. "No, I'm afraid I don't. But why do you ask?"

"It's nothing. Just curious. Thank you again, Celeste."

As Kate walked down the steps to her car, she heard Celeste call her name and she turned back.

"Why did you think you had to hide who you were?" Celeste said.

Kate forced herself to look directly at the woman as if she had nothing to hide. But she was sure that Celeste could see her heart pounding. "I'm not sure what you mean," she said casually.

"I know you are Bessie Howard's granddaughter. I heard through certain sources that someone with the name Tyler bought the house and was found to be related, which means you must be Jenny Howard's child. Are you?"

Kate felt her face turning red, embarrassed at being caught.

When Kate didn't answer, she said. "I'm not used to people lying to me. I think it changes a relationship, don't you?"

"I'm very sorry." Kate could have argued the point that she hadn't lied about not knowing the Howards. But she thought better of it. "I didn't mean to cause any trouble."

Celeste was silent, but the thin firm line of her mouth told Kate that she had not accepted her apology. "I'll have my assistant get back to you about covering my event. Perhaps it wouldn't be a good fit after all."

Kate turned and walked back to her car as she heard the front door close, hoping that she had not just made an enemy.

8

KATE GRIPPED THE STEERING WHEEL, her heart still
hammering in her chest. She hated confrontation, but was
indignant that Celeste had accused her of lying. She hadn't really
lied—had she? So yes, she may have hidden the real reason for
her visit, but the conversation led naturally to the questions she
had about Jenny and her boyfriends and Celeste didn't seem to
have a problem sharing what she knew. She seemed almost eager
to gossip about the boys from Winston-Salem Prep and about
the fact that Jenny left in the middle of her senior year. So Ms.
Duvall played a role in this, too.

By the time Kate pulled into the circular drive at Howard's
Walk, she had put the accusation behind her and refocused on
everything else she had learned from Celeste. She was sure she
had lost out on covering her art event and there was nothing she
could do about that. She could only take what she had learned
and find out what she could about this Davis person. It was still
a long shot, but at least she had a name to start with.

She went straight to her computer and searched for a
website that offered digital yearbooks from every high school in
the country. Kate set up an account and requested the yearbooks
from 1987, 1988, and 1989 for Winston-Salem Prep.

When the yearbooks were available, she began her
search. She wasn't sure exactly what she was looking for, but was
hopeful she would find a new clue.

She scanned through the digital pages of the 1987
yearbook. There were too many names with the first initials

of 'D' to be able to narrow the photos down to one particular person. She remembered that Jenny and Celeste might have dated football players, so she searched through photos of the football teams. Nothing caught her attention in yearbooks from 1987 or 1988. But when she looked through 1989's yearbook, she came across a photo of a newspaper article about the state championship football game for that year.

'Quarterback Davis Wingate led the team to their first state championship in ten years.'

Davis Wingate. There was a corresponding picture. He was dressed in a school football uniform and kneeled with his teammates. He was smiling, looking very confident as the winning quarterback. Kate could tell he was well-built and athletic even under the trappings of the uniform. According to Celeste, this was probably the last guy that Jenny dated before leaving town. What were the chances that there would be more than one student named Davis around the same age as Jenny? Chances were slim, and it was all Kate had to go on at the moment, so she refocused on the article.

Kate searched his features. There was something familiar about him, but she couldn't pinpoint it. She shook it off. Maybe she was just simply wishing for it and making something out of nothing. She knew her search was not over yet.

Kate immediately began to Google everything she could find about Davis Wingate. There were many results returned, and she diligently searched through each one for some clue that the person had graduated from Winston-Salem Preparatory School. Some were obviously too old or too young. Some were obituaries but she searched through those, too. She cross-referenced the possibilities against social media, taking copious notes. Finally, she narrowed it down to one person.

Davis Wingate was born July 1, 1971, in Winston-Salem, North Carolina. He was a graduate of Winston-Salem

Preparatory School in 1989 and was the owner of Wingate Winery in Pine Ridge, New York.

Kate's hands were shaking as she scrolled through the information on the screen. She hadn't thought it would be this easy. Of course, she could be assuming too much. There was a possibility that she was mistaken. But at least it was something.

Kate then began to dig deeper into the Wingate Winery and discovered more details about Davis Wingate. He attended North Carolina State University in Raleigh, North Carolina, and graduated in 1993 with a business degree. He then attended Cornell University in Ithaca, New York for his master's in viticulture studies from 1993 to 1995. Wingate worked at various wineries in New York State and France until returning to help run the Wingate Winery which had been bought by his father, Frank Wingate, in 2000. It appeared that when the elder Wingate died in 2017, Davis took over the responsibilities of the winery and now managed it with his wife, Marie.

She studied the photos of him as an adult from the winery's online presence. It was the same person as in the high school yearbook but in these photos, he was even bigger, brawnier, and intense, not the smiling high school senior from several years earlier. Kate then searched for anything she could find about the Wingates before they moved to New York State. It appeared they were a wealthy family, the father being successful in business in North Carolina and the mother, Delia, had been on the boards of several charitable organizations in Winston-Salem. She confirmed that Frank Wingate bought the winery near the popular tourist destination of Deep Lake and the town of Pine Ridge, New York.

Kate continued searching and taking notes until she heard the pocket door open. Ben joined her at her computer.

"You've been in here for a while. It's way past lunchtime. Are you hungry?"

"Not really. Look at this. I think I've found something."

Ben leaned over her shoulder and saw a name written on her notepad in large, bold print. "Davis Wingate. Who's he?"

"According to Celeste Duvall, he was the last guy that Jenny dated before she left home. Celeste said the girls from Eden Springs used to date guys from Winston-Salem Prep. Jenny was a cheerleader, so I guess it makes sense. The schools were football rivals according to her."

"Okay, so Celeste Duvall is the woman you went to see in Winston-Salem this morning? I guess the meeting went well?"

Kate frowned. "Well, that's a whole other story, but it turns out that she was friends with Jenny in high school. But she doesn't know what happened to her either."

"So how did you find this guy, Davis Wingate?"

"Celeste said Jenny dated a guy whose first name was Davis from Winston-Salem and I kept searching for the name and finally found this article in one of the Winston-Salem Prep yearbooks." She pulled up the photo on the computer. "They won the state championship that year and he was the quarterback. It's not a common name so it must be him."

"And where is he now?"

Kate showed him the other information she had found. "This is as far as I have gotten. But at least I have a name."

"I guess it's a good lead. So what do we do now?"

"I'm not sure exactly. But look at this." She opened the tab for the Wingate Winery website. "They're having a wine festival next week. The winery is near the town of Pine Ridge on Deep Lake."

"What are you thinking, Kate?" he asked guardedly. "I can see the wheels turning."

She shut down her computer, stood, and took both of his hands in hers. "Well ...."

He sighed. "Let's have some lunch and figure out if we have time to take a trip to Deep Lake," he said.

After lunch, Kate returned to her office. She and Ben had decided that they could take some time away from Howard's Walk for a quick trip and agreed that they deserved some time off anyway. But there was still one obstacle. She needed a cover if she really wanted to get to talk to Mr. Wingate. She could manage without one, but this would give her the opening she needed.

She accessed her email and typed a message to the generic business contact on the Wingate Winery website, introducing herself as a travel journalist who was planning a trip to Deep Lake and Pine Ridge over the week of the wine festival. She asked if she could interview Davis Wingate for her blog, listed several other wineries she had written about, and left her web address for them to verify her credentials. But she realized that he or someone on his staff might check out *The Wayfarer* before agreeing to an interview and learn more about her than she might want them to.

She opened her website in editor mode and searched for references to Howard's Walk and Eden Springs, anything personal that might alert them to who she was. Reluctantly, and with some effort and a bit of regret, she deleted what she found and republished it, knowing that it would just be a temporary change.

The email was completed but she could not manage to hit send. Was she doing the right thing? Was there enough evidence to warrant this intrusion into his life? If it ended up that she confronted him about the truth of who he was and he was not her father, the embarrassment would be unbearable. She went back over what she knew so far, and two things made the path clear for her. She had enough evidence that even if it turned out that they were not related, there might be some insight he could give that she couldn't get anywhere else. And, secondly, she and Ben deserved some time away from Howard's Walk. No matter what happened with Davis Wingate, the trip would give her great content for her blog. In the end, those were reasons enough for her. She took a deep breath and hit send.

Kate then Googled the rental situation for cottages on Deep Lake. The town of Pine Ridge was situated at the southern end of the lake and seemed charming. The lake itself was surrounded by hills covered with vineyards, reminding her of the picturesque wine country in France and Italy. She was immediately drawn to it from a visual perspective and hoped that the trip would work out.

There weren't a lot of rental openings even though summer had officially ended after Labor Day weekend. But she narrowed it down to cottages on the west side of the lake, closer to Wingate Winery. After making a few calls, she made a deposit on a cottage called *Summer Winds*. It had one bedroom and a beachfront with a dock. A motorboat and canoe were available, and it was only two miles from the town of Pine Ridge.

"A relaxing, cozy cottage on beautiful Deep Lake. All the amenities for the perfect getaway," the rental agency's website announced.

Kate read the description out loud and was already falling in love with the idea of a getaway with Ben at the quaint, lakeside cottage.

Later that evening, Kate's phone notified her of an email. It was from Suzy McNeill, a manager at the winery, who said Davis Wingate would be happy to do an interview with her. She said she would meet Kate on Monday, September 13 at 9 AM in the lobby of the winery, and she looked forward to meeting her.

Everything was falling into place. Her interview was scheduled, the cottage was rented, and Billy was back home with his mother. All the work at the gardens was covered for the next few days and finally, even though Kate knew it was secondary to her real reason for going, she and Ben were free to go on a much-needed vacation.

9

TWO DAYS LATER, Ben turned onto Pine Street, in Pine Ridge, New York, finally loosening his white-knuckle grip on the steering wheel of his truck. A drenching rain had followed them for the past two hours as they drove through the hills and valleys leading to the small lake town. Gray clouds hung like cement above them. Around them, a dense fog surged and retreated like a tide. Road markers and street signs were nearly invisible, and it was only the sound of the calm, reassuring voice from the GPS warning them of upcoming turns that kept them on the right roads.

Ben swiped at the windshield with his hand to clear the condensation and Kate reached over with the last paper towel on the roll to help. The truck's defogger had given out just as the rain started and they had battled with condensation inside since then.

Ben murmured his thanks to Kate and continued his slow crawl along Pine Street. He hit the brakes at a four-way stop as sheets of rain sluiced down the windshield, the wipers barely keeping up with the onslaught. Ben leaned forward, looked both ways, then crept through the intersection.

"Turn right onto Balsam Street, then turn left," the voice on the GPS announced serenely after two more blocks. Balsam Street took them past what appeared to be the town square. Kate squinted through the window and could make out a small gazebo in the center of it. She wished she could have had her first view of Pine Ridge on a sunnier day.

"Turn right onto Lake Street." Ben obeyed. *"Your destination is on the left."* The GPS voice was unconcerned with the downpour challenging them between the truck and the doorstep of the office where they were to meet their realtor, Molly Cameron.

"Thank you, Gertrude," Ben said to the lady in the GPS. He pulled into a parking spot in front of *Deep Lake Realty.*

It was a full minute before either of them could speak.

"Well, we're here," Ben said with no joy in his voice. He turned off the engine.

"Now how do we get inside without getting soaked?" Kate peered through the windshield and saw lights inside the office. "It looks like she's still here." She glanced at the time on her phone. "She said she'd wait for us." Kate had called when she realized they were going to be delayed. At the time, Molly's cheerful voice had reassured her that it was no problem.

There were only a few steps from the truck to the front door of the office, but the rain had still not let up. Ben reached into the back seat and grabbed their jackets. They struggled into them, pulled their hoods up, counted to three, and flung the doors open. Water sloshed around their ankles as they ran across the sidewalk.

Ben opened the door and a bell tinkled in greeting as they charged in. Two women looked up from their desks at the bedraggled visitors and jumped up to help them.

"Well, get inside and out of that rain," the shorter woman urged, "and take off those wet jackets. I'll hang them right over here."

Ben and Kate did as they were told, both glad to be out of their dripping wet coats.

"You must be Kate Tyler," the woman said, shaking Kate's damp hand. "I'm Molly Cameron. We spoke on the phone about the cottage, of course."

"Yes, and this is my boyfriend, Ben Evans," she said, linking her hand to Ben's.

"Nice to meet you, Ben. Well, I'm glad you made it here in one piece. This rain's been a doozy. You didn't have any trouble, I hope?" She wiped her hands on a flowing orange and purple skirt.

"The last two hours were the worst, but we made it okay," Ben said.

She ushered them to two chairs in front of a cluttered desk.

"Carol, get these folks some coffee. Or tea maybe?" she questioned them both.

"Tea please," they answered, and Carol hustled to the single-serve coffee maker in a room at the back of the office.

Molly settled heavily into a large office chair, squeaking it forward so that she could reach her desk. "So, you're from North Carolina, right?" she asked pushing aside messy piles of brochures and paper.

"Eden Springs," Kate answered. "It's a small town north of Winston-Salem."

"Never heard of it, but then I haven't traveled much out of the state. Why would I want to leave all this?" She waved her hand at the front door, setting off jangling silver and gold bracelets with the movement. A gust of wind rattled the pane-glass windows on the front of the building, and she frowned.

"Anyway," she said as she turned back to Kate and Ben, "welcome to Pine Ridge and Deep Lake. I'm glad you were able to find a cottage. Lots of folks still come to the lake in the fall and now with the wine festival, our rentals were almost all gone."

Carol was suddenly next to them, balancing two steaming mugs of tea on a small tray. They wrapped their hands around them and expressed their thanks.

"I just need a few forms signed," Molly said, searching her desk and drawers for a pen. She set a pair of bright red readers on her nose and peered through the rental documents before settling on several papers clipped together.

"Ah, here they are," she said, flipping to the last page and laying it on the desk in front of Kate. "Just sign here where it's tagged." She pointed at a blue-colored flag at the bottom of the page. Kate made a cursory look through the rest of the forms before signing since Molly had also sent them in an email the day before. She slid the packet back across the desk.

Molly twisted around behind her to reach a key organizer board, searched for a set labeled *Summer Winds,* and unhooked them. "Here are your keys," she said as she sorted through them, explaining each one. "This one's for the front and back doors, this one's for the storage shed on the beach, and this one's for the boat." She handed them to Kate. "Now all I need is the rest of your rental fee and we'll be all set."

Kate made a direct payment for the rest of their fee as Molly chattered about things to see and do in and around Deep Lake.

"Deep Lake Yacht Club is further down the lake and they're planning a regatta this week. It'll be the last one of the season. You don't want to miss that. And a Parade of Boats; that's always fun. There'll be music in the square this weekend. We have a nice little town band that plays in the gazebo; this will be their last performance of the year. All the restaurants are still open, of course. So you'll have plenty to do." She tapped a few keys on her keyboard to accept Kate's payment. "Oh, and don't forget to visit the wineries. The big event this week is the wine festival up at Wingate Winery. Art show, music, food, wine tastings, and wine competition. Delia Wingate has put on a great event every year for six years now since her husband passed. Are you planning on going to that?"

At hearing the name Wingate, Kate stiffened. She had been so focused on the drive to get to Pine Ridge that she had momentarily forgotten why she had come.

"Yes, we'll definitely want to do that." Kate wondered briefly if Molly might be a good source of information about the Wingates. "Do you know them, Molly? The Wingates?"

"Oh, sure," she said, waving her hand and setting off a new tinkling from her bracelets. "I remember when they first bought the winery. It's been quite a few years now. I knew the previous owners, the Tuttles, all my life. I'm born and raised in Pine Ridge, you know. It was hard to see them sell it when they retired. But Delia Wingate has done a good job there."

Kate was a bit puzzled; maybe she had assumed incorrectly that Davis Wingate was the driving force behind the success of the winery. And it seemed that the website emphasized that arrangement. But that wasn't the impression that Molly was giving.

Kate pulled a business card for *The Wayfarer* out of her pocket and laid it on the desk. "I'm going to be interviewing Davis Wingate while I'm here, for my blog. But maybe I should talk to Delia Wingate, too?"

Molly picked up the card, looking skeptical. "Well, I'm surprised you got an interview with Davis at all. You won't get one from his mother, that's for sure."

"Why's that?" Kate asked.

Molly leaned in. "Delia Wingate is in charge up there, make no mistake. Now, I'm not speaking ill of her. As I said, she's done a great job there and for Pine Ridge. But she's in charge and she likes it that way and has a lot of influence on what goes on in town and around the lake, ever since her husband Frank died. She's the matriarch now. But keeps to herself. Everything's about the business with her."

"What about the weather, Molly?" Ben asked. "This can't be good for all of those events."

"Oh, pish, this?" she said as if this were simply one of those April showers that brought May flowers. "This'll be out of here by tonight. They come through pretty strong since we're in a valley, but then they move on down the lake and are gone before we know it. You'll have a good week here, don't worry about that. Might be a bit chillier than what you're used to down south, but it's that time of year."

Ben and Kate said their goodbyes, put on their damp jackets, and headed back out to the truck. The rain had abated except for a lingering mist and fog, and Kate hoped that Molly was right about the weather.

Ben backed out of the parking space and followed Molly's directions down Lake Street to a Y in the road just outside of the town. It split off to the right onto Lake Road, which followed the lake's shoreline, and Hilltop Road on the left which appeared to lead up into the countryside, although at that moment the wet pavement leading up the hill disappeared into the dense fog.

"So that was interesting," Kate said as Ben took the road to their right. "I wonder how Suzy McNeill was able to get me an interview with Davis Wingate so easily. Maybe I could interview Delia Wingate. She doesn't sound very approachable, though."

"No, she doesn't. But it seems like she would be available because of the event. Maybe you can arrange something—if things work out, I mean."

"Sure," Kate replied and refocused on locating their cottage. A few minutes later, the sign for *Summer Winds* appeared on their right. Their parking spot was across the road from the lake, and Ben did a U-turn and pulled into it.

"Here we go again," Ben said, looking at the water rivulets running down the bank next to them and across the road from the receding rain.

They made their way to the back door of the cottage with their bags and went inside.

"Ben, what if this is a trap or something?"

He lifted an eyebrow. "A trap? The cottage?"

"No, not the cottage," she said, puzzled.

He shut the door and locked it. "Then what do you mean?"

Kate took off her wet shoes and set them aside on a small area rug. "What if Mrs. Wingate knows about this interview and is planning to sabotage it? Molly said she liked to be in control of things and here I come barging in at the last minute. I just don't like it."

"I think you'll be fine. The lady that set it up seemed okay, right?" Kate nodded. "So, you'll just go there on Monday and see what happens."

"I guess you're right."

He hugged her. "I'm just glad we're finally here. I'm beat. Let's get settled in. Molly said there was food in the refrigerator and coffee, right?" He opened the refrigerator and found cold cuts and salads. A bag of rolls was nearby on a butcher block island. He rubbed his hands together, eager to dive into a few meaty sandwiches.

Kate picked up their bags. "I'll unpack while you make something to eat?"

"Sounds good."

"And coffee, please!" she said over her shoulder as she found her way down the hall to the bedroom.

While Kate was finally beginning to relax from the stressful drive to Deep Lake, thoughts of the reason they were here crept into her mind. She might be getting closer to the truth of her origins. Or was she hoping for too much from this trip? Would she have to go home empty-handed with no answers for Billy?

10

EARLY THE NEXT MORNING, strands of mist rose wraith-like from Deep Lake's blue surface and the sun began to stream pinks and reds into the sky over the eastern hills. The brilliant hues of the emerging day slowly filtered into the cottage. The rain from the day before had passed through as Molly had predicted and if the sunrise was any indication, it was going to be a spectacular day.

Kate paused at the kitchen window. The day broke over the hills and the lake sparkled like diamonds as the mist slowly lifted. Water, whether a lake or a stream, or the ocean, always had a calming influence on her. Despite its ever-changing appearance in color and temperament, there was a constancy to it that was reassuring. Maybe Deep Lake was exactly the right place for her at this moment. Maybe the answers she sought were here, right in front of her.

She took the last sip of a protein shake and rinsed the glass in the kitchen's large farmhouse sink. The morning light filtering in through the windows of the living room brightened the small cottage and Kate took in details she hadn't noticed when they arrived the night before. The interior of their getaway spot was the perfect balance of modern convenience and cozy vintage decor. A small kitchen sat at one end of a long room extending across the cottage's front. The walls were white pine, the floor a dark shiny wood planking, and the low ceiling was finished with reclaimed wood planks. A sofa in the living area faced an expanse of windows that looked out over the lake.

Several white wicker chairs and rockers with chintz cushions were placed throughout the room. A tall vase of sunflowers sat on the dining room table, no doubt another thoughtful touch from Molly.

Kate planned on a long jog that morning and hoped the exertion would help center her. She tucked her ponytail into a ball cap, laced up her running shoes, and joined Ben on the wide deck that extended across the entire length of the cottage. He stood at the railing, already dressed and on his second cup of coffee.

"What a gorgeous morning," she said, taking in the sounds of small waves lapping onto the shale beach. A motorboat far out on the lake created a white-tipped wake that disappeared in the expanse of water before reaching the shore. She wrapped her arms around Ben's waist, and he clasped her hands.

"It is," Ben said. He turned around to face her. "Are you ready for your jog?"

"Yes, but I wish you could come with me."

"Wish I could, too, but I don't trust my knee yet. The long drive yesterday didn't help it, and Doc said no running for another couple of weeks."

"Okay. So, I need to find a good spot to run." Kate had decided that the shoreline itself was not the right route for a jog; too many cottages, docks, boats, and other lake paraphernalia to block her path. Lake Road, where their cottage was located, followed the length of Deep Lake on both sides and at most points didn't have enough shoulder for joggers to safely maneuver on foot, especially at sunrise.

She pulled a small map of the area out of her pocket, spread it out on the table, and pointed to a road marked with a county route number. "This road might work. It looks like it's out in the country without a lot of traffic. I'm ready if you are."

They climbed the rickety stairs up to the narrow two-lane Lake Road and crossed over it to Ben's truck. After backtracking to Pine Ridge, Kate directed him to turn right onto Hilltop Road. Ben negotiated several steep curves, but the road finally leveled out and the countryside opened up.

Kate rolled down her window. She was immediately hit with the lush aroma of ripened grapes. Acres of vineyards extended on either side of the road. Bunches of deep purple and pale green grapes hung heavily in the shade of the dark green grape leaves, nearing time for harvest. The sound of an occasional tractor floated to her from a distance. Men and women dotted the vineyards, walking between the grape rows and working among the vines.

Ben soon slowed the truck and parked on a widened place in the road where a sign pointed to a scenic overlook. They walked up a slight hill and stepped onto the flat roof of a small cement block building. A quaint wrought iron railing wrapped the perimeter of the roof.

From their perch on the overlook, past the slopes of rolling green hills, vineyards, and woods, Deep Lake spread out before them. It was a long narrow lake, seventeen miles from one end to the other as Kate had discovered in her research, so neither end of it was visible from their vantage point. An occasional cloud passed overhead, creating a shadow over the azure water. The entire colorful scene was displayed before them as if painted on a canvas.

They took selfies with the beautiful panorama in the background, and Ben took a video sweep of the lake while Kate narrated for her blog. After a few minutes of taking in the view, then stretching and tightening her laces, they left their perch on the overlook and Kate kissed Ben goodbye.

"You're sure you don't want me to wait for you here?" Ben asked.

"I'll be fine. Give me about an hour."

"Okay. I'm going into town to see if I can get the truck's defogger fixed," he said. "But call me when you're ready to be picked up."

Kate agreed and began her run along the edge of the macadam.

She ran steadily for about a mile when a movement to her right caught her attention. A cyclist sped out of a dirt driveway and swerved in front of her. She quickly stepped off the road to avoid being hit but lost her balance and fell sideways, unable to catch herself before falling. The cyclist didn't stop and soon disappeared around a curve in the road.

After the shock of the fall, Kate got her bearings and realized that she was sitting in a shallow ditch on a pile of wet grass and weeds. They had softened her landing but when she attempted to sit up, pain shot through her right ankle and wrist. She lowered herself back down into the grass and waited for the initial shock to wear off. After a while, she was finally able to maneuver herself into a better sitting position. Then, with her good leg and arm, she hauled herself back up to the road. She winced at putting weight on her ankle and glanced down to assess the damage. It was already beginning to swell. Nothing felt broken, but she knew she could never make it very far without some help and there was no one in sight. Other than the cyclist, she hadn't seen any other vehicles and there weren't any homes or businesses that she could see. She was surrounded by peaceful, wide-open, uninhabited, unhelpful countryside.

Kate noticed a small sign across the road and hobbled over to it. She was surprised to see that the road that the cyclist had careened out of was an entrance to the Wingate Winery. But this wasn't the entrance she had seen on the website when she had researched the place. It wasn't the entrance leading up to a grand building with a large patio across the front and a lawn tailor-made for festivals and events. This must have been the back entrance, the one that suppliers and grape trucks and out-of-control cyclists used.

She reached for her phone to call Ben but discovered that it was not in her pocket. She limped back across the road and saw it balanced on a few small branches just inches above the water. It appeared to be dry, but it was nowhere within her reach, especially in her condition.

As she debated a very small set of options, she noticed a man approaching on a golf cart. He bumped along the macadam, slowing as he came closer. The cart shuddered to a stop a few feet away and the man twisted himself out of the cart. He was tall, over six feet, with the wide shoulders and broad chest of a linebacker. She guessed he was in his forties and probably made his living working in one of the vineyards nearby since his clothes were dirt-stained and worn. He had a brownish-red beard and mustache, both neatly trimmed, but it was his eyes that caught her by surprise as he came closer. They reminded her of the azure color of the lake in the morning and seemed entirely out of place in the rugged image he projected.

Kate then realized with alarm who the man was. This was Davis Wingate himself. She wasn't prepared for an accidental meeting with the man who could be her father. She felt dizzy and faint as he came closer.

The man stepped forward quickly to catch her before she toppled to the ground, and she flinched at his firm grip. She noticed his assessment of the mud and grass splashed down her right side and the way she was favoring her right leg.

"Can I help you?" he said.

She almost refused but realized that would be a ridiculous move. With no way to call Ben, she had to accept his offer.

"Yes," she stammered. "I guess I could use some help. I was jogging and a cyclist came out of this driveway and almost hit me. I fell into the ditch trying to avoid him," she said, pointing behind her.

"Wait here," he said, and he walked back to the golf cart. He unhooked an attached trailer and pulled the cart up next to Kate.

"Is there someone you can call?" he asked as he helped her into the seat.

"Yes. But I'm afraid my phone fell into the ditch. I was afraid to reach for it."

Mr. Wingate peered into the ditch and inched his way down through the slippery weeds. He grabbed the phone, brushed it off, and handed it to Kate.

"You're lucky. Doesn't look like it got wet, so that's good," he said.

"Thank you. I'm sorry to put you to all this trouble."

"No problem."

She dialed Ben's number, and he answered on the first ring. She briefly explained where she was, but Mr. Wingate interrupted. "I think you need attention to that ankle. Ask him to come down this road to the winery," he said, pointing across the road. "We'll be on the patio down there at the house so he should be able to see you."

"He'll be here soon enough. I don't mind waiting here," she declared, not knowing who else she might run into at his house. She definitely was not prepared for that.

He shook his head. "You need to get some ice on it. We can take care of that down at the house."

When she began to object, he held up his hand. "No arguments."

Kate knew Ben was worried at this point, after overhearing her conversation with Mr. Wingate. "I heard what he said and he's probably right. I'll be there as soon as I can." Kate gave him general directions past where he had dropped her off and told him to look for the small sign to Wingate Winery on his right.

Mr. Wingate turned the cart around and they bumped and braked their way down the long, rutted dirt road towards a group of buildings Kate assumed were the working parts of the winery. She was already getting an idea of the type of man Mr. Wingate was. He was used to taking charge and fixing things. He was used to people doing what he expected them to do. And right now, she was at his mercy.

"I really appreciate the help, Mr. Wingate," Kate said.

He turned to her with a puzzled look on his face. "Have we met?"

"Uh, no, actually, we haven't but we're supposed to. Your manager, Suzy McNeill, set up an appointment for an interview tomorrow. I'm Kate Tyler, from *The Wayfarer*. It's my travel blog." She glanced over at him, waiting for a response, a facial expression, some hint of recognition. But he surprised her with a smile, barely visible underneath his bushy red beard. His eyes showed it too, crinkling at the edges.

"Well, if Suzy gave you the okay then I'm looking forward to it."

The mud and wet grass were beginning to dry on her joggers and Kate tried to brush off what she could. It was a sad attempt to restore some professionalism, and she realized that the moment had passed.

"I honestly didn't know I was at your back door," she said, trying to make light of the situation and hoping she wasn't coming across as trying too hard. But her voice sounded shrill and nervous to herself, and she took a deep breath to calm down.

"What exactly happened?" Mr. Wingate said.

"I was looking for a quiet road to do my morning jog and then this guy came out of nowhere."

He immediately apologized for the incident. "I think I know who was on the bike and I can take care of it if you like."

Kate wasn't sure what taking care of it meant to him, but she didn't think she would want to be on the receiving end.

"I just need to go home and get cleaned up." But they had already pulled into the paved driveway of a large house situated not far from the winery. He helped Kate to a chair on the patio and told her to wait there. She knew he expected her to comply.

He went into the house and soon returned with an ice pack and a roll of ace bandages. He lifted her leg onto a low table and laid the ice on it. "Leave that on for a while and then I'll wrap it up. Anything else hurting?"

Kate rotated her wrist gently and realized it was not hurting as much, so she said she was fine otherwise. He reached into a nearby cooler and pulled out a bottle of cold water and handed it to her.

"This isn't how I expected to be meeting you, Mr. Wingate," she said. "I'm sorry to be taking you away from your work."

He waved his hand. "No worries. And call me Davis. We can reschedule our interview if you need to."

"No," she said quickly, and thought he noticed her sharp reply. "I mean, I appreciate that. But I'd like to stay on track. I don't want you to have to rearrange your schedule."

He looked skeptical but agreed. "Let's take a look at that ankle. And don't worry. I'm on the Pine Ridge EMS squad as a volunteer so I know some first aid."

He took the ice pack off and had her stand and put a bit of weight on the leg. It felt better, but he insisted on wrapping it anyway. Soon she was able to walk around the patio to test it out.

The sound of Ben's truck slowly made its way down the driveway. She waved at him, and he pulled in next to the golf cart and got out. He hurried over to her.

"Kate, are you okay?"

"I'm fine, thanks to Davis. Davis, this is my boyfriend, Ben."

Davis Wingate reached out his hand and Ben shook it.

"Pleased to meet you, Ben."

Kate saw the look on Ben's face as if he were asking, *"Really? It's him?"*

"Uh, yes, sir. It's a pleasure to meet you. And thanks for helping Kate."

"No problem. Well, Kate, if you're okay, I have some things to attend to. Stay here as long as you need to, but I'll let Ben take it from here."

"Of course. And thank you so much. I'll see you tomorrow at nine?" Kate said.

"Tomorrow at nine," he said with a smile, got back into the golf cart, and headed back up the driveway to resume the work Kate had interrupted.

After Kate insisted she didn't want to wait there any longer, Ben helped her to the truck, and she carefully climbed inside.

"Wow, Kate," he said as he started the truck.

"Yes, wow. I can't believe this happened." She needed air and rolled her window down.

"Are you okay? I mean with meeting him like that?"

"I guess. I was so surprised it was actually him."

"He seems nice enough though," Ben suggested carefully.

She shook her head. "He doesn't know who I am so I guess he would be nice to anyone in that situation. Let's just go back to the cottage. I should get some more ice on this ankle."

Despite her doubts about the man, Kate realized that she had been given an unexpected insight into Davis Wingate, possibly the person at the heart of her search. That would be considered a gift for any interviewer, and she knew she shouldn't waste it.

A dip into a muddy ditch and a twisted ankle was a small price to pay.

11

BEN TURNED ONTO HILLTOP ROAD. Kate winced in pain with each pothole and Ben slowed the truck.

"Tell me what happened," he said, his eyes narrowed in concern.

Kate drew in a breath as she repositioned the ice pack on her ankle. "Some guy on a bike flew out of that dirt road, the one that went down to the winery, and he almost hit me. I was trying to get out of his way and fell into the ditch."

"Wait, you mean it was a motorcycle?"

"No," she reassured him. "A bicycle biker. It was an old one, too, from what I could tell. And he wasn't wearing a helmet. He didn't look like a serious biker."

"Serious or not, he was being reckless. And he must have seen you fall."

"Maybe. I'm not sure though. I was too busy trying to figure out what happened myself." Ben slowed to a stop at the intersection with Lake Road.

"We can find an urgent care clinic if you want to get an x-ray. There's probably one in town."

"No, let's just see how it goes this afternoon. I think I just need to keep it elevated and iced."

He nodded and turned left. After a few minutes, he pulled into the parking spot above *Summer Winds* and turned off the engine. He turned to face Kate.

"It must have been a shock to meet Davis Wingate like that. Do you want to talk about it?"

"I don't know." Kate shrugged. Then she tipped her head, her eyes quizzing him. "But you said he seemed nice. I'm not so sure about that. I was probably on his property and maybe that was one of his employees on the bike. Maybe he was just trying to cover his own butt. Maybe it was all an act."

"I guess that could be the case," Ben said carefully.

"And you saw the size of him. Just like Billy. Big and strong. And his eyes? They were blue, just like Billy's." A lump formed in her throat, and she fought back tears.

Ben got out of the truck and walked to the passenger side door. "Okay, so all that could be true," he said, helping Kate maneuver herself to the ground. "But it could be a coincidence, right? I mean, you can't be sure, at least not yet."

She glared at him. "No, Ben. I think this is a man who likes to be in control of people. He takes charge. He makes things go his way. I can tell."

Ben's look told her he wasn't following what she was saying. "But how is that connected to ...," he started.

Frustrated, Kate snapped back. "He takes charge. What he wants is what he gets. And what he doesn't want, he probably just throws it aside."

Ben placed his hands on her shoulders. "But he doesn't know who you are. He was helping you when you were hurt. That counts for something, right? And I can read between the lines of what you're saying. He was what, seventeen years old when this happened? Maybe it wasn't his choice at all. Maybe he didn't have a choice but to leave his name off the birth certificate. And, besides, you don't know yet if it's even him."

Kate shook his hands off. He wasn't understanding what she was going through. He couldn't possibly understand how she felt. There was a connection to this man. She wasn't imagining it. She had experienced this when she met Billy for the first time, as if there were an invisible thread that stretched between them. Of course, she couldn't be sure yet. But if Davis Wingate was connected to her, she didn't want that thread to break. Not yet. There was too much at stake.

The throbbing in her ankle matched her heartbeat and she took a deep breath. She knew Ben meant well and always wanted the best for her. But at the moment she had more immediate concerns.

Ben said, "Kate, look, I know this is hard for you. I get that. But I'm not the enemy here. You know that, right?"

Reluctantly, she nodded. "I know." She looked both ways up and down the road. "Right now, I just need to take care of my ankle." They waited for a car to pass. Ben helped her across the road, and they navigated the steep steps to the main floor of *Summer Winds*. She hobbled to the deck, settling into a chaise lounge to stretch out her leg. Ben brought her a fresh makeshift ice pack wrapped in a towel and arranged it on her ankle.

He leaned up against the railing. "You haven't said how Davis happened to come along."

"Everything happened so fast," she said. "I had just managed to get myself out of the ditch and he drove up in a golf cart. I don't think he saw what happened, but he stopped when he saw me standing there. I mean, I looked like I had just crawled out of a ditch, right?"

Kate saw a brief smile cross Ben's face and was grateful for it. He knew her well enough to realize that she had to work through this in her own head before she could admit that he had a good point, too. He was reasonable when she was reactionary, and calm in the midst of her panic.

"Are you sure you want to do the interview tomorrow with everything that's happened?"

"Oh, yes, I'm sure," Kate said vehemently.

Ben sighed. "You could have rescheduled."

"No. I'm lucky I got an appointment with him at all with everything he has going on right now. I'll be fine." She saw the concerned look on Ben's face and reached out her hand to him. He took it and sat down on the lounge chair next to her.

"I'm sorry, Ben. This has all been a lot for me to take in."

"It's okay. I know it's been hard."

"I'm glad you'll be there, too, for the wine classes." Ben had signed up for the Introduction to Winemaking class at the winery that was part of the six-day festival. He and Kate had been thinking of planting a few rows of grapevines on the property and making their own wine with the Howard's Walk label, but neither one of them knew much about the process. He jumped at the chance to sign up.

"Me, too. But right now, I'm hungry. How about you?"

Kate wobbled her hand. "Not very, but I guess I should eat something."

Ben retreated to the kitchen and soon returned with toasted bagels and cream cheese from the supply Molly had left for them. After they finished eating, Ben carried their plates into the kitchen. Kate picked up a pair of binoculars from the table beside her. She hadn't noticed it before, but off to the left, in the middle of the lake, there was an island. It appeared to be uninhabited as she scanned across it, although she knew there could be cottages or houses on the other side. There were no docks or boat ramps leading into the water that she could see. The shoreline was strewn with large boulders that would prevent an easy landing.

She lowered the binoculars and closed her eyes. A light breeze with the promise of autumn flitted across her face. They had been at the cottage for less than twenty-four hours and already things had gone sideways, and she and Ben were at odds with each other. She hated that feeling. This trip together was a luxury and was the first time since they met that they had been able to get away together for more than a weekend.

Have we already ruined our time together? Ben was the most understanding man she had ever known. He was thoughtful but not afraid to say what was on his mind and he was as invested in this trip as she was. She was determined to make it up to him.

She opened her eyes and flexed her ankle. The ice pack fell off and she stood tentatively, putting as little weight on her leg as possible. The swelling had gone down a bit, and she walked to the deck railing, testing it out.

She heard Ben behind her. "Feeling better?"

She nodded. "I'm not running a marathon any time soon but the swelling's gone down."

She limped around the deck. Ben had brought more ice and she reluctantly sat down again and laid it over her ankle. He pulled another lounge chair next to her and stretched out onto it.

"Sometimes it's hard to slow down and just take a day off," he mused. "We've been going non-stop for the last year without a lot of breaks. Maybe we just need to sit here, relax, and enjoy the view today. No agenda, no worries. Tomorrow will be here soon enough."

"I was thinking the same thing, actually. We'll take time to explore the lake and see what Pine Ridge has to offer when my ankle is better. Maybe we can take the boat over to that island," she said, handing the binoculars to Ben. "See, over there, up the lake a ways."

"Looks deserted," he said.

"I thought so, too. I wonder what it's called." She searched for information about it on her phone. "What a coincidence," she said and held the phone out for Ben to see what she had found.

"Wingate Island," he said, handing the binoculars back to her. "I guess we shouldn't be surprised."

12

THE NEXT MORNING, Kate checked herself in the bedroom's full-length mirror. Today was the day she would interview Davis Wingate. She didn't know where it would lead but from the time she woke up, she had been trying to talk herself into a confident and professional state of mind. She tugged a dark blue skirt into place, re-tucked a cream-colored blouse, and shrugged into a light blue sweater. Taking another look in the mirror, she rearranged her clothes and tucked a stray wisp of hair into place. The swelling in her ankle had mostly subsided overnight and she was able to slip on a pair of flats. Professional yet approachable was the look she was going for. She hoped she had gotten it right.

In the mirror, she noticed Ben walking up behind her.

"Wow, you look great," he said, nuzzling her neck. "I like your hair up this way."

"Thank you," she said, still pulling at her skirt. "It only took me about an hour to get it right."

"Well, it was worth it. You're going to knock his socks off."

She shook her head. "All I want to do is redeem myself from the mess I was yesterday. That wasn't the look I wanted to have at our first meeting."

"You're going to be great." He turned her to face him. "Have you thought about how you'll do the interview yet?"

"Just all afternoon and all night. Maybe it was good that I'd met him already, even though it wasn't under the best of circumstances. But it's not something I can prepare for. I guess

I'll have to wing it." She sighed in frustration and adjusted her blouse again.

"Hey, listen, you've got this. And I'll be nearby."

"Thanks. That helps." She smiled at him. "But you're right. I'm a professional. I've done this a million times. I do have questions about the winery, and I can easily work my way into asking him a bit about his personal life. I might not get all the answers I want today but maybe I can get to know him better, right?"

"Right. Now, I should be there by nine for my first class. Are you ready?"

"As ready as I'll ever be." She checked herself one more time in the mirror and didn't find anything else to fix. She grabbed her tote bag and they left the cottage.

Ben followed Kate's directions to the public entrance of the winery and parked the truck.

They got out and walked across a paved parking lot toward three large buildings that sat side by side up a slight hill. The land gradually sloped away from the buildings down through acres of vineyards, fallow fields, then woods, and eventually, to Deep Lake, about a mile away. She scanned the view with her camera, narrating for her blog as she went. The lake was like glass that morning, a bright blue that matched the color of the sky. The air was crisp and fresh but from where they stood, it held a fruity aroma from the acres of ripening grapes surrounding them. Kate breathed it in deeply, committing it to memory.

Soon, they took a wide stone stairway up to a patio that stretched across the front of the most imposing structure in the middle of the three buildings Kate assumed was the main winery. Bright yellow chrysanthemums in large clay pots brought color to the stone terrace. Several small glass tables with red umbrellas had been set up, and Kate imagined that guests would soon be settling in to enjoy a glass of wine with the stunning view of

Deep Lake and the rolling hills just beginning to show a hint of fall colors.

"Is he meeting you inside?" Ben asked as he put his hand on Kate's back.

"No, I'm supposed to meet Suzy McNeill, the woman I emailed to arrange the interview. She said she would meet me in the main lobby at nine."

"Let's go then," Ben said.

Ben pulled on the ornate handle of the heavily carved entry door, and they stepped into a large room filled with wine and gift displays and seating areas of comfortable leather couches and chairs. High-top tables were interspersed throughout the room for wine tastings. Built-in wine racks stretched across the back wall of the space, the highly polished wood reflecting the sunlight pouring in from large windows at each end of the room.

A clock in the distance rang out the hour. At the last chime, a woman approached them, hands outstretched and smiling.

"You must be Kate Tyler," she said, shaking Kate's hand. "I'm Suzy McNeill. And this is?" she asked, looking at Ben.

"This is my boyfriend, Ben Evans."

Suzy shook his hand warmly. She was a petite woman; Kate guessed her to be in her early sixties with white hair cut in a style that gave her a much younger look. Her smile reached her eyes as she talked, and Kate immediately felt at ease.

"Welcome to Wingate Winery. I'm so pleased to meet you both. Mr. Wingate isn't quite ready yet and apologizes for the delay, but he'll be with you shortly. In the meantime, why don't we have a seat over here." She led them to a couch nearby.

"Ms. McNeill, I'm scheduled for the Winemaking Class," Ben said before they sat down. "Can you direct me to where that will be?"

"Please, call me Suzy. And of course. It's right down that hall," she said, pointing to her left. "You'll see the Cabernet Room where they'll be gathering. I know you'll enjoy it."

Ben thanked her, gave Kate a look of encouragement and a quick hug, and said he would see her later.

Suzy motioned for Kate to take a seat and sat down next to her. "Now, Kate, tell me a bit about yourself."

Kate knew from their email exchange that Suzy was a manager at the winery, overseeing the tasting room and personal schedule for Davis Wingate. She seemed well suited for the job; efficient, friendly, and very likable. But Kate knew she could not be completely open with the woman, or anyone at the winery for that matter, and gave only a vague version of her background. Suzy told her what the expectations were for coverage of the festival, which were reasonable. Kate knew her obligation was to focus on her reporting as much as her real reason for being there at the winery.

They hadn't talked for long when a young woman approached. She was as tall as Kate and model thin. Her blond hair was long and straight with bangs that were casually tied back from her face with a simple rubber band.

"Abby, I'm so glad you stopped by." Suzy turned to introduce Kate. "This is Kate Tyler, from *The Wayfarer*. She'll be interviewing your father. Kate, this is Mr. Wingate's daughter, Abby."

A daughter? Kate was at a loss for words and tried to hide her surprise. For some reason, she had never entertained the thought that there might be other children in the picture, and having this young woman standing in front of her now threw her off. But Abby grinned, grabbed Kate's hand, pulled her to her feet, and hugged her tightly as if they were old friends.

"I'm so glad to meet you!" she said after releasing Kate. "I'd love to travel and do what you do. Well, that would be my dream job, but I've only been to a few places out of the country.

And only to visit wineries with my mom and dad. I mean, that was great and all but there's so much more I want to see and experience."

As Abby rambled on, Kate guessed that she was in her mid-twenties. Her big blue eyes sparkled with enthusiasm. She wore a fuzzy white cropped sweater with slim-leg jeans and boots, a style that suited her. Kate couldn't help but smile at Abby's eagerness and the way she engaged with her so quickly. She realized Abby was still talking and refocused.

"Are you going to be here long? Maybe we can talk about how I could get into the business?"

Kate had to think quickly. In truth, she had no idea how long she would be staying or under what circumstances it might be. But Abby was too eager for Kate to refuse her request.

"Of course," she assured her. "I should be here for a few more days. I'm sure we can find a time to get together."

"Thank you so much!" Abby said eagerly.

Kate noticed Suzy checking her phone.

"Well, I think Mr. Wingate is ready for your interview now, Kate," Suzy said. "Would you follow me, please?"

Kate did. Abby walked along with them.

"Dad said I could sit in on the interview," Abby declared. "I hope you don't mind."

Kate was deflated at that news. This changed everything, and she hadn't even gotten started. But she put a smile on her face and hoped it looked genuine.

"Sure, that would be great!"

The three women walked down a long hallway and stopped at the last door on the left. Suzy knocked and entered. Davis Wingate stood up from a large roll-top desk and greeted them. The work clothes were gone, traded in for khaki pants and a white shirt. But it reinforced Kate's opinion of him; a man of many sides and one who was comfortable leading a successful winery, yet not afraid to get his hands dirty in the soil of a vineyard.

He stood, kissed Abby on the cheek, and shook hands with Kate. "Good morning, Ms. Tyler. I hope your ankle is better?"

"It is, thank you. And please, call me Kate." She managed to get the words out as her mind raced, so conflicted with thoughts about how to act and what to say. There was no road map for this moment. Yesterday, she had been carried along by the sudden events after her run-in with the cyclist. Now she was face to face with him again and needed to be coherent and inquisitive and professional. But she felt none of those things.

"Thanks again for helping me out yesterday. You were a lifesaver," she said, at least thinking to start with a bit of well-deserved gratitude.

"No problem at all. Glad I could help. And I apologize for the incident." He moved to a small round table near a large window that looked out over a few short rows of grapes. The table was set with two bottles of wine, a plate of cheese and crackers, and three wine glasses.

"Dad," Abby started eagerly as they sat. "Kate said she and I could get together and talk about the travel business sometime."

Davis smiled indulgently at his daughter. "That sounds great, Abby." He turned back to Kate. "My daughter thinks the world is waiting for her. But I'm hoping that you might be honest about what it takes to do the type of work you do. I don't imagine it's all you see in the blogs and magazines."

"Well, you're right about that," Kate agreed. "It can be challenging at times. But," she said, unable to suppress a smile towards Abby, "if it's something you love to do, then it's not really work." Kate understood the need to wander, discover new places, and meet new people. She had always known deep down in her bones that it was going to be part of her life and was lucky that no one had ever tried to crush her dreams. She would hate to see that happen to Abby.

"See Dad? That's what you always say about the winery. 'Find your passion, or do what you love to do, and you'll never work a day in your life'."

"Yes, I have said that. But," he reached for one of the bottles on the table, "Kate is here for an interview. And I never sit down with a guest without offering a glass of wine. I have a dry Riesling and a Cabernet Franc. Any preference if it's not too early for you?"

"I would love a small glass, thanks," Kate agreed, thinking it would be rude to refuse. "I think the Riesling would be perfect. Can you tell me about it?"

He uncorked the bottle. As Kate watched, she realized that Davis Wingate was a man of opposites. His build, six foot two inches of broad shoulders and muscular tattooed arms, a beard, and short cropped hair, reminded her of a Scottish warrior who should have been holding a shield and spear instead of wine in fine crystal. But this was his world, and she found herself intrigued by him, regardless of who he might or might not be in her life.

"Of course. This is a 2020 vintage, made from Riesling grapes we grow here on the estate, aged in stainless steel; it's an off-dry wine, not too dry and not too sweet, and pairs well with spicy dishes." He poured a glass for himself and then for Abby.

Kate nodded as she sipped. "I'm no expert but I do know that sometimes Rieslings are used for ice wines. Do you also make those?"

"You're right. We do produce small batches of ice wine from our Rieslings. Please, have some cheese and crackers."

Kate's stomach was in knots, as she struggled to make casual conversation. She wasn't sure how she would react to the wine at that hour of the morning. But she took another small sip and a bite of a cracker to be polite. Her hand shook as she returned the glass to the table, and she hoped Davis hadn't noticed. But he was continuing with an explanation of ice wines as he swirled the Riesling in his glass.

"Ice wines are made from grapes that have been frozen while still on the vine. The water in the grape freezes and this gives a more concentrated grape juice. We press the must, which is the fruit juice that contains the skins, seeds, and stems of the grapes, so the juice is more concentrated and very sweet. Then ...."

"Dad," Abby interrupted, "isn't Kate here to interview you? Right, Kate?"

"Oh, no, Abby, this is perfect," Kate assured her. "It's fascinating." She pulled a small tape recorder out of her tote. "Do you mind if I use this for the rest of our interview?"

Davis said he didn't mind at all, and Kate turned it on. As he finished talking about ice wines, she gathered her thoughts again and started with questions about the wine festival that week.

"I read that it was also a fundraiser. Can you tell me about that?"

Davis revealed that the funds raised would go to scholarships for students at Cornell University in their viticulture program.

"There are so many talented young people that want to study wine growing but don't have the funds to do it. This helps."

Kate made a note in her notebook. *Generous philanthropist.*

"It's called the Frank Wingate Scholarship, in memory of my father. He passed away in 2017."

"I'm so sorry to hear that. But what a wonderful legacy."

Davis nodded and continued to talk about all the events that had been planned for the Frank L. Wingate Wine Festival and Competition: wine tastings, a wine judging event for local vintners, and art created by local artists celebrating the beauty of Deep Lake. And of course, the winemaking classes. Kate mentioned that her boyfriend Ben had enrolled in them and almost made the mistake of telling Davis why he was taking them. But she caught herself. Davis didn't need to know that it was for the Gardens at Howard's Walk. Besides, this interview was about him, not her.

"The judging is really just a chance for all of us to get together in friendly rivalry and learn from the judges," he continued. "We're all here to help each other when we need it."

A generous philanthropist. No doubt a leader in the area wine industry. A member of the Pine Ridge EMS Squad and fixer of sprained ankles. Was there anything wrong with this man? Kate needed to delve further into his personal life. She decided to try another approach.

"How did you decide to go into the winemaking business?"

"Well, as you may or may not know, I grew up in North Carolina. I had traveled some in Europe as a teenager and fell in love with wines and winemaking. At that time, North Carolina didn't have much of a wine industry, nothing like what they have now. So, after I got my degree in business, I went on to Cornell University here in Ithaca, New York, to study viticulture and learned that the European grapes did very well here in the area around Deep Lake. I had never expected to own a winery. I planned to be a winemaker, maybe in France or Italy. And I did that for a few years. But my parents had a different idea. My father bought Tuttle's Winery, renamed it Wingate Winery, hired the best winemaker he could, and revamped everything. And it's grown to what you see here today."

"So it's a family-owned and run business?"

"Yes, my wife Marie and I and my mother, Delia. And of course, Abby will, if she chooses to go that direction."

Abby frowned. "Maybe someday, Dad. But while I'm young, traveling the world is what I really want to do."

Kate searched her brain for more questions. With Abby there, she couldn't follow the line of questioning that she had hoped to. Even if it had led to her being asked to leave the property and never come back, she felt emboldened enough to take the opening if it had presented itself. But she simply could not find a way to pursue it now. Not with Abby there. She let it go and went on with a generic line of questions.

"What wine are you most proud of? Is there one that you will be entering into the competition?"

Davis talked for a few more minutes about his wines but Kate saw him glance at his watch. It had been almost an hour. She had plenty to write about in her blog, but her real goal for the morning had been completely defeated. When Davis finished talking, she turned off the recorder.

"I've taken up enough of your time. Thank you so much. I can't wait to write this up for my blog. It should drop tomorrow."

"You are staying for the festival, right?" Abby said.

"Of course. I wouldn't miss it." The truth was, she couldn't leave Deep Lake yet. She had to find another way to get the information she was after. It wasn't for her; it was for Billy, and she couldn't let him down.

13

AFTER LEAVING DAVIS'S OFFICE, Kate followed Abby down the dark paneled hall to the lobby. As they walked, Kate noticed a gallery of photos along one wall, some black and white from an earlier era at the winery, long before it was bought by the Wingate family, and color photos from more recent years. She paused and looked at one of the framed pictures, a family photo, Kate presumed, of the Wingate clan.

Abby stopped next to her. "I was just a baby in this picture. That's my mom holding me, and my dad of course," she explained, pointing to the younger couple. She moved her finger across the photo. "This is Nana Delia and Papa Frank. And that's Uncle Briggs in the middle."

"You have an uncle?" Kate asked, immediately thinking that this man might be another source of information.

"Yes, Dad's younger brother."

"He didn't mention him during the interview. Does he work at the winery, too?"

Abby hesitated. "No, at least not all the time. Just sometimes when he's around." She reached out to touch the photo again, a wistful look on her face. "He travels a lot. In fact, he's away now."

Kate studied the features of everyone in the picture. They were all smiling and appeared happy except for the man Abby pointed out as her Uncle Briggs. He had a faraway look, not engaged with the photographer at all. Unlike everyone else in the picture. Kate wondered why Abby seemed sad when speaking of him.

"I would love to talk to him, too," Kate said as casually as she could. "Do you think he'll be here for the festival this week?"

"Oh, no, I don't think so," Abby said shaking her head. "He's not great with …."

"With what?" she prompted when Abby hesitated.

"Oh, you know, big events, things like that. Anyway," Abby changed the subject, "I'll show you the way out." They reached the lobby, and she brightened a bit. "I hope we can get together again, Kate. I have some things to do for the festival or I'd stay, and we could talk more now."

"No problem, Abby. It was nice meeting you and we'll plan something, okay? I'll be back for the festival tomorrow."

"Great! See you then," she said as she hurried away.

Kate went out the front doors to the stone patio and looked over the scene in front of her. The activity on the lawn had increased since they had arrived earlier. Vendors were setting up their booths with temporary counters for serving wines. Tiny white lights rimmed the edges of their tents to create a festive atmosphere. Racks of white folding chairs were strewn about the lawn waiting to be set up. She found a small table away from the hubbub where she could wait for Ben. She texted him to let him know she was done with her interview and where to meet her.

The sky was still a bright blue that morning. It was warm, probably unusually warm for the middle of September in that part of New York state. She checked the weather app on her phone and saw only a small chance of rain for the next couple of days, which was great news for the festival.

She took a few moments to relax and think about the interview. She pulled out her journal and realized she hadn't written much. There weren't any huge revelations in her recorded interview either. It wasn't her best work. She'd been too distracted, trying to think ahead and not slip up with any information about herself. Davis had been generous with his time. He appeared at ease talking about the winery and the festival, and even some about himself. Abby was a sweet young woman, and obviously the apple of her father's eye. She was lucky. Kate felt a twinge of envy but tamped it down. It wasn't Abby's fault that she knew who her father was, unlike Kate, who was on the search for hers. She figured Abby was about seven years younger than she was, around twenty-four or twenty-five probably. She had the same fair features as Becky, but she also resembled the woman Abby identified as her mother in the photograph.

Stop it, Kate, she said to herself. You are reading too much into this. You still don't know the truth.

Her phone pinged. Ben texted that he would be done soon. Kate opened the journal to a blank page and began to sketch the scene in front of her. Vineyards, rolling hills, and a swath of Deep Lake. She made some notes on the Riesling she had tried and sketched the label from memory.

Ben soon joined her. "How did it go?" He sat in the chair next to her.

"Well, I hadn't expected Davis's daughter Abby to sit in with us, so I'm not sure."

"His daughter?" He looked around and lowered his voice. "But I guess we shouldn't be surprised. Were you able to learn anything?"

"Learned a bit about the history of the winery and the wine. We had a nice crisp 2020 Riesling. I learned how Abby wants to be a travel journalist like me. Davis Wingate is a philanthropist and raises money for scholarships over at Cornell in memory of his father. He indulges his daughter in a lot of ways ...." Her voice trailed off.

Ben leaned back in his chair. He laid a folder from his winemaking class on the table and reached for Kate's hand.

"You couldn't have done anything differently, Kate. I can tell you didn't want to dig too deep with her there. I don't blame you for that. You did the right thing. Will you be able to meet with him again?"

"Not sure. But I will be spending time with Abby, at her request. She wants to pick my brain about the travel business. Yay for me," she said, faking a smile.

Kate's gaze drifted over the beautiful property in front of her. "I'll just have to find another way of getting what I need, I guess. Oh, I did learn something interesting, though. I saw a family picture in the hallway. Davis has a younger brother, Briggs. Funny I don't remember seeing his name anywhere in my research. But Abby confirmed it was her uncle."

"Will you be able to talk to him?"

"No. She said he's not planning on being here this week for the festival. He travels a lot, and only works at the winery when he comes here, which didn't sound like it was very often."

"That's funny. I overheard one of the people in our class say that someone by the name of Briggs should be along in a couple of days to help with something; I don't remember what it was exactly. But I'm sure that was the name they said. Maybe it was another Briggs?"

"It's not a common name but I suppose it could be, or maybe someone's last name. Abby seemed sad when she talked about him. And she said he didn't like crowds so that's why he wouldn't be here this week. But at least I know to keep an eye out for him in case he does show up. How was your first class?"

"Great. I enjoyed it. I asked a lot of questions about what grapes worked well in the South and how the growing climate was different. And I was careful not to say North Carolina although they did ask where each of us was from and why we were taking the class. I knew I couldn't reveal much so I was pretty vague."

"Thank you for that. I'm glad you thought of it." She tipped her head and asked, "So, are we going into the winemaking business?"

Ben raised his eyebrows. "We might be doing just that."

Kate flipped through the pages of her journal, studying the smattering of notes she had written during the interview.

"Kate?" Ben said, after a long silence.

"Hmmm?" she murmured, not lifting her eyes from the pages.

"I'm thinking that instead of starting our own winery, I might buy this one. What do you think?"

Kate's head jerked up, panicked. "Wait, what?"

Ben grinned. "I said, let's get some lunch in Pine Ridge, explore the town, take some time for us."

Kate sighed and put away her journal. "I'm up for that, but I still need to prep for tomorrow and post to the blog," she said. "And don't scare me like that again."

⁓

Shortly after Davis's interview with Kate concluded, a meeting began in a large conference room next to his office. Delia Wingate sat at one end of a long table with Davis at the other. His wife Marie took a seat beside him while Suzy McNeill sat across from her with the groundskeeper, Terrance, and the family's personal chef, Marcelle.

Delia began the meeting. "Terrance, I noticed that the east lawn was not mowed as I asked. We'll have a lot of foot traffic through that area so please see that it's taken care of."

"Yes, Ms. Wingate," he replied.

"And I don't like the signs that have been erected. The branding is not correct for the Wingate Winery. Suzy can work with you on that. Please fix them by tomorrow."

"Yes, ma'am."

Delia turned her attention to the chef.

"Chef Marcelle, how are the preparations going for the judge's reception Wednesday night?"

"Very good, Ms. Wingate. We had to make a substitution for some of the offerings but I'm sure you'll be pleased."

She shook her head. "No, no, the food must be as we discussed. If it's the Snapper Crudo that's the problem, tell the supplier to find another source or find it yourself. I must have the snapper."

"Of course."

The door opened and Abby tiptoed around the table to sit next to her mother.

"Sorry, I'm late," she mumbled.

Delia glared at her but turned her attention to her daughter-in-law.

"Marie, I'm still seeing equipment in the vineyards that should be removed before tomorrow. That's what the barns are for. I want no obstruction of the views of the lake or the vineyards this year. And Davis, have you done your final walk-through of the winery?"

"Yes, Mother. Everything's in order."

"I hope so. The judges will want a tour, of course. And the vendors? I hate that they will be clogging up the front lawn, but I suppose it's expected. I hope we have enough trash cans nearby. Suzy, have the brochures and programs arrived?"

"Yes, Delia. Everything's ready."

Delia nodded, then turned her attention to the only person who hadn't given a report.

"Abby? Are you listening?" she said sharply.

Abby raised her head.

"Mother," Davis said as a warning.

"I'm sorry, Nana. Yes, I'm listening," Abby said as she put her phone down.

"Good. I have an assignment for you. Suzy and the caterers need help setting up the reception for the judges

Wednesday evening. They seem to be short-handed. They'll need you all afternoon and to help during the reception."

Suzy interrupted. "I think we're fine, Delia. Abby was scheduled to greet the judges, right?"

"Yes, but I'll do that myself. Davis, you had planned on being there, too, correct?"

"Yes, but with Abby."

"She's needed in the reception area," she said, dismissing their objections with a wave of her hand. "I have one final announcement. We have added a judge to the competition."

Davis sat up straighter in his chair. "But we had them all lined up. Why are we adding a new one?"

"This is something I've been working on behind the scenes and we are very fortunate to have Renee Scott from Scott Hill Vineyards in California joining us. I realize it's last minute but it's quite a coup. She is now a Master Sommelier and we're lucky to have her. Their restaurant, *Les Collines du Vin*, is a 2-star Michelin now."

"I agree it's wonderful to have her with us," Suzy interjected, "but this is a last-minute change. We've put out all of our publicity already."

"Do a social media blast, emails, all of that. I've emailed you her CV. Just add an insert to the brochures. That's your area. Her presence will bring in even more people once they know that she'll be here. She'll be joining the panel discussion on Thursday as well. It will be wonderful for the festival to have a judge of her caliber. I want every accommodation to be made. I've arranged a suite for her at the Pine Tree Bed and Breakfast and a driver while she's here. Melinda at Pine Tree made up a gift basket per my instructions, all local goods. I told her what was expected during Ms. Scott's stay."

"That's all very nice, Delia," Marie said, "but this is more than we are doing for the other judges. They may not take kindly to that kind of favoritism."

"If they want the same accommodations, they should add something more impressive to their resumes," she replied, coldly. "No. We need to treat Ms. Scott extraordinarily well while she's here. It will pay off in the long run, you'll see. That's all for now. Let's get busy."

Everyone filed out of the room except Abby. When Davis saw her linger, he and Marie stayed behind, too.

"Nana, I'm happy to help Suzy but she said they had enough help. I really wanted to be there with Dad to meet the judges. It's really important to me."

"I agree with Abby on this one, Mother," Davis said. "You'll be there, of course. But Marie and Abby and I should be there to greet everyone, too. It shows we appreciate them coming, as a family. We are a family-run winery after all."

"I have already said I would be there." Delia looked at him over her reading glasses. "No, my mind's made up. Abby, when you show me that you can take on these responsibilities, you will be given more. You were late for an important meeting. Promptness and dependability are everything in business. Now, let's move on. We have a lot to do and very little time." Despite using a cane, Delia swept from the room.

14

WHEN KATE AND BEN ARRIVED at the winery the next morning, the festival was already well underway. The aroma of donuts, beignets, and croissants from the food trucks filled the air, ready for the early arrivals. The sky was once again a bright blue, without a cloud in sight. A soft breeze brought the smell of ripened grapes over the lawn. It was a perfect opening day for the festival.

Ben set off for his second winemaking class and Kate strolled around the grounds, her camera always ready. She recorded a few videos, guiding her blog viewers through the festival events, the history of the winery, and grape growing in the area. She highlighted the view of the lake but knew that she would need to get close-up coverage of that for her blog. She spoke to the people at each of the wine-tasting booths and tried several different wines.

An event board had been added near the steps to the winery, boasting of the wine competition and the art show and giving the locations for each of the events. There were face painting booths and a bouncy house in another area for the children; it was a festival for the whole family. She was always on the lookout for Davis or Abby, and she thought she might recognize the uncle if he showed up. But she saw none of the Wingate family.

Kate was browsing through a box of prints and renderings of Deep Lake at an artist's booth, and considering which ones to buy when she heard a voice behind her.

"Well, Kate Tyler. I guess I shouldn't be surprised to see you here."

Kate recognized the drawl and raised her head. But it couldn't be. She turned slowly.

"Celeste." Her body stiffened at seeing the woman standing in front of her. But this was no mirage. This was Celeste Duvall in the flesh.

"Yes. Happy to see me?"

Kate took a deep breath to calm herself. She could not think of any reason why Celeste would be at this wine festival. After the conversation she had with her in Winston-Salem and knowing that Celeste knew that she was the owner of Howard's Walk and the daughter of Jenny Howard, to find the woman here at the Wingate Winery was a shattering turn of events. She steeled herself for the conversation that was sure to follow.

"Of course," Kate managed to get the lie out. "Why wouldn't I be?" By Celeste's tone of voice and the smirk on her face, Kate knew that her intentions were not going to be helpful to her, but she still needed to know what her game was. Kate began to walk away from the booth, away from anyone who could overhear the conversation. "But I am surprised. How did you happen to hear about the wine festival?"

Celeste followed her. "After we met, I did remember Davis's last name. Funny how it came back to me after all these years. I hadn't thought about them in so long, but your questions made me curious, so I did some research. And I learned that his family had this winery and was hosting this lovely wine festival and I thought, why not take a quick trip north? I enjoy wine and I did need to get away from the heat for a bit. And wouldn't you know it, but it so happens that Delia Wingate, that's Davis's mother. Have you met her?" Kate shook her head. "Well, it turns out that she and I have a lot in common. We're both lovers of the arts, especially women artists, although she favors the European. We spoke on the phone and when I asked, she graciously offered to loan me a painting by Berthe Morisot. Well, I was thrilled of course because it will now be the centerpiece of my show. So I said that I would come to the festival so we could meet and take care of the details. Such a generous woman to offer that, wouldn't you say?"

Like mother, like son.

"Yes, that's very generous of her."

"It is. And it's all for a good cause, of course. But what brings you here, Kate? If you don't mind my asking?"

"I'm covering the event. For *The Wayfarer.*"

Celeste stopped walking and stepped in front of Kate. Kate backed up a step. Her personal space was being invaded and she didn't like it.

"I suppose that's partly true," Celeste said. "But isn't it a coincidence that you came to me under the guise of covering my art show and yet we started talking about Jenny Howard, and who she might have been dating in high school? When I gave you Davis's name, you asked for his last name, too, which of course at the time I couldn't remember. And now here you are, at the Wingate Winery, under the guise of covering their wine festival, having every opportunity to speak to and get to know Davis Wingate himself. Very clever, Kate. Very clever indeed."

"I don't know what you're getting at, Celeste. I'm doing exactly what I said I would be doing. This is for my blog."

Celeste gave a thin condescending smile. "Of course, dear. Of course. Well, I have an appointment with Delia. Good luck, Kate. I hope you find everything you're looking for here at Deep Lake."

Celeste walked away. Kate felt weak in the knees and slowly found her way to a table.

Things could not have gotten any worse. Celeste was on to her and now she was going to meet with Delia Wingate, the woman who supposedly did not grant interviews and the last person that Kate wanted Celeste to meet.

☙✗❧

Delia Wingate led the way to her office from the lobby with her guest, Celeste Duvall, following. Delia was a tall woman with angular features. A halo of thick white hair hinted at her age, but her face was smooth and unlined. She was dressed in loose-fitting black pants and a generously cut gray blouse. It seemed that her pink skin had never seen the sun of a summer's day and yet she ruled the vineyards as if she had plucked every grape from the vines and stomped them to a pulp herself. Each step was aided with a magnificently carved wooden cane, but her back was as straight as a soldier at attention, and she held her head high as she walked.

In her office, Delia motioned for Celeste to take a seat, then carefully lowered herself into a high-backed chair of dark carved mahogany. She leaned her cane against a desk of matching wood with intricate carvings of leaves and grapes in bas-relief across the front. She folded her thin manicured hands neatly in front of her. The late morning sun shone into the room through a floor-to-ceiling window behind her and cast a pleasant glow into the room.

Celeste also sat with her hands folded, her legs crossed at her thick ankles as daintily as she could manage.

Delia had rather enjoyed the visit so far. Celeste Duvall was who she said she was; she had looked into her background quickly but efficiently before granting her a meeting. The painting she had offered to loan Celeste for her art show was sufficient to gain a gush of appreciation from the woman. The piece was quite valuable, and Celeste was thrilled when it was offered. But she also knew that the Duvall-Benedicts did carry some weight in the art world, so it would be good exposure for the Wingate Winery name as well. And so the agreement was made.

She was also well aware that Celeste Duvall thought she was gaining a friend of similar taste and social status. Delia's secret enjoyment came from knowing that it was not the case at all, but simply another thread in a wide net of acquaintances she had cultivated over the years; often useful but if they proved to be ineffective in helping her get what she wanted, they could easily be ignored.

Soon the conversation turned tedious. Delia feigned interest as Celeste blathered on and on about her homes in Winston-Salem and Nags Head and Grandfather Mountain.

"I'm sure you will have a wonderful art event," Delia interrupted in an imperious tone. "You have gathered some impressive pieces and I'm happy to loan the Morisot to your show." She stood and came around to the front of the desk. "I'm afraid I'm terribly busy though, and I must cut our lovely conversation short. I'm sure you understand."

Celeste quickly rose to her feet. "Of course, I know what it takes to put on an event of this magnitude. I've done it so many times myself. And I do appreciate your time. But if I may say one more thing, Delia."

How long would this go on? Delia wondered. *The woman doesn't know when it's polite to leave.*

But she smiled and said, "Of course. What is it?"

"Well, it is rather an awkward thing to mention, but I feel I must."

Delia's interest was elsewhere but she asked Celeste to continue.

"I know how challenging it can be to protect your privacy with a successful business such as yours. Believe me, I deal with that all the time. So I hope I'm not overstepping my bounds when I tell you that there's someone here who is not being honest with you, someone who is trying to make a connection to your family when there is none. Of course, I can't be sure, but regardless, her intentions are not what they appear."

"What on earth are you talking about?" Delia asked, surprised at this turn in the conversation. "Who is this person?"

"Her name is Kate Tyler."

Delia's face paled at hearing a name that had been unspoken in her presence for over thirty years. She gripped the edge of her desk to steady herself and turned away to mask the shock on her face. "Go on."

"She's here under the pretense of covering your wine festival for her little online blog, but I know for a fact that she's here for other reasons. She came to me, in Winston-Salem just five days ago offering to write an article about my art show. She'd done some coverage for me in the past and I liked her work, so I agreed. We talked some more, and I learned that she had inherited Howard's Walk in Eden Springs. She claimed she didn't know the Howards who had owned it originally. But that turned out to be a lie."

"And why is that?" Delia asked, carefully. She was slowly putting the pieces together from a casual comment Davis had made. He said that he was being interviewed by a young woman on Monday. But no name was mentioned. Now it was beginning to make sense. She slowly returned to her seat behind the desk, so Celeste wouldn't see the weakness she was feeling.

"Because Kate Tyler is the granddaughter of Bessie and Enoch Howard. I grew up in Eden Springs and still have some connections there. I recalled hearing that a young woman who was adopted at birth had turned up to claim an inheritance of Howard's Walk from her sister who had bought the place just before dying in a car accident. A sad thing, too, since the girls had also lost their adoptive parents in a car accident several years before that."

Delia absorbed this news through a veil of disbelief as if some portal had opened to a past life that she thought had long been buried. Why was this happening? Why now after all she had done to put it all in the past?

This conversation had to end. She slipped on a familiar mask of indifference and interrupted something Celeste was saying about car accidents.

"Ms. Duvall, I can't imagine why you are telling me this. We haven't had any connection to that area in many, many years."

"Of course, Delia, as I said, I've had to deal with interlopers in my past. I had no idea she would be here. It was such a shock when we met on your front lawn just now. I simply came for the wine festival and a little getaway and of course your incredibly generous offer of the Morisot. At any rate, I felt I had to tell you about her. You do with it what you will, of course."

"I'm sure it has nothing to do with us, but thank you for telling me. Would you mind, though?" She motioned Celeste to walk with her to the window overlooking the front of the winery. "Is she anywhere here? Can you point her out?"

Celeste joined Delia and scanned the people on the lawn. "There." She saw Kate at a table and pointed at her. "Just sitting down now, by the Castle Vineyard booth; long auburn hair, jeans, and a loose green sweater. That's her."

"Well," Delia said, with an air of indifference. "I'm sure it's nothing." She took Celeste by the elbow and guided her to the door. "I'll have Ms. McNeill take care of the details for the loan of the painting. She'll be in touch. Thank you for coming, Ms. Duvall."

Celeste's last words to Delia were lost as the door was closed. Unthinking, she walked quickly back to the window. But a hitch in her hip stopped her, reminding her that she had left her cane at her desk, and she held on to a couple of well-placed chairs to continue.

The woman must think I'm an idiot, she thought. There's more to this story. She's the one who leaked the connection to us. I'm sure of it. It's no coincidence that she's here at the same time as ...

Delia Wingate could not even say the name. She had controlled herself in Celeste's presence, but the information the woman had shared was shattering that self-control. Celeste

Duvall was a gossip and a conniver. She wasn't there to do any favors for the Wingates. Delia knew her type. She came from a small rural town, probably married well, and now thought herself an equal to people like the Wingates.

Thirty-two years. She had protected the family and especially her son for thirty-two years. Who knew what this young woman wanted if she even were a Howard? There was no proof. But the name was certainly correct.

The situation was intolerable. She could not allow this young woman, or anyone for that matter, to disrupt what she and her husband Frank had built, what she was leaving as a legacy to her sons. And she couldn't imagine how the woman had been able to get permission to cover the wine festival.

Delia glanced out the window again. The young woman was hurrying away toward the parking lot. *Good riddance*, Delia thought.

Delia picked up her phone and dialed a number. A man finally answered.

"Mother? Is everything okay?"

"Yes, of course, it is, Briggs. Everything is fine. I wondered if you were still planning on coming this week?"

"Yes, I am, why?"

"Well, dear, maybe it's better if you don't come; maybe wait until later this month."

"Why would I do that? The festival is this week and I told Davis I'd help him."

"No, dear, that won't be necessary. I'll talk to him about it. I ... I just think you should stay away for a bit."

"What's going on, Mother? You're telling me I shouldn't come but won't tell me why?"

"I'm sorry, Briggs. Please trust me on this."

He sighed. "No, Mother, not this time. I'm coming just like I promised Davis I would. I'll see you soon." And he ended the call.

Delia's hand shook as she replaced the phone on its charger. Briggs had never talked to her that way. She had done everything in her power since high school to protect him, especially after his time in the army. He was her pride and joy as a young boy but, unlike Davis, difficult and headstrong. And the military destroyed him. He was never the same after he came home from deployment. She would never allow anyone to interfere with his life now. Especially someone from his past. Someone who deserved to stay there.

She knew she couldn't stop Briggs from coming. She needed to talk to Davis, but he had other responsibilities at the moment and couldn't be disturbed. She would talk to him later. Right now, she needed other options.

A plan began to form in her mind.

15

KATE FUMBLED WITH HER PHONE, incapable of entering her password. She sat at a small table near a wine vendor's booth to catch her breath.

"Focus," she told herself, as she tried for the third time to input four numbers that would help her reach Ben. Voices around her had faded into the distance and she was aware of nothing but her own breathing.

She had watched in shock as Celeste entered the winery for her meeting with Delia. Kate had no idea what that horrible woman might say. But she feared the worst.

As Kate finally punched in Ben's number, she scanned the front of the winery. Two women, framed by a tall window, looked out over the booths and tents on the lawn. One of the women, hidden by the room's shadows, could have been Celeste. Kate wasn't sure. But the other woman's eyes seemed to settle on her. Was this Delia Wingate? Even from that distance, Kate felt her icy stare.

Kate grabbed her bag. She needed to escape. She hurried to the parking lot to Ben's truck and got in, desperate for Ben to answer his phone.

"Kate?" He said in a whisper. "I'm still in class."

"Ben, please come. I'm in the truck. I need to get out of here. Please hurry."

"I'll be right there."

Ben soon hopped into the truck and with one glance at Kate, immediately began to talk calmly and quietly to her.

She was pale and her face was covered in a sheen of sweat. Her eyes were squeezed shut and her chest rose and fell with deep breaths. He grabbed a towel from the seat behind him, laid it on her lap, then turned the air conditioner on high and pulled out of the parking lot.

He told her they would be home soon and to just keep breathing. When they reached the cottage, Kate's eyes were still closed but her breathing had slowed to normal.

"Kate, can you talk to me?"

She nodded but no words came out.

"Do you want to sit here or go down to the cottage?"

"Sit here," she managed to say.

"Okay." He turned the fan down a notch and held her hand.

A few minutes passed and Kate finally opened her eyes. She squeezed Ben's hand.

"I'm sorry I pulled you out of your class. But ...."

"It's no problem. What happened?"

"Celeste Duvall was there. At the winery."

Ben had a puzzled look on his face. "The lady from Winston-Salem? How ...?"

"She's on to me," she whispered, barely able to get the words out. "She put everything together, the questions I was asking her, everything, and she thinks she knows why I'm here. And to make things worse, she knows Delia Wingate now. I think she might have told her who I really am."

"Why would she do that? What reason could she have?"

Kate shook her head. "I don't think she expected to see me here, either. But now she thinks she knows the real reason I'm here and she thinks I manipulated her at her house, saying I was covering her art show, which I did want to do, but then I got her to talk about Jenny. Now she thinks I'm doing the same thing here, using my cover as a blogger to find out more about Davis Wingate."

"Well," Ben started.

She glared at him. "Yes, Ben, I know that's exactly what I'm doing. You don't need to remind me." Kate got out of the truck, slammed the door, and quickly walked across the road and down the steps to the cottage. She stormed out onto the deck and sat in a chair with her head in her hands. Ben joined her a few moments later with a bottle of water.

"Here," he said, handing her the bottle.

"I'm sorry Ben. I'm not mad at you. This whole thing is blowing up in my face. Why did I even come here? Nothing's going right."

"Kate, listen to me." He pulled up a deck chair next to her. "You're doing this for Billy, of course. But maybe you're thinking you can stay outside of it all, emotionally, I mean. You were hoping to come here, ask some questions, find some answers, and go home. One way or the other, you were thinking of it as a fact-finding mission."

Kate shook her head. "No. That's not it at all."

He pressed on. "But we didn't know how it would go, right? It wasn't anything we could plan out exactly."

Kate sighed and leaned back in the deck chair. "I guess you're right about that."

"So, even if Celeste tells this Delia person or even Davis himself what she thinks she knows, so what? You can still talk to them about it, maybe just a little earlier or in a different way than you expected to."

Kate twisted the cap off of the bottle of water and took several gulps.

"You haven't accomplished what you came here for. You aren't sure Celeste will tell Delia anything. Yes, she might have been a little miffed after you met with her. But what would she have to gain by telling the Wingates anything? And you haven't met this uncle yet and you haven't had a chance to talk to Davis like you wanted to. It might be hard, but maybe you need to go to Davis again and confront him. We knew this would be hard, but it's for Billy. If it turns out that the Wingates are nothing to you, then we'll have to go back to square one and start over."

"I can't even think about starting over right now." She took a deep breath. "But you're right. I'm not done here. I know that. But it was such a shock to see Celeste. It felt like my heart just stopped. And I don't even know if I could get another meeting with Davis or not. I guess I came at the worst time, right in the middle of his festival."

"Well, we're here now. We've got a few more days. Let's stay and you can plan on talking to him again. We have the cottage for the rest of the week."

A cool breeze blew in off the lake and Kate shivered. "I'm going to change my clothes. Maybe we can go for a boat ride or something. I need to get my mind off this."

"Sounds good," Ben agreed.

Kate was feeling better after thinking about what Ben said. He had a way of cutting through the chaos and reaching her. She knew he was right. She wasn't done at Deep Lake yet.

A few minutes later, Ben came into the bedroom. "Kate, there's someone here that wants to see you."

Kate's first reaction was expecting Davis or even Delia Wingate herself to be standing at their door, threatening them with bodily harm if they didn't leave immediately. But she knew Ben would never have allowed anything like that to happen.

"Who is it?"

"She says her name's Abby. She's down at the dock."

It wasn't who Kate wanted to see at the moment, but it was better than confronting any of the other Wingates. She quickly finished getting dressed and followed Ben out to the deck. Abby waved at them from an outboard motorboat tied up at the dock. Kate waved back. "Did you talk to her?" Kate asked Ben.

"I went down after she stopped at the dock and waved at me. Is this Abby Wingate?"

"The one and only."

Kate and Ben took the steps down to the lower deck and across the lawn to the dock.

"Hi, Kate! Sorry to stop by like this but I had to get away from all the craziness at the winery for a while, and I thought you both might like to go for a boat ride. I can show you around the lake."

Did she read my mind? Kate wondered. *And how did she find me?* But it was a beautiful day and the gentle rocking of the boat against the dock was beckoning her.

"We were just talking about taking the boat out. But sure, we'd love for you to show us around."

"Great! Hop in!"

"So how did you find us, Abby?" Kate asked as she stepped into the boat.

"Oh, I used to work with Molly, your realtor. I know most of the cottages on the lake and when she said someone that was here for the wine festival had rented *Summer Winds*, I took a chance. Well, I stopped at a couple of places. But I finally found you!" Her eager face suddenly dropped. "I hope that's okay."

Kate clearly understood now that she was in a small town with small-town gossipers where everyone knew everyone else's business, not unlike Eden Springs. She needed to remember that.

"It's okay, Abby. Don't worry about it," Kate reassured her. Ben cast off the last line from the dock cleat and hopped into the boat. Abby slowly idled out into the lake. Once clear, she pushed the throttle forward.

"You can put on your life jackets if you want," she called out over the noise of the engines. "I never use them, even though Dad tells me to all the time." Abby seemed to be in her element on the water. She drove the boat fast, but the lake was clear of any other traffic, and she took advantage of it.

"I'm taking you to the Lake House," she shouted, her voice barely understood over the sound of the wind and the boat bouncing over the waves. Kate simply nodded, struggled into her life jacket, and hung on to the seat and Ben. It wasn't that she was afraid of the water; she was an experienced swimmer and even spent a summer as a lifeguard at a popular resort. But when she wasn't in control of a boat herself? That was another story.

As Kate relaxed, she had to admit that the view from the boat was completely different than what she could see from their cottage. The shore was lined with homes of all sizes, from tiny cabins to McMansions. A few hotels dotted the shoreline. They passed a restaurant with outdoor seating; boats were lined up at the docks to fill their gas tanks. The boat flew along at the only speed that Abby seemed to know—fast—but Kate welcomed the freedom she was feeling and, after the stress of the morning, decided to enjoy the moment.

Abby suddenly slowed the boat as the wail of sirens reverberated across the water. They all looked toward the sound and soon several rescue boats came into view, moving fast to an emergency on the lake toward Pine Ridge.

"Does this happen often?" Ben asked.

"Not so much this time of year after the summer people are gone," Abby said. "But when there are storms, it's always busy."

"Are storms common? We came through a bad one the day we arrived."

"No, those are soakers, but sometimes we get thunder and lightning storms that can be pretty scary. When they hit, watch out. They come in fast and hard. It's not good to be out on the lake then. But the rescue squad does a good job of being there when we need them."

Abby picked up her speed again for a while but soon slowed the boat and pulled alongside a long wooden dock.

"Here we are," Abby announced. "This is the Lake House. Let's go in."

The Lake House was a three-story structure with decks spread across the top two floors and a stone patio on the first floor that reminded Kate of theirs at Howard's Walk. Each floor had a view of the lake through floor-to-ceiling glass windows; Kate knew it would be a spectacular sight.

Abby had started walking up a terraced stone path to the house and Kate hurried to catch up while Ben tied the boat to the dock. "We don't want to intrude," Kate called out to Abby, suddenly concerned that there might be someone from the family there.

"You won't be. Everybody's at the festival." Abby turned as Kate caught up to her. "Come on, let me show you around," Abby urged.

Kate hoped that Abby was right. She didn't want to run into anyone else unexpectedly that day. They entered the house through a sliding glass door into a living room large enough to hold the entire cottage of *Summer Winds*.

"White or red?" she asked over her shoulder as she headed to a bar at the back of the room.

Kate and Ben looked at each other, agreeing at the same moment that a drink would be welcomed. "Red," they said in unison.

Abby pulled a bottle from a wine refrigerator behind the bar and opened it. "My favorite is this red blend we did last year. Our winemaker, Audrey, let me help her create it. Mom and Dad like it, too." She poured three generous glasses and handed two to Kate and Ben.

Kate took a sip and smiled. "Abby, this is very good."

"You have a talent for this," Ben added.

"Really? Thanks! It was fun but I don't know if that's what I want to do with my life. So, tell me about what you do, Kate. Where have you traveled? I checked your website. I help

Suzy with the winery website, so I know something about creating one and adding content, and all that. I liked the videos you posted from Rye, England, last year. You made me want to go there."

Kate wondered if she would be able to get a word in with Abby's rambling. She hoped for a break soon. She took another sip of wine and sat at the bar.

"I want to go to Paris and Rome and Greece. And Patagonia. I'd really like to go there. What do you think?"

Finally, a break. "Well, I would recommend that you start with one location, maybe even something here in the US or Canada before going to Europe or South America. Focus on a place you've never been to so it will be fresh to you and your readers. Like you're both discovering it at the same time. Of course, you need a blog or a website first. But it sounds like you have some ideas for that." Abby nodded eagerly. "Check out other travel websites and decide what will make yours unique. Have a niche, like 'single girl traveling', or 'hidden destination gems', depending on what you like to do when you travel."

"Oh, like I could focus on wineries since I know something about them, and winemaking, just to start, right?"

"Exactly." Kate was encouraged that Abby was coming up with her own ideas about a unique take on the business. "How many young travel bloggers have experience in the winemaking industry? But it's something that people of all ages like. That might be just the niche you need to get started."

"I see," Abby said thoughtfully. "Oh, maybe I could start right here on Deep Lake! 'Hometown Girl and her Favorite Wineries' or something like that!" she said, waving her hand through the air as if showing off a headline.

Kate smiled at Abby's eagerness. Her only doubt was that she might be more of a homebody than she realized. The travel business could be challenging, as Kate knew all too well. She had some wonderful experiences on her trips but also some frightening ones, including the trip to England, although that part never made it into her blog. Even so, she wouldn't have traded her experiences for anything. Only time would tell if Abby was made of the right stuff for it. It was something she had to learn for herself.

After an hour of Abby drawing out Kate's thoughts about her profession and another glass of wine for each of them, Kate knew it was time to go. The stress of the morning had crept back into her thoughts, and she had work to do. On their way out, Kate noticed another grouping of photographs on the fireplace mantel and walked closer. One was of Davis and Briggs in the vineyard, with several crates piled with grapes at their feet. Kate took the opportunity to ask about her uncle again.

"Is this your dad and your uncle?"

"Yes. It was taken a few years ago when Uncle Briggs was around more. He's a bit of a loner. But he's been that way since ...."

"Since when?" Kate asked gently. This was the second time that Abby was hesitant to talk about her uncle. But she didn't seem like the type to keep things hidden and Kate wondered if it was something that she might need to open up about.

"He was in Mogadishu. 1993. In the Army. And just before that, he was in the Gulf War."

"Abby, I'm so sorry. That was a terrible time for all of the service men and women there."

"We're lucky to have him back at all. But I miss ... well, I miss my uncle."

Kate suddenly understood. Many members of the military did not come back whole after their tours of duty. It was clear now that Briggs was one of them. Physically, he was present. But mentally and emotionally? Kate could only imagine what it must have been like.

"I'm sorry, Abby. I didn't mean to upset you."

Abby brightened a bit. "It's okay. We get to see him sometimes. That all happened before I was born, but sometimes I can see what he must have been like. Dad says he was a great guy and a great brother. He still is, but you know what I mean."

Kate knew exactly what she meant. She knew what it was like to have a brother that was not completely present. Billy was a light in her world, but he lived in his own and always would. She suddenly knew she needed to talk to Mimi as soon as they got back to the cottage.

After a moment, Ben said, "I think we should be getting back, Abby." She nodded and led them back down to the dock.

The trip back was more subdued. Abby took her time. The air had cooled and yet she stood without a coat or jacket at the wheel, letting the wind pour over her, oblivious to the chill. Kate snuggled up to Ben. This was not like the warm autumn weather in North Carolina.

Abby steered the boat to the middle of the lake. She slowed and pointed off to her left to the rock-ringed Wingate Island Kate and Ben had noticed earlier.

"You should be able to see this from your cottage, but that's Wingate Island. We own it but nobody lives there. It's hard to get to because of the rocks and all." She turned the wheel, gunned the engine and they were soon back at *Summer Winds*.

Kate and Ben thanked Abby for the boat ride and the wine.

"No. I should be thanking you," she said. "You've given me a lot of ideas to think about. Hey, would you two like to come to our reception tomorrow afternoon? It's at the winery, for the judges and staff, well, everyone that's there really. I'd love for you to come, and I know Dad wouldn't mind."

Kate didn't hesitate to decline. She knew she wouldn't be able to handle it. And she wasn't sure if 'Dad' would have the final say in it anyway. "That's so nice of you, Abby, but we wouldn't want to intrude. Maybe some other time."

Abby looked disappointed but acquiesced.

"It really would be okay, but I understand." She pulled out her phone. "Here's my phone number in case you change your mind. I hope you'll come by tomorrow."

Kate said they would be at the festival although she wasn't sure what her next steps would be in her search for her birth father. But maybe the winery was not the place to continue her search at that point. Something was missing, but she couldn't put her finger on it.

16

"WELL, THAT WAS INTERESTING," Ben said as they took the steps up to the cottage.

"I'm glad you got to see what I experienced in the interview. She's okay, really sweet, just a bit flighty. But she'll figure it out." They reached the door and Kate unlocked it and stepped inside. "She got me to thinking about Billy though. I think I'll give Mimi a call."

"Shall I put on some burgers?"

Kate gave him a thumbs-up. She pulled out her phone and dialed Mimi's number.

After several rings, Mimi answered. "Kate, it's so good to hear from you. How is your trip going?"

Kate hated to lie, but there was no reason to upset Mimi. She had enough on her hands.

"It's fine. The weather's great. How are you? And Billy?"

"Well, Kate, I probably should have called you, but I didn't want you to worry."

Kate's face fell and she sat down. "Why, what's going on? Is Billy okay?"

"He's fine but I had to ask Doc Bartlett to come out to the house the other day. Billy wasn't feeling good, and Sara thought Doc should see him. And I knew I couldn't take him or go with him, even if Sara drove, so I asked him to come out here to the house, and he did."

"So what did he say?"

"I think it's just a stomach bug, but doc changed one of his medicines. Billy doesn't like taking them, but I make sure he does. I think he's wondering what's going on. He's not used to being sick, you know."

"I know. I'm sorry I'm not there to help, Mimi."

"Don't you worry about it, Kate. You are where you're supposed to be. I guess I should ask if you've found out anything."

"No, not yet. I mean I've learned a lot but not anything specific. I'm sorry Mimi. I'm doing my best."

"Of course, you are, dear. I know that. And don't worry about Billy. He's back to his old self today."

"Okay. We should be home by this weekend if everything goes well. So take care, Mimi. And give our love to Billy."

"Will do, Kate. Same to you. Bye-bye."

Kate ended the call and went out onto the deck where Ben was seasoning the burgers.

"How's everyone back home?" Ben asked.

"Billy was sick, and Mimi had to call Doc Bartlett. He's better now. Ben, I can't put this off any longer. I have to talk to Davis. As soon as possible."

"Okay. Let's do it then."

The smell of burgers on the grill whetted Kate's appetite and she dove into one as soon as they were ready.

"I still feel like we're overlooking something," Kate said in between bites. "Something obvious. I mean, what if I'm completely wrong? What if it isn't Davis at all?" She spooned a helping of potato salad onto her plate. "Am I just wasting my time here?"

"Well, I'll play devil's advocate. We know Celeste doesn't have your best interest at heart. Maybe she was steering you wrong, either intentionally or unintentionally, when you talked to her at her house in Winston-Salem."

"I guess that's possible. But it does seem logical that if the Eden Springs girls liked to date guys from Winston-Salem Prep that it might be one of them."

"We could look through the yearbooks again. Maybe that will trigger something?"

Kate went inside and got her laptop. In a few moments she had the yearbooks pulled up again.

"Let's check Davis's junior year," Ben suggested.

They scanned the photos and names of all of the classes and finally found something.

"Hey, look, here's Briggs as a sophomore." Kate looked at the photo of a cute, happy kid, no doubt popular with his classmates, especially the girls. It was a shocking change from this yearbook picture to the ones she saw at the Lake House. There was a heartbreaking metamorphosis from a carefree teenager to a troubled man who had seen too much war and destruction. Who knew what demons had crept into young Briggs's psyche over the course of his life?

Kate made some notes and then exited that yearbook. She then opened one for Davis's senior year and searched until she found Briggs's picture as a junior.

At the same time, they both said, "What about Briggs's senior year?" and Kate quickly accessed the next yearbook.

There was no photo of Briggs in the senior class of Winston-Salem Prep.

"Just like Jenny," Kate whispered, staring at the place on the screen where Briggs Wingate's senior picture should have been. She sat back in her chair. "We know what happened to Jenny." She looked up at Ben. "What if the same thing happened to Briggs? He left school sometime between his junior and senior years. Maybe he joined the army then? I wonder if we could find out," she said, almost to herself. On a hunch, she googled the name, Briggs Wingate.

There were no hits.

"No social media, no nothing?" Ben asked. Kate kept scrolling through the names. "Bob Wingate, Brian Wingate, Brigadier General Wisner ... nothing. No Briggs Wingate anywhere." Just to double-check, she searched for Davis Wingate as she had before she left Howard's Walk and found his name in several results, but mainly for Wingate Winery.

"It's like Briggs dropped off the face of the earth in his senior year in high school," she said. "He's probably in some army database but we don't have access to that. I guess I have more questions for Davis than I thought."

Kate and Ben searched the internet further for any information on Briggs Wingate, but every attempt was a dead end. Kate stood up to stretch the kinks out of her back from being hunched over her laptop when her phone rang. It was a number she didn't recognize, and normally she would have let it go to voice mail, but it was the local area code for Deep Lake, and out of curiosity, she answered it.

"Hello?"

"Is this Kate Tyler?" The voice was unfamiliar. It was a woman, but her words sounded more like a demand than a question.

Kate hesitated but finally said, "Yes. And who is this?"

"This is Delia Wingate of Wingate Winery. I wonder if we could meet this afternoon. I believe we have some things to discuss."

Kate quickly put the call on speaker and waved Ben over to her.

"Of course. Where can I meet you?"

"I'll be at Romano's Trattoria in Pine Ridge at four o'clock. We'll speak then." And she hung up.

"I wonder what that's all about," Ben said.

Kate shook her head, a puzzled look on her face. "I don't know. So first of all, how did she get my number? Did she get it from Celeste?"

Ben shrugged. "Or maybe from Suzy McNeill?"

"Maybe. I did give it to Suzy along with my email address. But as far as I know, Delia Wingate didn't know who I was unless Celeste told her."

"Maybe she told her. But we're still not sure."

"Oh, I'm sure," Kate insisted. "She might have known about my interview with Davis." She sighed. "I guess it doesn't matter how she got it, but she did."

"Molly did say that Delia was in charge at the winery, right?" Ben said, reminding Kate about how the realtor described her. "I think she called her the 'matriarch.'"

"She did but she also said she was all about business and kept to herself. So why does she want to meet with me? I don't have a good feeling about this. She didn't sound friendly at all on the phone."

In her head, Kate ran through all of the many reasons Delia Wingate might want to meet with her. Most of them had unpleasant implications, but there was one outcome of a conversation with her that might end well. She glanced at her watch.

"I need to freshen up before I meet with her. I'll shower and change my clothes and be out in time to go into town."

Kate had hoped to speak to Davis again and get the answers she needed. But now a different opportunity had presented itself. Maybe it was Delia Wingate who held the answers she was looking for.

She let the hot water run over her, thinking through what had brought her to this point. Ben was right. They could not have planned out how this trip would play out. A simple clue had led her to this point. Actually, it had happened more quickly than she had expected. Maybe now the work of peeling back the layers of secrets and identities and truth had just begun.

They arrived at the restaurant promptly at four o'clock. Ben waited for a few minutes in the truck while Kate went inside.

He said he would come in later and find a discreet place at the bar to be nearby.

Kate told the host she was meeting someone, and the young woman took her directly to a booth at the back of the restaurant where Delia Wingate was waiting.

Kate hadn't been able to clearly see who was in the window with Celeste earlier. But there was no doubt this was the same woman. She looked up as she saw Kate approach but made no effort to rise or greet her at all. She simply waved her hand at the seat across from her and Kate slid silently into the booth.

Kate was ready to greet this woman with an open mind. Delia Wingate might be the person who could supply the answers to her questions. She was prepared to have a civil conversation with her, but as the seconds passed and Kate felt Delia's eyes assessing her, judging her, she decided there was no room for small talk and got right to the point.

"What is it that you wanted to talk to me about?"

Delia raised an eyebrow at Kate's directness. She folded her hands in front of her on the table. "It appears that you have been getting to know my family since yesterday. I know that you are a blogger and have an interest in the wine festival, but I have an idea that is not the only reason you are here. Is that correct?"

Kate tried to calm her nervousness. Under the table, her legs were shaking, and she hoped it was not evident to Ms. Wingate. The woman was an intimidating figure.

"I did come to cover the festival for my blog, yes. I'm not sure what else you are talking about ...."

"Oh, please, Ms. Tyler." She waved her hand dismissively. "Don't waste my time or yours. You have an ulterior motive to get information about my family. I know who you are. You are the granddaughter of Enoch and Bessie Howard, and you live at Howard's Walk in Eden Springs, North Carolina. Do you deny that?"

Out of the corner of her eye, Kate saw Ben take a seat at the bar. He nodded at her, and her resolve returned. Celeste had obviously said something to Delia, so there was no need to hide her purpose there any longer.

She leaned in and calmly said, "No, I don't deny that Ms. Wingate. And as you probably know, as the granddaughter of Bessie and Enoch Howard, I am also one of the daughters of Jenny Howard, who on August 16, 1990, at the age of seventeen, had triplets, triplets who were split up and adopted by two different families after both of their parents gave them up. And I have lived with the fact that I never knew who my father was or what happened to my mother. So I will not apologize to you or anyone for trying to find my birth father. That's what this is about, isn't it? Celeste Duvall told you, didn't she? And, for the record, I have not approached anyone in your family about this. So just the fact that you are here, in private, telling me I have an ulterior motive, speaks volumes. So do you want to know the rest of this story from me or just rely on what a gossip told you?"

Kate could see that she hit a nerve. Delia sat back in her seat. Her lips were a thin line and her eyes widened. Her breathing quickened and Kate knew she had made a dent in the woman's armor.

Delia crossed her arms. "Go ahead then. Tell me the rest of your story."

Kate took a deep breath and said, "Billy, my biological triplet brother, who also lives in Eden Springs, has been diagnosed with Berger's Disease. His doctor said it was important that I find out our family medical history, since he may need a kidney transplant someday. But, since I never knew who that was," she said pointedly, "I had to do some digging. And it led me here." She delivered the final blow. "So which one is it, Ms. Wingate? Is Davis our father? Or is it Briggs?"

Delia flinched at hearing Briggs' name. A server approached with two glasses of water and started to ask if they would be ordering anything, but Delia waved her away.

With what appeared to be a great effort, Delia responded. "I am sorry to hear about your brother. I understand why you began your search. But," she said, looking Kate directly in the eye, "neither Davis nor Briggs is your father, and it is ridiculous to even think that."

Kate interrupted. "Why did Briggs leave high school in his senior year?"

Delia scowled. "What makes you think he did?"

"No picture in his senior yearbook."

Delia seemed to consider this. Then a thin smile came across her face. "Is that what you are basing your assumptions on? A picture that isn't in a yearbook?"

For a brief moment, Kate felt unsure of herself. But she had her reasons for thinking Briggs might be her father instead of Davis. And it was the right call.

"Yes."

"Well, now I see why you are confused. It was an oversight on the school's part, one I always regretted but could never seem to get rectified. A young man's senior year is so important, don't you think? I'm sure your brother's senior year was special to him, too."

The woman's casual answer was intended once again to dismiss Kate's concerns for her brother, and it infuriated her.

Kate grabbed her phone and scrolled to a photo of her and Billy. It was a picture of them in the gardens, both with happy grins on their faces and dirt on their overalls and jeans. She faced it across the table to Delia.

"No, his senior year wasn't special. Billy never made it to high school. Billy can't even read at a third-grade level."

Delia took in a sharp breath and sat back as if in revulsion at seeing Billy in the picture. She turned her head away. Kate was now thoroughly disgusted with the woman across from her.

"This is why I'm here. Because Billy can't do this on his own. If it's the last thing I ever do, I will find our father."

Delia took a sip of water, her hand shaking as she set the glass down on the table. She reached for her bag and pulled out a pen and what appeared to be a checkbook.

"Ms. Tyler," she said, her tone lowered as people passed by the booth. "I will have to insist that you stop this pointless search here at Deep Lake. You will leave and not come back anywhere near this town or the winery. Do you understand?"

"I won't agree to that. I have a right to speak to your sons about this and that's what I plan to do."

"I think you will change your mind." Delia wrote something on a check, tore it out of the book, and held it up in her hand. "What your brother is going through is heartbreaking of course. Perhaps this will help." She slid the check across the table.

Kate picked it up and read the amount of fifty thousand dollars. She threw it back down on the table.

"I don't want your money."

"You can cash this check or not, Ms. Tyler. It's entirely up to you. But do not come back to Deep Lake. Ever again."

Delia Wingate stood, picked up her cane, and walked haltingly out of the restaurant. A moment later, Ben slid into the booth.

"Kate, what happened? What did she say to you?"

Kate picked up the check from the table and crumpled it into a ball. She relayed what Delia had said to her.

"So she's denying that either Davis or Briggs is your father, and she wrote you a check for fifty thousand dollars?"

Kate nodded and flattened the wrinkled piece of paper on the table. "I can't believe she just wrote a check for that much money like it was nothing."

"What are you going to do with it?"

"I'll never cash it. But I think I hit a nerve when I mentioned Briggs's name. She actually flinched. She can deny it all she wants but now I know need to talk to Davis and Briggs. She wants me to leave town but there's no way I'll do that. Not before I find answers."

17

DELIA WALKED INTO HER OFFICE and locked the door behind her. She threw her car keys on her desk and her coat on a nearby chair. She was surprised at the young woman's reaction to her offer. It was a very generous amount of money that would help her brother with his medical expenses, and yet she had rejected it. Perhaps she had misjudged her. She had backbone, something that Delia usually admired in people. But regardless, Kate Tyler had lied to her to achieve her goal. This was unforgivable. If she wouldn't accept money, then another tactic was needed to get this woman out of their lives.

She sat down and shuffled distractedly through a pile of papers awaiting her attention. Invoices, advertisement samples, and images of new bottle labels were scattered across her desk. She pushed them aside and picked up a framed photograph of her family on a rare day when they were all together at the winery. She and Frank, Davis, and Briggs. It was one of those days that was a turning point although none of them knew it at the moment the picture was taken.

It was harvest time. After the family photo was taken, Frank had gone back to the vineyards to work. Much later, he had returned to the house a little more tired than usual but then, after supper, he had gone back out into the vineyards. "For one last look," he had said, not knowing how prophetic his statement would be. He collapsed, away from the house, away from anyone who could help. When he hadn't returned, Davis went out to look for him. By the time he found his father, it was too late.

He was buried two days later, and then everyone went back to work. There was a threat of an early frost and too much depended on getting the grapes harvested. There was no time to grieve, only time to move on.

Delia had lost a partner when Frank died, but she soon found that she was in her element. She put all of her energies into running the winery and she ran it with an iron fist.

Delia and her husband had started the winery twenty-two years ago. Davis had graduated from his master's program at Cornell and briefly worked in France and was still learning the business. But they convinced him to return to the States and join them at the newly named Wingate Winery.

Davis had the technical knowledge, her husband had the management skills, and she had a vision of what the winery could mean for her family and future generations. Through sheer determination, they had taken a floundering winery and vineyards and brought it all into the twenty-first century. They tore out the old non-producing vineyards, planted new hybrid grapes, and bought more land as it became available. Davis began using new winemaking techniques and Delia updated the brand. And they succeeded. Despite downturns in the economy, despite reinventing both themselves and the new brand of Wingate Winery, they had succeeded, even beyond her expectations.

Despite Frank's death, the winery continued to thrive. Davis was doing a magnificent job as the head winemaker. His wife Marie had taken over managing the vineyards and now they were the best they had ever been. But the all-consuming day-to-day work was now taking its toll on Delia. She was tired. It was harder for her to envision what the winery would be like in twenty years, or even ten. She was seventy-six years old, and the future was becoming less clear to her. She had finally admitted to herself that she might need to step away. Not retire completely, of course. She could never see herself doing that. It was time to start thinking about handing over the reins. But to whom?

Delia stood and walked to the fireplace. With a flick of a switch, the flames ignited, sending a warm glow into the room. She settled on a sofa to feel the warmth of the fire. She had already pondered some solutions. Another winemaker could be hired. She could find another vineyard manager. Davis and Marie could certainly handle everything on that front. Suzy McNeill and her staff would carry on as they always had.

Her thoughts then turned to her sons. They were only a year apart in age and she had given up a part of herself as they grew, burying her own hopes and dreams and adapting herself to the raising of two boys who were following in their father's footsteps to manhood.

Her sons reminded her so much of Frank. Loud, quick to anger, prone to fighting, and to win. She remembered their explosions of growth in childhood and youth, outgrowing their joints and limbs and skin. Like trying to control lava spilling out of a volcano, she lost her ability to contain them. She wanted to try tenderness with her boys, but she could never seem to raise it in herself. So, there was no gentleness in their upbringing.

Davis, as the older brother, would not be ignored, and Briggs seemed to ignore him at every turn. Davis tried to advise him, but his advice was rejected. Briggs made mistakes and Davis pushed him back into a better way. They fought with each other, often ending in bloody mouths, black eyes, and bruised knuckles. But they fought because they truly loved each other and their size predicted that this is how they would end their differences, with marks on them as clear reminders of who won and who lost. Delia couldn't separate them when they wrestled their anger out on each other. She could only bandage their wounds and ice their bruises.

Except for a few physical trophy-like scars, Briggs almost made it through his high school years. But a mistake was made, and a series of events followed that set him on a course for his life that no one in the family could ever have imagined.

She had desperately wanted Briggs to be part of the Wingate Winery team. But she finally realized that it would never happen. And it was all because of her. She was the one who insisted that he be sent off to military school halfway through his senior year in high school. He needed to be as far away from the situation he had created as possible. She knew he hated her for it. Sending him away as she did was like severing a limb. But she had to take back the control she had lost in raising him. She and Frank made the impossible decision to send him to military school in New England for the rest of his senior year and longer if needed. She found out later that Davis had kept in touch with him after he left home. To her knowledge, they never fought again.

After Briggs graduated, he enlisted in the Army. She remembered with regret the words he said to her that day. *'You wanted me in the military, then that's where I'll stay.'* But it wasn't what she wanted. She was only trying to protect him, to remove him from what she considered to be a scandal that would surely affect everyone in the family and ruin his chances in life. She thought that some time away, away from the rumors and the shame, would do him good. But it changed him in a way that she never expected. He became his own man. He went his own way. She guessed later that rejection from a family could do that, and the military became his family. Then came the Gulf War and immediately after that, Mogadishu, Somalia. Those deployments broke him, and he was never the same. Davis changed too, understanding how one mistake can change the trajectory of a life.

Delia finally learned to live with her decision. But once she realized the enormity of how that one choice altered Briggs's life, her new role was to protect him, as she thought she had done by sending him away. She could no longer control him, so she did everything in her power to shield him.

Briggs eventually reconciled with the family to some degree and when Delia tried to convince him to join them at the winery, he made an honest attempt. But he could never stay long. He always had to be on the move. He suffered from post-traumatic stress disorder from his time in the military and said he couldn't put the family through the tortured times that he experienced. It was something he had to deal with on his own. So he stayed away, for months and even years at a time. Davis said she should leave him alone; he would come back when he wanted to. But she knew it was all her fault. She had driven him away and now this had happened to him. He was broken, and she had a hand in it.

Now there was Kate Tyler. Delia had thought that was all behind them. And suddenly she appears, at the very time Delia thought hers and Frank's legacy at Wingate Winery was settled. Even without Briggs working there, it was secure and thriving. Then this woman shows up and starts asking questions. Delia had dealt with people like her before. Trying to take something from her, from the family and the business. She was always on the alert for it. It could happen too easily. And Kate Tyler was a perfect example. She said she just wanted to know who her father was. But Delia could sense it was more than that. Kate said she didn't want the fifty thousand dollars. But she would probably be back tomorrow, once she had thought about it, and ask for more. If indeed her brother needed a kidney transplant, the money would help her accomplish that. It was silly of her to reject the offer. And Briggs never needed to know that one of his biological daughters by Jenny Howard had been looking for him. That was all that mattered. She would protect her son until the day she died. But she needed an ally. It was time to inform Davis as to what was happening.

Delia picked up the phone and dialed Davis's cell number. He answered on the second ring.

"Yes, Mother?"

"Davis, I need you to come to my office. There's something I need to discuss with you."

"There's a lot going on right now, Mother, I—"

She interrupted impatiently. "Please, Davis. It's important."

After a sigh, Davis agreed to come. "Of course, then. I'll be there in a few minutes."

When he arrived, he took a seat across the desk from Delia. "What's this all about, Mother?"

His mother proceeded to tell him everything she knew about who Kate Tyler was or claimed to be except for one very important part. She did not want to tell him about Billy, at least not unless she had to. She would hold back that information for now. Davis's compassionate side would win out in any discussion about that. She simply said the woman was looking for her father.

She told him that she had asked Briggs not to come but he was coming anyway and that he didn't know about Kate yet. And she said that she had written a check to Kate Tyler for fifty thousand dollars to make her go away.

Davis sank further into his chair, a look of disbelief on his face.

"Mother, I can't believe you've done this! What were you thinking?"

"I was thinking," she said emphatically, "as always, that the family and the winery need to be protected. Briggs needs to be protected. You know how he is. This would destroy him."

"How do you know that? Yes, Briggs has his problems, but you can't protect him from everything, and you shouldn't think you need to protect him from this. This should be his decision, Mother, not yours."

She shook her head. "No, I don't agree. All that we've built here? She could take it all away, and I will never let that happen."

"I think you're exaggerating. She didn't seem like that type of person at all."

"Oh? She came here under false pretenses. She also got information from a woman in Winston-Salem, also under false pretenses, who led her directly to us. She has lied to get what she wants. She has lied to you and Suzy. No, she is nothing to us and it will stay that way."

"Briggs still needs to know."

She silenced Davis with a wave of a silver-ringed hand, a movement that was all too familiar to her son. "No. I forbid it. I didn't even want to tell you, but she might approach you again, even though I told her to leave Deep Lake and never come back."

He paused for the span of a heartbeat and then began again, shaking his head in disgust. "Mother, you have tried to manipulate the situation when you had no right to. Not for me, nor Briggs. If it turns out that Kate Tyler isn't who she claims to be or if she starts asking for anything other than knowing who her father is, then we'll deal with it. We have attorneys for that sort of thing."

Delia knew her son was right. The family and winery were probably well protected legally. She had grown to respect her oldest son over the years for his wisdom in family issues. His intentions were always the best when it came to her and Briggs and his own family. She still debated telling him about Billy, but she didn't want to lie to him. She stood and steadied herself, one hand on the back of her chair. She took a deep breath.

"But she does want more than that."

"What is it, then?" Davis asked guardedly.

"It seems that her brother, one of the triplets, might need a kidney. But Briggs has enough health problems ...."

Davis held up his hand to stop her. "So let me make sure I understand. Her brother, one of the triplets, who is also Briggs's son from what you are telling me, might need a kidney someday, but we're not sure. And Briggs may or may not be a match. And yes, she may or may not be fabricating the whole thing. Both of them would need to be tested to confirm paternity at the very least before any decisions are made." He leaned forward. "Either way, Mother, it's up to Briggs to decide. I can help him work through it if I need to and if he wants me to."

Delia was now visibly shaken, realizing that her son was right.

"I thought this was all behind us," she said quietly. "The children went to good homes. They had a good life. I never thought ...."

"No, none of us did. But I have to say, if I were Kate, or if Briggs needed something like this, I probably would do the same thing she's doing. I would do everything in my power to help my brother. Just like you would do everything you could to help your son. Right, Mother? You've already proven you would do that."

She turned away from him, staring out the window at the vineyards and lake, the place where they had made their home so many years ago.

"Mother, I'll handle this from now on. Do you understand?"

Davis left the room without waiting for a reply. Delia knew her son would do what he thought was necessary to control the situation. The risks were still too great to ignore but the festival needed her attention, too. She pushed thoughts of Kate Tyler out of her mind.

18

BRIGGS WINGATE PULLED HIS MOTORCYCLE to the side of the road, removed his helmet, and dug out his cell phone. There was a missed message from his brother, Davis. He called him back.

"Hey Briggs, did you listen to my message?" Davis asked without a greeting.

"You know I never listen to messages. But I saw it was you. What's up?"

"Where are you?"

Briggs looked around. "About seventy miles from you. Just passed Lake Bremer. I'm stopping for the night pretty soon."

"Okay. Are you going to the cottage tomorrow?"

"Yeah, but why the twenty questions?"

"I need to talk to you. I'll meet you there, okay?"

"Sure." He shifted the phone to his other ear as a group of bikers blew past him. "Listen, does this have anything to do with Mother asking me not to come home?"

Davis sounded hesitant. "I'll explain everything. Just let me know when you'll be getting there tomorrow. I'll see you at the cottage. Don't talk to Mother before we meet."

Briggs ended the call. He knew something was going on. His mother would never tell him not to come home. But she had. And now Davis wanted to talk to him first. Yes, something was up.

He put his helmet back on, motioned to the biker behind him, and turned out onto the road. Several miles later, the two men pulled into the parking lot of a small motel and took a room for the night.

Briggs called Davis about fifteen minutes before he arrived at the cottage the next morning. He parked his bike just off the road next to his brother's truck and told the biker who had pulled in behind him to do the same. He breathed in the scent of pine trees and listened to the familiar slap of modest waves against the shale beach. He shook off the strain of the long ride and let the sounds and scents of the place settle in.

The faded sign on the peak of the cottage facing the road said *Sunny Days*. The sign and the cottage both needed paint but Briggs preferred things with rough edges, and he had made Davis promise to keep it as it had always been. Davis had fulfilled that promise except for some minor repairs over the years to keep it livable. Their mother had no say in any decisions about the cottage although she had tried on many occasions, calling it an eyesore and a blight on the family. Briggs was the only one who wanted to stay there as far as the rest of the family knew. But Briggs knew Abby occasionally used it as a getaway when she couldn't take things at what they all called 'the big house' anymore.

So it had been maintained as a summer cottage, heated by a wood stove and a fireplace in colder weather and rotating fans in the living room and bedroom to blow the heat around in the summer. Besides those two rooms, there was one bathroom and a simple kitchen.

Sunny Days had been owned by the Wingates for over fifty years. Every summer, the family used to drive up to Deep Lake from Winston-Salem, and Briggs remembered those months as some of the best in his life. Swimming, canoeing, fishing, and sailing, evenings by a bonfire, almost every meal cooked on a charcoal grill on the beach. The cottage had never been his mother's favorite place, and she had often stayed behind in Winston-Salem for most of the summer. But Frank and his boys led a simple life for a brief time and loved it. On his infrequent visits to Deep Lake now, *Sunny Days* was where he stayed; never at the big house where his mother ruled.

Then his father bought the winery and moved everyone there. Everyone except him, of course. Unlike his brother Davis, who had always been in good graces with his parents, Briggs had felt he was not a part of the family ever since his mother sent him away to Blackstone Military Academy. It always puzzled him how a mother could think that rejection was a form of protection, but that was the truth of it. Delia Wingate was nothing if not determined to control and manipulate everything in her line of sight. She believed she needed to protect Briggs from his own poor choices, but he knew it was just as important for her to protect the family name, to shield the great southern Wingates from any hint of impropriety and scandal. Over the years, he believed she had finally been able to look forward to his visits, but he had purposely kept his distance as much as possible. Nothing had ever been fully resolved between them.

He couldn't figure out how Davis managed to survive working so closely with her all these years, but he seemed to be thriving. He and his brother were just two very different men who had made very different choices in life.

He took the wooden steps down to the small four-room building, a backpack slung over his shoulder, and found Davis on the weathered deck facing the lake. They hugged briefly.

Davis nodded at the young man accompanying his brother. Evan was tall and lanky, with a head of blonde hair that needed a cut and ripped jeans that needed patching, but he had a genuine smile that Davis remembered from the few times he had visited with Briggs before.

"You remember my stepson, Evan," Briggs said.

Davis took Evan's outstretched hand. "Sure. It's been a few years though."

He turned back to Briggs. "You look good."

"I doubt it but thanks anyway."

Briggs shed his scarf and leather jacket and raked his hand through a head of graying hair. He hadn't shaved in a couple of days. His face was browned by the sun and chapped by the wind.

Davis already had a cold beer waiting. He opened it and they clinked bottles. He offered one to Evan, but the young man held up his hand.

"Don't drink the stuff," he said, and Davis returned it to the cooler.

"How've you been? We haven't heard from you in a while."

Briggs sat on a dirty plastic deck chair, stretched his legs out, and rested them on the railing. He looked at his brother with a raised eyebrow.

"Were you expecting to hear from me?"

Davis smiled. "No, I guess not."

They sat in uncomfortable silence for a few moments.

"Hey, Evan, do me a favor?" Briggs said. "Go into town and get some steaks or something for tonight, whatever you want. Me and Davis have got some catching up to do." He took a few ten dollar bills out of his wallet and handed them over to Evan.

"Sure, no problem."

"I wasn't expecting Evan to come," Davis said after he heard the sound of Evan's bike fade away down the road.

"I didn't think it would be a problem. Is it?"

"No, not at all. It's great. I know Abby will be happy to see him again." Abby and Evan were close in age and had connected when Briggs had brought him along on earlier visits. Briggs knew that texting was frequent between Abby and Evan, phone calls less so, but they had kept the connection alive over the years.

"So, your ex doesn't mind you taking him on these trips then?"

"Nah. She hardly knows he's gone." He took a long pull at his beer. "You know, I've messed up a lot of things, but I think maybe I did something right with Evan while his mom and I were together. And after, too. I was never great with kids, but he's different. He's a good kid and we get along."

"No other relationships then?"

"The road is my mistress," Briggs laughed, raising his beer to the sky in a mock toast. "Clichéd but true. So, what's going on? Mother never asks me not to come. Is she sick or something?"

Davis shook his head. "No, nothing like that. But there is something I need to tell you about." But he said nothing and stared out over the water.

Davis pulled on his beard. To Briggs, that was a sure sign of nerves. "Well, let's have it then," he prompted.

"A young woman has been here, at Deep Lake, looking for her father."

Briggs stiffened. He wrapped his hands tightly around his beer bottle. "Is that so?"

"Yes. Her name is Kate Tyler. She's from Eden Springs, North Carolina."

A few long moments passed in silence.

"Well, damn," Briggs finally said. "After all these years."

Briggs knew the name Tyler. Davis had told him, after many years had gone by, that his two girls had been adopted by the Tylers and the boy by another family. But he had buried the information deep in his memory ... until now. He controlled himself by focusing on the rocks guarding Wingate Island across the lake. A Lightning sailboat sliced through the water across his line of vision, its ballooning sail stretched to the limit with the prevailing winds from the lake. He wished he could plant his feet on it right at that moment. Instead, he was landbound and restricted to the discussion with his brother. He tapped his fingers against the glass bottle. The road was only a few steps away.

"Is she still here?"

"I'm not sure. Mother ...."

Briggs interrupted. "Mother tried to get rid of her, didn't she? Did she give her money? Or just tell her to get out of town and never come back."

"Yes, and yes."

"So how much does this woman know?" Briggs asked, his emotions still in check.

"I'm not sure about that either. Mother didn't tell her it was you, of course. She's not even sure she is who she claims to be."

"Easy enough to find out though, right?"

"Yes, it would be. She's got information on Howard's Walk, though, and claims she's the granddaughter of Bessie and Enoch Howard and the daughter of Jenny Howard. She knew dates. Knew there were triplets. Seems to be the right age."

"So, what do you think? Is she telling the truth?"

After a moment, Davis said, "Yes. I think she is who she says she is."

"So why now? Why after all these years?"

"I'm not sure. I haven't talked to her directly about it. We've met, but that was before I knew about this. I just heard it from Mother yesterday. She thinks she's after something, of course. She didn't want you to know anything about it. But I told her I would handle it now."

Briggs nodded. "I'm not surprised." He got up and leaned up against the deck railing facing Davis. "So here we are."

"I'd understand if you wanted to get back on the road, Briggs. We can manage here. I'm glad you came but under the circumstances ...."

Briggs drank down the rest of his beer and pried the top off of another one. He shook his head. "I brought Evan, though. He wants to help out and see Abby. I don't want to disappoint him by leaving." He seemed to make a decision. "Maybe there's a reason for this. Maybe we're meant to meet now. So if it happens, it happens. But I'll tell you one thing. I won't be unhappy if our paths don't cross while I'm here. And I'm not going out of my way to meet her, understand?"

Davis nodded and tossed his empty beer bottle into a bucket on the deck. "I've got to get back to work. You'll be okay?"

"I'll be fine, brother. One day at a time, right?"

⚮

Delia Wingate's words still occupied Kate's thoughts the next day like sharp barbs darting in and out of her brain. She paced the deck of the cottage, rubbing her aching temples, but nothing could scour away the revulsion she had for Delia and what she had tried to do. The woman thought she could buy her silence, offer a bribe for her to disappear, and never come back. And all in the name of helping Billy? It was disgusting.

After Ben left for his class, which he offered to skip, Kate called Mimi. She said Billy was doing okay but a tremor in her voice told Kate she was worried. His health problems weren't going to go away. Delia's shameful attempt at ameliorating her own guilty conscience, if she even had one, was not going to sway Kate from getting what she needed from the Wingates.

Kate grabbed her windbreaker, slipped into a pair of clogs, and hurried down the steps to the water. The outboard was thumping against the dock, like a horse chomping at the bit to be let free. It was the first time she would be taking the boat out by herself, but the pull of the lake and the temptation to escape across the waves was too much to resist. She put on a life jacket and backed the boat out into the open water.

The lake was empty except for a clutch of sailboats preparing for the regatta that afternoon. They raced full out, not an inch of sail unfilled, their crews straining fearlessly against the pull of the sails to balance and control their vessels for maximum speed. Kate knew she had to let them pass but it was thrilling just to watch those beautiful boats, like colorful sea creatures, skimming across the waves. They flew by her in a glorious parade, then faded silently into the distance.

Kate urged the boat forward again, dipping in and out of several small coves. There were few signs of life along the shore except for two men swimming out to a floating dock, their strong strokes slicing through the waves as if in a race. Their laughter floated across the water as they reached the dock and climbed on. The men were different in age, maybe a father and son. Kate brought her hand up to wave, but they turned to face the shore and she let it drop.

She turned out into the lake again and headed to Wingate Island, curious to see it up close, and it gave her a focus to point to. Abby warned that it was a dangerous spot because of the large boulders lining the shore. But Kate was confident she could stay well away from those.

She slowed the boat as she approached, rocking with waves that grew larger as she neared the shore. As she idled there, she studied the landscape. The island was covered with pine trees and stunted shrub growth. There were no buildings on it or docks leading out to the water. The boulders blocked any hope of landing, so she slowly circled the island and discovered the same terrain on the other side.

As she brought the boat around to head back to the cottage, she misjudged her location and realized she was dangerously close to the rocks. She nudged the throttle forward and turned the wheel to head into the waves instead of sitting broadside against them. Her lack of experience with the boat made her struggle against the relentless push and pull of the surf, but she was finally able to maneuver out into calmer, deeper water. A few feet closer and she would have felt helpless against the wind and waves pushing her where she didn't want to go. She didn't like the feeling and pushed hard on the throttle, flying along a clear path back to the *Summer Winds*.

19

EVAN SOON RETURNED to *Sunny Days* with steaks, potatoes, and corn on the cob for their meal that night. He put the food in the refrigerator and then looked for Briggs. He saw him doing laps in the water and changed into his trunks to join him. After a chilly race to the floating dock, Evan broached the subject of seeing Abby.

"I'd really like to get together with her today. And I can help do whatever you or Davis need me to do."

Briggs knew that seeing Abby was one of the reasons Evan wanted to come along and that was fine with him. Abby was a sweet girl, his favorite and only niece, and Evan was a nice kid. The two had become friends over the years. He didn't want to pull her away from her work at the winery for too long though, especially with the festival going on. Davis wouldn't care but his mother would not appreciate that at all. There were some old friends he used to work with in the vineyards and he wanted to catch up with them. But doing all that meant a trip to the winery and after talking with Davis earlier, he wasn't sure he was ready for that.

"What do you think, Briggs? Can we go up to the winery today? Or we can ask Abby to come down here?"

"Nah, she'll be busy." Evan's face fell and he dove into the water. He turned and treaded water as Briggs considered it for another minute. "But I guess we can head up that way," he called out. He dove in and raced Evan back to shore.

About thirty minutes later, the two men pulled their bikes off to the side of Hilltop Road, just above the winery. Davis wasn't in sight, nor was Abby. Or his mother. He would have to reach Abby without sounding any alarms. He knew how she would react to hearing that they were there, but all he wanted her to do was break away for a few minutes to say hello to him and Evan. But that would be hard for a young woman with her enthusiasm.

Evan had waited patiently for Briggs's next move but then said, "I can call her. Or ...."

"Yeah, that should work. But, Evan," he said putting his hand on Evan's arm, "we don't know who she's with, so let her know she shouldn't let anyone else know we're both here. At least not yet, okay?"

"Yeah, sure, no problem." Evan made the call and while Briggs didn't hear any shrieks of joy from Abby on the other end of the phone, he did see her burst out onto the patio and race up the long driveway toward them.

"Uncle Briggs! Evan!" she squealed, giving them each a hug. "You came!"

"You didn't think we'd miss the fun, did you?" Briggs said, smiling.

"I wasn't sure. And I wasn't expecting you to come," she said turning to Evan. "But I'm glad you did!"

"Me, too. You look great," he said shyly.

"You, too," she said, lightly punching his arm. "Well, come on inside and we'll find everybody," she said, trying to pull them both in the direction of the winery.

"Hold on there, Abby. Not so fast," Briggs said, standing his ground. "We just got in this morning. There's plenty of time for that. I'd like to go out to the vineyards and see the crew first. Let's ease into this, okay?"

"Sure, Uncle Briggs. I have to go help Suzy set up for the judge's reception. Hey, maybe Evan can help?"

Briggs chuckled to himself. The girl just didn't get it.

"Eeease into it, okay?" He dipped his hand through the air and Abby did the same. It was an old habit between the two of them and Abby knew exactly what it meant.

"Okay, I get it," she said, rolling her eyes. "But maybe we can all get together for the Parade of Boats at the Lake House tonight? Please say you'll come!"

Evan and Abby looked at him with such hope that he couldn't refuse. He would control that situation by arriving after everyone else.

"Sure," he relented. "That sounds good. We'll see everyone then. But Abby, your grandmother has a lot going on right now. So don't tell her I'm here yet, okay? In fact, don't tell anyone yet."

"Well, okay. But I know everyone will want to see you."

"I know. I guess I'll see you later then."

She hugged her uncle and Evan again. "I'm so glad you're here," she said, grinning.

They watched as she ran back down the driveway, raising puffs of dust as she went. She turned and raised her hand in a slight wave, then went inside.

Briggs scanned his eyes over the nearby vineyards. He had wanted to catch up with some old friends that worked there but once again, his proximity to the winery gave him second thoughts and he couldn't see anyone working in the grapes at the moment.

"If it's okay with you, I think we should head back to the cottage," Briggs said as he put on his helmet and started his motorcycle.

"Sure, Briggs, if that's what you want," Evan answered. But Briggs had already driven off and Evan hurried to catch up.

ༀ

Later that afternoon, Delia looked out over the eager crowd gathered in front of the winery. She was pleased with the numbers so far. Attendance was better than last year, and the vendors had reported increased sales for the first day of the festival over previous years. Guests clustered patiently on the lawn holding glasses of their favorite wines and bags of their purchases. And, best of all, she realized that the noise from the children's play area was just a thrum in the distance.

The entire scene was calm but expectant; a cloudless blue sky overhead, a gentle breeze that wafted the enticing aroma of grapes into the air. Delia felt a quiver of excitement at meeting her special guest for the first time.

She was extremely satisfied with what she had achieved so far. The arrival of the judges and the reception that followed had, over the years, become a highly anticipated event, and for good reason. It was a chance to rub shoulders with the movers and shakers of the area's wine industry and other local celebrities while enjoying superior wines and food.

Right on schedule, at three fifteen, the first judge arrived. Taylor Hammond, a notable wine connoisseur who wrote for *The World of Wine* magazine, had published three well-respected books on the subject of wine and was a regular judge on the wine competition circuit. He was a small, fussy man, with slicked-back hair and a pencil-thin mustache. He carried an umbrella and tapped the stone steps as he ascended. He turned and waved at the applauding crowd then turned and awkwardly shook hands with Delia, their competing walking aids getting in the way. It was embarrassing, although he didn't seem to notice, and she hoped that no one else did either.

Next to arrive, promptly at three thirty was Kelly O'Doul, a large man with a booming voice who could have been Davis's twin. The two were old friends from their years at Cornell and hugged each other heartily. O'Doul bowed to Delia, which she outwardly scorned but secretly found flattering. Then a kiss on both cheeks was too much, she thought, but who was she to complain?

O'Doul was known throughout the United States as a top consultant when starting a winery or when marketing new wines. He was a favorite on the competition circuit because of his generous and constructive advice to all the winemakers, and he had been coming to the festival since its inception. He also won a round of enthusiastic applause from the audience.

Delia checked her watch. It was nearing three-forty-five and there was no sign of the third and final judge. The minutes ticked by. Davis announced that one more judge was arriving shortly and that everyone should be patient and enjoy another glass of wine. Four o'clock came and finally, far down the road, a large black limousine could be seen making its way up the winding turns to the winery.

"Davis, this must be Renee Scott," she whispered with a critical look at her son. "You could have worn a suit, you know." Davis looked down at his crisp white shirt, khakis, and leather shoes and shook his head.

The limousine slowly came to a stop in front of the winery. A uniformed driver got out and opened the back door. Everyone turned to watch a woman take his hand and step out of the limousine.

She was a beautiful woman, with dark shoulder-length hair and fine features. She wore a navy-blue jacket over a creamy white shell and a knee-length skirt. Pearls peeked out from beneath the buttoned jacket. A wide-brimmed hat dipped down over one eye. And Delia was sure that the stylish ankle-strap sandals she wore were by Jimmy Choo. She was stunning, and for a moment the crowd was silent. But she gave a quick wave which garnered an enthusiastic round of applause.

After a nudge from his mother, Davis came down the steps to escort her. The woman took his arm and as she navigated the steps slowly. Delia noticed a slight limp on her right side. She wondered briefly if the limp was from a recent accident and thought it must have been the reason she chose the low-heeled

Jimmy Choo's instead of high-heeled pumps, which would have been a more appropriate choice of footwear. But Delia put this faux pas out of her mind and held out her hand as Renee Scott reached the patio.

"Ms. Scott. Welcome to Wingate Winery. It is a pleasure to have you here. I'm so grateful that you were able to come."

Renee Scott nodded. "Pleased to meet you, Delia Wingate, is it?"

"Oh, yes, yes, of course," Delia gushed. "I should have introduced myself. And this is my son Davis Wingate."

"Pleasure to have you here with us, Ms. Scott. Shall we go in?" Davis asked.

Ms. Scott nodded. Davis offered his arm again, but she waved it away.

"Thank you but that won't be necessary," she said softly.

"I hope your accommodations are satisfactory at the bed and breakfast?" Delia inquired as they walked across the lobby of the winery, the other judges and guests trailing behind.

"Actually, I found the room to be rather small, so I made my own arrangements. I hope you don't mind."

"Oh," Delia said, startled at that bit of news. "Of course, I don't mind at all," she stammered. But she did mind, and thought it was very inconsiderate of Ms. Scott after all the trouble she went to. The room she chose was perfectly fine, and she knew it to be the largest one in the B&B. But she let it go. A woman of Renee Scott's caliber was used to having only the best.

They arrived at the entrance to the reception hall and Davis escorted their guests in. A group of locals including winemakers, winery and vineyard owners, the mayor of Pine Ridge, the Chamber of Commerce President, and Yacht Club leaders, had assembled around a podium at the front of the room. Everyone from outside gathered in the room as well, and Delia stepped up to the podium to say a few words.

She tapped on the podium's microphone. "May I have your attention, please?" she said. The room quickly quieted.

"I'd like to thank you all for coming. Especially our three judges whom I would like to introduce at this time."

She went through the biographies of Hammond and O'Doul, leaving Ms. Scott for last. Davis nudged her as she went into the second minute of her final introduction.

Delia quickly got the hint and finished her speech, ending with, "There's plenty of food and wine, so please enjoy."

Delia watched as guests huddled around Renee Scott, greeting her. The woman's cool demeanor seemed to change as she engaged with the guests. Even the other judges came to greet her. She hadn't needed to move one inch from where she first stood in the room. She was like a magnet, drawing everyone to her. For a brief moment, Delia hoped she hadn't made a mistake by inviting her, at great personal expense, no less. She put her personal feelings aside and decided that the most important thing right now was a successful event.

She looked around the room. Guests were lining up at the tables of food and sampling Wingate wines. Third in line was that awful woman Celeste Duvall, piling her plate high with hors d'oeuvres and balancing a glass of wine, full to the brim.

She heard Abby's laughter as she chatted with her father's friend O'Doul. So Abby had gotten her way, after all, she thought. The room had been set up to perfection, but that was probably all Suzy's doing.

Abby was spoiled as far as she was concerned. Her parents gave her too much rope. At her age, she should be taking on responsibilities at the winery. It was her legacy, after all. The only grandchild she had. Except for .... she pushed the thought from her mind. At least Kate Tyler had enough sense not to show her face here. She should have left town as Delia had told her to. She made a mental note to ask the realtor if they had turned in their keys to the cottage yet.

20

CELESTE DUVALL WAS THOROUGHLY ENJOYING the festival so far. Delia Wingate had been a pleasure to meet, although she did feel slightly dismissed at the end of their first meeting. No matter. Celeste had gotten what she came for and more. The loan of the painting for her art show was confirmed. Kate Tyler thought she could fool her, but she was wrong, and Celeste felt entirely justified to warn Delia about her. It was definitely the right thing to do.

Celeste slipped into the reception area quite unnoticed. She didn't want to run into Kate or her boyfriend again. She knew Kate wouldn't want to see her either, but she just wasn't up to another confrontation. She was there to enjoy the food and wine, so she filled her plate with an array of hors d'oeuvres and accepted a glass of Riesling from the bartender. She slipped behind one of the high-top tables off to the side and studied the room.

Not far away, a small gaggle of fans had gathered around Renee Scott. From where Celeste stood, they seemed to be enthralled with this so-called celebrity. But as she watched, she sensed something was off.

There was something odd about the way Renee Scott was standing, favoring her right leg. Celeste had noticed a limp when Renee walked up the steps to the winery earlier. Davis Wingate had offered her his arm to lean on, which she accepted. Perhaps she was recovering from a recent injury. Celeste thought a closer look might quench her curiosity.

But just as she began to approach, the woman raised her right hand to push her hair back, revealing a raised, mottled scar that extended across her hand and wrist. Surprisingly, instead of trying to hide it, she had chosen to wear large diamond rings on her fingers and a stack of gold bracelets which brought more attention to the disfigurement. It was somehow familiar to Celeste. And the limp. It was familiar too.

But it couldn't be. This was Renee Scott from California, a well-known and respected wine expert, here at Wingate Winery to judge a wine competition. They certainly had never met before.

Just then the woman tipped her head just so and smiled.

Celeste gasped and hurried from the room. Renee Scott was not who she pretended to be.

21

BY FIVE O'CLOCK, the judge's reception had ended, and Delia began to make her way through the crowded lobby to greet the outside vendors and the owners of the neighboring wineries.

Everyone was in high spirits, and this lifted her own. She was chided for surprising them with a third judge, especially one the caliber of Renee Scott. But Delia took their reproach in the spirit it was intended knowing that the area wines, and especially her own, would stand up well to any scrutiny, even that of the new judge.

Delia felt a buzzing from her phone. She dipped her hand into her pocket to retrieve it. The number wasn't one she recognized, but the sender had added her name.

> I would like to meet you at Salisbury House B&B on Lake Street in Pine Ridge at noon tomorrow. Is this convenient? Renee Scott

Delia wondered how Ms. Scott got her personal cell number but the text made her smile, nonetheless. No doubt the woman wanted to apologize for her rude behavior when she arrived. It was wrong of her to find her own accommodations after everything had been arranged, and Delia was sure she had now realized her mistake.

She responded.

I will meet you there at noon.

Delia finished making her rounds, then escaped down the long hallway off the lobby to the patio of their private residence where her family was waiting.

"Well, that went well," Delia said, uncharacteristically upbeat as she greeted Davis, Marie, and Abby. "Everyone seemed pleased with the introductions and being able to chat with Ms. Scott at the reception. You see," she pointed her finger at Davis, "it was the right call to invite her." She lowered herself into a cushioned patio chair.

"Yes, Mother, you were right," Davis nodded in agreement, handing her a glass of wine.

"Nana," Abby chimed in, "we're all going to the Parade of Boats tonight, right? We've never missed it."

"Of course, dear," Delia agreed, surprising everyone with her enthusiastic response. "I've even asked chef to send supper down for us."

"This is great," Abby gushed. She turned to her grandmother. "Nana, can we invite Kate and Ben to the parade tonight? Maybe they would enjoy—"

"No!" Delia interrupted, startled by hearing Kate's name coming from Abby. Could she be talking about Kate Tyler? Delia knew from her conversation with Celeste Duvall that Kate Tyler was there covering the festival and thought she was probably the person who had interviewed Davis. But she couldn't think of any scenario that would explain how Abby knew her and, from her tone, thought they were friendly enough to be invited to a family gathering. No logical reason came to her, but she needed to squelch the idea immediately.

Davis said he would take care of things after she first spoke to him about Kate Tyler. But had that happened yet? And what did he mean by 'taking care of things'? This was why she needed to be in control of everything that went on at the winery and in the family. She was regretting that she had not insisted he stay out of it.

But Davis quickly interjected. "Mother, Abby was with me during the interview on Monday."

"I see," Delia murmured. Now it made sense. She didn't know who this Ben person was that Abby wanted to invite, too, probably a boyfriend. But she really didn't care. The casual tone of Davis's response and a slight shake of his head reassured her that Abby knew nothing about who Kate might be and Delia softened her tone. "Let's just keep this as a family night, all right, dear?" she said hoping that this would put Kate and Ben out of her mind.

Abby looked at her father for support. "Daddy, I think it would be fun."

"I'm with your grandmother on this one, Abby," Davis said. "We're all tired from today so it will be a good time to relax and not have to entertain guests, okay?"

"Well, it's not, but whatever."

There was a slight rustle behind her, and Delia turned, shading her eyes.

"Mind if we join you?"

"Uncle Briggs!" Abby exclaimed. She ran to greet him and hugged Evan, clutching his arm as Briggs shook hands with his brother and kissed Marie.

Delia stayed seated, stunned that Briggs was actually there. She wondered when he had arrived; she was sure Davis knew but had kept that secret. She would have to address it with him later.

Briggs leaned down to kiss her cheek. "Mother," he said.

"Briggs," she said softly, glancing at Davis. "I wasn't sure you were coming or not."

"I said I would. Anyway, I'm like a bad penny," he said evenly. "I always turn up." He pulled Evan out of Abby's grip. "You all remember Evan?"

"Of course, welcome to our home," Delia said, shaking the hand Evan offered. "It's lovely to have you here," she managed to say, even though she thought it was the worst thing imaginable. The young man was poorly dressed in ripped jeans, a tee shirt, a leather jacket, and hair that needed a proper cut. She caught Abby out of the corner of her eye and noticed the wide smile on her face. Was that for her uncle, or this motorcyclist he brought with him? Probably the latter, she thought sadly. She knew Evan was Briggs's stepson from a disastrous marriage. He was well rid of that woman. But was this really what Briggs needed? An extra burden to add to his other problems? She thought not.

Abby turned eagerly to her stepcousin. "We're all going to the Parade of Boats on the lake tonight. Are you coming?"

Evan looked at Briggs who nodded. "I guess we are."

"Great, can I ride down to the lake with you on your bike?"

Delia cringed but Evan looked to Davis, who gave his approval.

"Sure, that'd be great," Evan said.

"Okay, I'll get my jacket and meet you up by the road." As she ran into the winery, she called, "See you all down at the lake!"

Evan excused himself after Briggs reminded him to use the extra helmet for Abby.

Marie set her wine glass down. "Delia, I told the kitchen staff that we'd pick up dinner and take it with us instead of sending it down later. Briggs, could you help me with that?"

Briggs eased himself away from the door as she approached him. "I'd love to, Marie," he said, following her inside.

"Does he know?" Delia asked when she was alone with Davis.

He nodded. "I told him yesterday."

"And how did he take it?" She braced herself for his answer.

"I believe he said he'd take it one day at a time, as usual."

She let out a breath. "I should have handled this myself. Now, we don't know what will happen."

"Not everything is in our control, Mother. You know that as well as I do."

"What exactly are you trying to say, Davis? You think I have handled this badly, don't you?"

"I just think there comes a time when we must let go of things. I'll see you at the Lake House later." Davis left Delia alone on the patio and went inside.

Delia sipped her wine. The sun was sinking in the west, and she shaded her eyes at the glare. Davis didn't understand how much a mother worries about her children or the lengths they would go to protect them, no matter their age. Some needed more protection than others. And the presence of Kate Tyler at Deep Lake simply proved she was right.

The next morning, after breakfast at a small café in Pine Ridge, Ben and Kate returned to the winery and made their way to the conference room for the judges' panel discussion. It was open to questions from the audience and replaced the final winemaking class that would have been held that morning. They found two seats at the back and sat down.

At the front of the room, the three judges, Hammond, O'Doul, and Scott, sat at a long table with Marie Wingate who acted as moderator. She began with a brief reintroduction of the panel and gave guidelines for the question-and-answer period.

As the discussion began, Ben glanced across the room and noticed Celeste Duvall enter. He nudged Kate and pointed in Celeste's direction.

"I'll wait outside," she whispered, quietly exiting the room through another door. Ben kept an eye on Celeste until he was sure she hadn't noticed Kate leaving.

An hour later, the question-and-answer time was over and Ben texted Kate to let her know he wanted to speak to the panelists, especially Ms. Scott and Mr. O'Doul. He told her Celeste was still in the room. Kate responded that she would get something to drink and wait for him outside.

Ben went to the end of the line of people waiting to speak to the judges, hoping it would give him more time with them. He heard a voice next to him.

"You're Ben, right? Kate's friend?"

He turned and came face to face with Celeste Duvall.

"Yes," he said curtly and stepped forward as the line moved.

"Excellent panel today. Especially Renee Scott, don't you think?"

"I guess so." Ben was torn between engaging her or being unfriendly, wondering which would keep her in the room so she wasn't out hunting for Kate.

"I did an internet search on her last night," Celeste said, keeping her voice low. "She received her Master Sommelier certification recently. Very impressive. Funny, there isn't much other information about her. She lives in California now and married an older wealthy man with a winery. Just stepped into it, I guess. She hasn't lost all of her Southern accent though. North Carolina, I think. It comes through once in a while. Did you notice?"

"Not really." Five more steps and he could be rid of her.

"I do know something that you might not be aware of. Now she goes by the name Renee. But I know that her full name is Jennifer Renee Scott. I'm thinking that maybe she didn't want people to use a nickname like Jenny, so she's using her middle name." She chuckled. "I should call her Jenny when I talk to her. I wonder how she would react?"

The name Jenny, which Celeste seemed to emphasize when she said it, rattled around in Ben's brain for only a brief second before settling on what she was trying to tell him. Jenny from North Carolina. He paled at her words. This woman truly knew no bounds. But could he believe her?

"Well," she said, "I guess now might not be a good time to approach her about it. Have a nice day, Ben. And say hi to Kate for me, will you?" Celeste turned and walked out of the room.

Ben felt rooted to the floor. He felt a tap on his back from someone behind him and he took another step forward, trying to absorb what Celeste Duvall had just told him. He looked up and saw Renee Scott excuse herself and walk out of the room. Ben took in as much about her appearance as he could, including her limp, committing it to memory.

Then he bolted from the room in search of Kate. When he didn't see her, he took out his phone and called her. "Where are you?" he asked, out of breath.

"I didn't want to be out front where I might run into Celeste, so I went back behind the winery for a walk. I'm at the spot on the road where I had the accident. It's pretty quiet up here, but it looks like it's going to rain."

"Okay, wait there, I'll come to you."

"Are you okay? You sound frantic."

"Just stay where you are. I'll be there in a minute."

Kate was surprised to see him running full tilt up the driveway a moment later.

"You look even worse than you sounded on the phone," Kate said when he reached her. "What's wrong?"

Before he could catch his breath to answer, two men pushing motorcycles approached them and Kate and Ben turned in their direction.

Kate gasped. It was the face of the older man that first startled her, handsome but ruddy with an unshaven gray beard, and a wild shock of uncombed hair, a mix of gray and black. He wore a heavy scarf around his neck and a black leather biker's jacket. His eyes were dark, and they narrowed as he looked at her, as if quizzing his mind at what he was seeing.

This was the man in the photos that Abby had shown her. This was Briggs Wingate. Kate desperately needed something to hold on to.

"I'm Ben Evans," Ben said, breaking the silence that had been lengthening since the men stopped in front of them. "And this is Kate Tyler."

After a long moment, the man cleared his throat. "Briggs Wingate. I'm Davis's brother." He pointed to the young man with him. "This is Evan, my stepson." His voice was raspy and deep. The introductions were oddly formal considering the situation they found themselves in. It seemed that no one knew what to do next.

"Are you okay?" Evan turned to Briggs with a concerned look on his face when no one else spoke.

"Yeah, Evan. All good." But to Kate, he looked like a man who might bolt at any second. She was very sure he knew who she was already. And this reality collided with everything she had suspected up to this point.

Kate knew she might never get another chance to talk to him. She took a deep breath and let it all out rapid-fire.

"I don't know exactly what or if Davis told you, but my brother Billy has Berger's disease. Our doctor has said we may need to find a kidney donor someday. He said it was important to know our family's medical history. But of course, I never knew anything about that." Kate's heart was pounding as she pulled out her phone and found the photo of Billy. Her words poured out in a nervous torrent. "I never needed to search for my biological parents, and I never wanted anything from them before and I still don't. Except for what I need to help Billy. But my search led me here, to you." She held her phone out to him, her hand shaking. "This is Billy. He can't do this for himself. He could get very sick."

Briggs held a curious gaze on the photo. The screen was damp from the mist that had settled around them, distorting the photo. But there was truth in what she was asking him.

"I know Jenny Howard is my mother, but I've never met her, and I have no idea where she is, or if she's even alive. So I need to know … are you my father?"

The sky began to darken, and the mist turned into heavy drops of rain, pounding against the dry dirt of the driveway. Time seemed to stop there on Hilltop Road. Maybe the clouds stopped moving across the sky. Maybe the birds stopped flying and maybe the wind stopped. Maybe Kate's own heart stopped as she grasped what she had just asked the man.

There was an imperceptible nod of his head before in one swift motion, he jumped on his motorcycle, turned, and roared off down the road.

"Briggs!" Evan shouted after him, but he was long gone. Evan turned to Kate, his eyes flashing. "What the hell, lady? Do you know what you just did?"

Kate couldn't answer. Tears poured down her face, indistinguishable from the rain.

"Listen, Evan," Ben said, "maybe you can go after him."

"No, man, I can't!" Evan's voice echoed the frustration he was feeling. "My bike's dead. That's why we were walking here."

"I've got a truck," Ben offered. "We can use that."

"No, thanks," he scowled and shook his head. "You've done enough damage already." He laid his bike down in the grass and ran the rest of the way down to the winery. Ben and Kate stood by helplessly as the sky changed from gray to black.

22

AT NOON, Delia asked for Renee Scott's room number at the reception desk of the Salisbury House B&B, informing the clerk that they had an appointment. The room was on the first floor and Delia soon found it and knocked on the door. Renee Scott opened it a moment later.

"Thank you for coming," Renee said, and motioned for Delia to take a seat in one of the comfortable chairs in front of the room's fireplace. Delia noticed the slight limp again and debated whether to ask if it was something she needed to have addressed while she was here, but then thought better of it. She didn't want to embarrass her guest. Especially if she was going to apologize for her earlier behavior.

"I hope everything has been satisfactory so far, Ms. Scott?" Delia began.

"Yes, quite, thank you."

"I'm sorry I missed the panel discussion. I trust it went well?"

"Yes, very well."

There was a pause during which Delia expected her guest to begin her apologies. But she was silent.

"So, Ms. Scott, is there something you wanted to discuss with me?"

The woman chuckled. "I guess I have done what I set out to do in my life."

Delia wasn't sure what she meant but said, "You've been very successful. And we're glad to have you here. But is there something more we can do for you?"

The woman shook her head. "Not really. Actually, I've been anticipating this meeting for years. But I wanted to wait until after I became a Master Sommelier to meet you ... again."

"I'm afraid I'm confused," Delia said with a pleasant smile. "I'm sure we've never met."

"It's been many years. And under less than pleasant circumstances."

Delia studied the woman. "I'm sorry, but I have no idea what you're talking about. I'm sure we've never met," she repeated firmly. "And I don't like your tone."

Renee chose to remain standing. "February 28, 1990. I met you at Howard's Walk. You and your husband stopped by for a ... visit ... with me," she paused, and then continued with some resolve, "and my parents. Enoch and Bessie Howard."

Delia's face turned pale. "No. You're mistaken. I never ... we never ... who are you?" she said, stumbling over her words.

"My name is Jennifer Renee Howard. My married name is Scott, of course. I decided to use my middle name for professional purposes."

"Why are you here?" Delia said through gritted teeth. "What do you want from me?"

"Just to see the look on your face, Delia. So that you could see that I was not the loser teenager you thought I was, the one you said ruined your son's life. That I had made something of myself despite everything." She gave a hollow laugh. "And how fitting it was that you begged me to come here and be the prize catch of your little wine festival. I did it all on my own, Delia. Without anyone's help. It turns out I'm not the country trash you thought I was."

Delia shook her head. "No, I never thought that," she whispered.

"Yes, those were your exact words, Delia. Country trash. I imagine you used a few other choice names for me behind my back, too."

"I don't believe you. You don't look at all like ... like Jenny Howard."

"I've grown up, haven't I? Dyed my hair, had a nose job. But some things never go away." She pulled up her sleeve. "Some scars never disappear, Delia."

Delia now saw the burn scars on Renee's hand and wrist. And she recalled the limp. It all came back to her. There was a fall from a deck at a beach party, Jenny broke her ankle badly and burned her hand in a bonfire all those years ago. Or so she was told weeks later when it came out that Renee—Jenny—was pregnant by her son Briggs. All signs that this woman was who she said she was. Was that the night it happened? Was that the night that ruined her son's life? No, all of their lives?

Delia stood. The room was suddenly cold and dark, everything swimming around her, and she grabbed the back of her chair. She closed her eyes tightly to reorient herself, then finally opened them. The woman was still there, a thin smile playing on her lips.

Delia could not let her get away with this. Two could play this game.

"So, you two are in this together, I see?" Delia asked.

"I beg your pardon?" Renee asked with a light laugh. "I came here on my own."

"Oh, so you don't know?"

"Know what?" Renee said, impatiently.

"There is someone else here who wants to destroy this family. Someone you never expected to see here, either, I would say."

"What are you talking about?" Her eyes narrowed. "You aren't making any sense."

"A young woman came here looking for her father. As a matter of fact, she's here right now." Delia couldn't be sure if Kate was still there, but it didn't matter. The shocked look on Renee's face was satisfaction enough. Now she would turn the knife. "And you've met her before. She's your daughter."

"No. I don't believe you," Renee whispered, her face a pale mask of astonishment.

"Oh, you can believe me. And you're probably wondering, which daughter? Well, I'll let you figure that out yourself. That is, if you want to meet her."

Renee began to shake. "You're a wicked person, Delia Wingate. You haven't changed a bit."

"I'm just protecting my family, Ms. Scott." She reached for her cane. "I'll leave now. And don't worry about staying around to judge the competition. We no longer need your services."

Renee sank onto the couch, her hand on her heart. Delia took one last look at her and walked out the door, slamming it behind her.

Thirty minutes later, Jennifer Renee Howard Scott carefully made her way out of the B&B through a light rain to the waiting limousine. She grabbed the railing as she descended, her right ankle feeling weaker than usual. The driver opened the door, and she got in.

"Take me to the airport, John." The man nodded.

Renee clutched at her coat, her hands shaking, her breaths quickening. Delia Wingate hadn't changed a bit. She was still the controlling, vindictive, hateful person Renee knew as a teenager. The names that the woman had hurled at her when it was discovered that she was pregnant by Briggs were despicable. She shouldn't have been alone with her ever, but Delia managed to arrange it, just once. No one, not even her parents, believed that Delia could have spewed such hate at her, so she suffered with it alone. According to Delia Wingate, Jenny was to blame for getting pregnant. Her son had nothing to do with it, of course.

Jenny had trapped him, seduced him. She must have gotten him drunk at that party. The words 'country trash' were used several times. Jenny had ruined him, not the other way around.

Not only did Jenny physically suffer broken bones and burns from her fall from the balcony that night at the beach party, but she also carried scars on her body from giving birth to the triplets and emotional scars from giving them up. She had scars from the hate that Delia Wingate wounded her with, and scars from losing Briggs Wingate, her first love. She carried those scars throughout her life, trying to erase them with success in her career, a marriage to a wealthy man, and possessions she believed could never be taken away from her, ever. She had lost her innocence that night in more ways than one, and that had put her on the path she chose.

She knew what had happened to Briggs. His mother sent him away, just as Jenny was sent away. She knew that he had been in the military and that it had changed him.

Scars. Everyone carried them, some more obvious than others, but they were there just the same.

Her mind turned to the news that Delia dropped on her. It was too hard to believe. She was probably lying to her, trying to hurt her again. But what if it were true? What if one of the girls was there, trying to find Briggs? And why, after all these years? And which daughter was it? Renee had agreed that she wouldn't know anything about the families her children went to. Her mother Bessie had assured her only that they were good families, and she knew her mother wouldn't have lied to her about that. But she knew she could never return to Eden Springs. So she found her own way.

Her path was never easy after the triplets were born, but she eventually graduated from college and moved to California where she met her husband. She finally felt as if she had made it; she was successful and wealthy. Maybe she drove herself to that success just to spite her past. Her husband knew everything about her life before she met him and knew that she wanted to put it all behind her. He loved her for the woman she was now, not the seventeen-year-old that she had been so many years ago. She left that girl behind like so much country trash.

Renee slid open the onboard bar and found a small, chilled bottle of champagne and two glasses. She opened the bottle and poured a glass, drinking it down quickly, then refilled it as the limousine carried her away from Pine Ridge.

Her trip to Deep Lake and the Wingate Winery was ill-conceived. She could see that now. It hadn't served the purpose she wanted it to, which was to teach Delia Wingate a lesson. She realized it was an immature move on her part, but she had been driven to it for years. Then Delia Wingate had reached out to her, personally, to invite her to the festival. Call it fate but it was an opportunity she couldn't resist. Maybe it was meant to be. Or maybe being that close to one of her daughters was her punishment for thinking she needed to have revenge on Delia Wingate.

Now she had a decision to make. What should she do with the information that one of her children was in Pine Ridge? Anything? Nothing? Briggs might be there at the festival, too, and her daughter might eventually meet him although she knew Delia would do everything in her power to prevent that from happening. And what if she had run into Briggs? She knew that was a risk when she accepted the invitation to be a judge at the competition. But she had been there for only a short time; no one would have recognized her. She even fooled Delia until she revealed herself. So she had kept an eye out for Briggs and had prayed she would be able to avoid any meeting with him. She had put all of her feelings for him behind her years ago but seeing him would only distract her from her real goal. She was sure Briggs didn't want to see her either.

Renee saw flashes of the lake through the tree line as they drove towards the interstate. The wind whipped up a surge of white caps on the water and a steady rain beat against the windshield. The driver slowed down at a stop sign and as he did, Renee caught a glimpse of a family running along the beach through the rain, arms stretched wide. This might have been her life if things had been different. If different choices had been made, she and Briggs might still be together and happy, with a family like that.

What if? What if she returned to Deep Lake and changed what had just happened? She might never have this chance again and couldn't help thinking that maybe this ill-conceived, random reunion was meant to be. Her stomach knotted up as she considered it.

What would happen?

∽⚬∾

Briggs raced away from Evan, Kate, and Ben, taking the curves of Hilltop Road at dangerous speeds. He turned sharply onto Lake Road, hunched over the handlebars of his motorcycle. He tried to block out the images of Kate Tyler looking at him, asking the question, "Are you my father?" The events that had put him on this path happened a lifetime ago. He thought the memories had faded enough that they would someday disappear, but they had only been buried, like so much other trauma in his life. And now they had come roaring to the surface.

Ripped away from everything he knew in the middle of his senior year in high school when he had plans and dreams, friends and family—it had been taken from him in the blink of an eye. He knew his objections to leaving Winston-Salem would be overruled. His mother had made up her mind and there was no questioning it. He guessed his father agreed with her although he had never actually said so. His brother took up on his behalf, but there was no changing the decision. He was sent to military school at a huge expense, he was sure. He graduated, but he knew that the diploma had also been paid for by Wingate money. He was hated by his peers at the academy and was bullied so badly as the new kid, the kid who must have done something terrible to be sent there in his senior year, that he began to hate himself.

He was supposed to enroll in college, but the military school had drilled into him that his only use was being a soldier. They did an excellent job of that. He enlisted in the Army where he eventually found a new family—his fellow soldiers. Other than his brother Davis, they were as close a group as he had ever known. They would have given their lives for him, and he would have done the same. And he almost did.

1991. The Gulf War. 1993. Mogadishu, Somalia. He had seen and experienced things that changed him. Since the day his mother told him what he was going to do, at the age of seventeen, because of a mistake he and Jenny had made, he had known nothing but a battered existence, physically and emotionally. The academy was wrong. He was not cut out to be a soldier. But a soldier he became. And when the army stopped putting him into battles, he created his own. Always fighting this demon or that one. Drinking, drugs, homelessness. It was the only way he knew to escape the torture of his mind.

He didn't hate the woman named Kate for asking the question. She had every right to know the answers. But the knowledge that he had hidden inside himself all those years, that he was able to push away because time had passed and because he had convinced himself that the triplets were better off without him in their lives, now it was blowing up through him like a land mine. Now she said they needed him. All he knew to do then was run, as he always did, as far away and as fast as he could.

Briggs was suddenly aware of rain hitting his face. He passed into a rainstorm as if through a curtain. The road was already thick with leaves and dangerously slick. He felt himself sliding around a curve, but he didn't slow down. He righted himself and picked up speed, barreling down a straightaway. The rain grew heavier, whipped by the wind, pounding at his face, and blurring his vision. He swiped at his eyes and at that moment, rounded a curve that took him straight into the path of an oncoming car. He jerked the bike to the right as the car tried to swerve away from him, but it was too late. He felt himself flying through the air, his arms outstretched as if grasping for a lifeline. He hit the ground hard and fast.

23

"WHAT HAVE I DONE?" Kate whispered as Ben held her.

"Let's go back to the cottage. There's nothing you can do now," Ben said.

"I shouldn't have just blurted it out like that. What was I thinking? I need to get out of here," she said, and they hurried down the driveway to the parking lot of the winery. She wrenched open the door to the truck and climbed inside. They drove in silence back to *Summer Winds*.

It had begun to rain hard, and Ben started a fire to warm the chilly cottage. Kate curled up on the couch and wrapped a blanket around herself. She was barely aware of the flickering fire and the sounds of large drops of rain splattering against the patio doors and the deck.

"Here," Ben said, handing Kate a cup of hot tea. "This will warm you up."

"Thanks," she murmured. She felt him sit down close to her and she put her head on his shoulder. She sipped the hot tea quickly, barely feeling the heat as it coursed through her.

"I've ruined everything, haven't I?" Her hands began to shake, and Ben took the cup from her and set it on the coffee table. He shifted so he could look at her.

"No, Kate, you didn't. There's no game plan for this, for what you're trying to do. You didn't even know he was going to be there. It was all a shock. If he ran, then he has to deal with that."

"Maybe Delia was right. Maybe we just need to go home."

"That's always been up to you."

"Abby said he wasn't the same after his time in the military. And he looked ... broken. What if this pushes him over the edge? What if he does something crazy now? It sounded like his stepson was worried. I wouldn't be able to live with myself if something happened to him."

"It was probably just too much for Briggs at the moment and he felt like he had to get away."

"Maybe you're right. I hope so. Evan was really mad at me. I don't blame him." Kate suddenly felt the blood rush from her face. "Oh, no! He'll probably tell Davis or maybe even Delia. This is bad, Ben. This is so bad," she whispered, her eyes flooding with tears.

Ben sat silently next to her, his presence the only comfort he could give her. Eventually, the strain of the day caught up to her and she dozed off. Ben stretched her out on the sofa and covered her with a blanket.

His heart broke for her at that moment. He hated that she was in such pain; he loved her and couldn't bear that she was going through this. But he felt helpless to change anything or even offer advice.

He hadn't had the chance to tell Kate about what Celeste had said to him. It would destroy her if she knew Renee, or Jenny, was there at the winery, too. He wanted to be honest with her, but he couldn't believe that this news would be good for her right now. He had to keep it from her until the time was right.

Kate awoke as the afternoon sun dipped behind the hills far across Deep Lake, drawing shadows across the room. The rain had stopped but wisps of mist lay in patches over the water. Her eyes were red, and her face was still damp from her tears. She tried to run her fingers through her hair but only met knots and soon gave up. She pulled the blanket around her and joined Ben at the kitchen table.

Ben had warmed up soup and ladled out a bowl for her. She ate slowly and finally laid her spoon down before finishing.

"Have you decided what you want to do?" Ben asked.

She coughed, her voice rough from sleep. "I guess we should go back home. There's nothing more we can do here. I don't want to talk to anyone, but I feel like I should tell Abby at least. I'll call her to let her know." She sighed in resignation at the fact that it was time to leave Deep Lake. "We can leave in the morning."

After Kate gathered her strength to make the call, she dialed Abby's number. She was surprised when she heard her voice. It sounded as if she had been crying.

"Abby, it's Kate. Are you all right?"

"No," she mumbled.

"What's wrong? What's happened?"

"Uncle Briggs has been in an accident. We're here at the hospital. He's still unconscious. They said it might be a head injury."

Kate gasped and put the phone on speaker, motioning to Ben. "What happened?"

"I'm not sure but he was on his motorcycle, and it had started to rain and apparently he hit a car, or the car hit him, I'm not sure. I think he broke some bones, too."

"Abby, what hospital is it? I want to come."

"Of course. It's Pine Lake Community Hospital. I don't know the address ...." she said as her voice trailed off.

"Don't worry, I'll find it. Is ... is your dad there?"

"Yes, and Nana, too, and Mom. They're a mess. I'd love for you to be here if you can."

"Of course. We're leaving now. Just hang in there, Abby. Everything will be okay."

"Thanks, Kate. Look, I've got to go. I think the doctor just came out." The line went dead.

Kate slumped into a chair. "This is all my fault!"

"No, Kate, you have to stop thinking like that. It was an accident. It was raining."

"But if he hadn't been upset, this might not have happened. Maybe I shouldn't go to the hospital. It's probably a bad idea."

"But you've already promised Abby. Sounds like she might need a shoulder to cry on, too. Listen, if it gets too hard, we can leave, okay?"

Kate nodded.

Kate and Ben followed the directions on their phone to the emergency entrance of the hospital. As the doors opened in front of them, Kate had flashbacks to another trip to an emergency room after another accident—that of her sister Becky. She staggered under the weight of that realization, but shoved it down deep inside her. That was then and this was now. And Abby needed her. She bravely forced herself to walk through the automatic doors.

They found Abby sitting in the Emergency Department waiting room. Kate quickly wrapped Abby in a hug. Evan was with her and stood, glaring at Kate, but Abby didn't seem to notice as she introduced him. She said she didn't have any new information to share.

"Thanks for coming though. We can't all be in there with him. Dad's with him now and Mom and Nana went to get some coffee. I think it's going to be a long night."

Just then, Davis approached them. He scowled at Kate. "What are you doing here?"

"Dad," Abby said, looking puzzled. "They came because I asked them to."

"Kate, I need to speak with you. Privately," he said, his voice firm.

"Dad!" Abby persisted.

"It's okay Abby," Kate said, understanding that Abby must still have been unaware of her connection to the family. "I need to talk to your dad, too. It's okay." She nodded at Ben and walked away with Davis.

"You shouldn't be here," Davis started. "If Mother sees you ... well, she's upset enough right now."

"I understand but ...."

"I know who you are, Kate. Now I need to know what happened. Evan told me that you saw Briggs. But I want to hear it from you. What did you say to him? I need to know everything that happened."

Kate was experiencing too much emotion to try to reason how Davis knew who she was or how much he might already know about why she was there. But he said he knew who she was, and that spoke volumes.

She relayed the brief conversation she had had with Briggs. "He really didn't say much though. Then he just took off on his motorcycle." She debated whether she should tell Davis that she had asked Briggs if he was her father. Maybe it was Evan that had told him after witnessing the conversation at the winery with Briggs, or maybe it was Delia. She was tired of all of the secrets. "And yes, I told him about Billy and asked him directly if he was my father. I guess you know about Billy now, too. Seeing Briggs was as much of a shock for me as it must have been for him. You think I'm to blame for all of this, don't you?"

Davis sighed and looked away. "Not entirely, of course. I wanted to be there when and if you met."

"I'm so sorry that he's been hurt. If I had any part in that, I'm sorry for that, too. I never intended for any of this to happen."

He nodded. "My concern is for my family: Briggs and Abby, and my mother. So you need to leave before Mother sees you. She doesn't know you met with him, and she doesn't need to know. Do you understand?"

"Of course." Kate turned to leave and go back to the waiting room. "I want to know how he's doing though. Will you take my calls?"

He hesitated. "Yes, but only me. Please do not call Abby either. We need to put this all behind us."

Easier said than done, Kate thought, but she kept it to herself. Ben was sitting alone in the waiting room and Kate motioned for him to follow her.

Ben took Kate's hand as they walked down the sidewalk toward the parking garage. A few moments later, a woman walked past them. Kate kept walking but reacted to Ben's grip on her arm as he stopped her.

"What?" she asked him when she saw the bewildered look on his face. "Ben, what's wrong?"

He opened his mouth to speak but nothing came out. He turned around and blurted out loudly, "Jenny Howard?"

The woman stopped, then slowly turned around. Kate pulled her arm out of Ben's grip.

"What did you just say?" He shook his head. "Ben, answer me!"

The woman slowly approached them. Kate finally recognized her as one of the judges from the winery. She turned back to Ben.

"Ben, what did you just say?" she asked again. He still could not speak.

"It's okay, Ben. You don't have to explain," the woman said.

"Yes, he does," Kate exclaimed. "He just said 'Jenny Howard' and you ... you turned around," her voice trailed off to a whisper. "What's going on here?"

"Could we sit down?" Renee asked and pointed to a bench in a small garden area just off the sidewalk.

"Good idea," said Ben, finally finding his voice, and he led Kate to the bench. Renee sat but Kate remained standing, her arms tightly clutched to her stomach.

"My name is Renee Scott. Why did you just call me Jenny Howard ... Ben, is it?"

He nodded. "Yes, I'm Ben Evans. And this is Kate Tyler," he said.

"Yes, Ben. Tell us why you did that," Kate said tersely.

"I saw you in the panel discussion earlier," Ben said carefully. "I was approached by someone who led me to believe that you might be ... that you are ...."

"Jenny Howard?" Kate laughed. "That's ridiculous! Who in the world would have said such a thing?"

"Celeste Duvall."

Renee's face blanched.

"What did she say to you?" Kate whispered, a sick feeling rising up through her.

"She said she did an internet search on you," he said, addressing Renee. "You live in California and married a rich older man who owned a winery. But she said you hadn't lost your southern, specifically North Carolina, accent and asked if I had noticed it. I said I didn't but then she said she knew your full name was Jennifer Renee Scott. She sort of laughed and wondered if she should call you Jenny and how you would react. The name's familiar to me, of course." He paused for their reaction, but Kate and Renee were silent. "Look, I know that Celeste Duvall knows Kate and I know that she also knew Jenny Howard in high school. If I'm wrong, and if Celeste Duvall was wrong, I am very, very sorry. But I think we're owed the truth here, once and for all. Let's just clear this up, okay?"

The woman took a deep breath. Her color had returned. She took a tissue out of her purse and dabbed her upper lip, sniffing slightly.

"Are you the young woman who is searching for her father here at Deep Lake?" Renee said to Kate.

Kate nodded slowly. "How did you know?"

"Delia Wingate told me. I met with her today for reasons I won't go into now, and she told me one of my daughters was looking for her father." Renee twisted the tissue in her hands.

She glanced between Kate and Ben. "I agree, we need to clear things up. It's time to be honest. I turned around when you called my name because I am Jenny Howard."

Kate gripped Ben's hand, her nails digging into his skin. "No, no, no," she repeated, shaking her head. "No, this isn't possible. How? Why?" She swallowed hard. "Why are you here at the hospital?"

"After talking to Delia, I was going to leave and go back to California. I was on my way to the airport. But I decided I couldn't leave things the way they were. I knew Briggs was probably at the winery or somewhere close by. My plan when I first came to Deep Lake was to avoid him. I had only meant to meet with Delia. But then she said someone was there looking for her father. I was shocked, to say the least. So instead of going to the airport, I went back to the winery to try to find Briggs. That's when I found out that he was in a motorcycle accident and had been taken to the hospital. I assume that's why you're here, too." Renee ran her hand through her hair. "Anyway, I realize I'm probably not welcome here, not if Delia has anything to say about it. But, right or wrong, I felt I had to come." She looked at them pleadingly. "I never wanted any harm to come to him. You have to believe me. I guess I thought maybe there was something I could do. But now ...."

Kate turned and walked away, her hands jammed in her jeans pockets. She tried to control herself but could feel the weight of what just happened pressing in on her. Besides the shock of learning that Renee Scott was really Jenny Howard, Ben had kept this from her. He had spoken to Celeste without telling her. She wasn't prepared for this meeting like she could have been. She couldn't forgive him for not telling her.

Ben came up behind her and put his hand on her shoulder. "Kate," he said. She shook his hand off, but he persisted. "That's why I was trying to find you when Briggs and Evan came up to us on the road. That was a shock for both of us. There wasn't time to tell you."

"We were at the cottage for a long time after that. You could have told me then," she said through gritted teeth.

He turned her to face him and raised her chin so that her eyes finally met his. "I had no idea we would run into Renee here. My first thought was that you didn't need any more stress on you. Are you trying to tell me that I should have told you what Celeste Duvall hinted at? For all I knew, she was just trying to cause trouble again. I did what I thought was best and I'd do it again the same way."

She shrugged him away for a second time. "That doesn't make me feel any better. You should have told me." She walked back to Renee and pulled out her phone. She found a picture of Billy, the one she had been showing to anyone who would listen. Now she held it out to Renee, simply praying that it might make a difference this time.

"This is my brother, Billy. Your son." She gave the same reasons for why she was here looking for her father as she had told Briggs. The story was the same. She was beginning to wonder if anyone except her really cared.

"I'm so sorry, Kate," Renee said. "I had no idea about your lives after," she paused, "after you were born. That's the way my parents, your grandparents, wanted it. Maybe that's no excuse but it's the truth. I wasn't supposed to know what happened to the three of you except that you went to good homes. But I need to know; what about your sister?"

"She's dead," Kate declared. The woman sank back on the bench, tears welling up in her eyes. She covered her mouth with her hand to stifle a sob. Kate's anger simmered, somehow feeling that she needed to punish this woman for what she had done by leaving them. She knew it was wrong, but she couldn't stop herself.

"She was killed in a car accident three years ago," Ben said trying to soften Kate's bluntness.

Renee dabbed at her eyes, seeming to gain control of her emotions. "I'm so very sorry. I see you've both had a lot to deal with lately." She stood. "But I know that I'm not welcome here. I'm sure the Wingates have no interest in seeing me. I should have known better than to come here. I hope Briggs will be okay. And I hope you find what you need to help Billy." She turned and walked to a limousine waiting at the curb.

Kate watched her walk away, then squeezed her eyes shut, trying to put the scene out of her mind. But it was now forever fixed in her, just as she had watched Briggs leave her. Finally, she was able to speak, and all of her pent-up anger, hurt, and disappointment suddenly burst from her.

"She just leaves? Just like that?" she cried out, tears pouring down her face. She turned and ran down the sidewalk.

24

KATE FELT BEN'S STRONG HAND on her shoulder as he caught up to her. He slowed her to a walk, wrapped his arm around her waist, and guided her through the maze of sidewalks and elevators to the 2C parking deck.

They had left her—again. First her father and then her mother. One more way of simply saying, *we don't want you.* The realization triggered a jagged pain that twisted her insides, and she grabbed her stomach, pushing in on the hurt, desperate for it to go away, once and for all.

Kate was angry with Ben too, but she didn't have the strength to shake him off again. She knew she couldn't have found her way alone. She wasn't seeing or comprehending the spaces around her.

They reached the truck and she managed to climb inside. She felt the seatbelt tighten and heard the click of the latch. Ben pulled out of the parking spot, glancing behind him but then turned to look at Kate.

"Kate," she heard him say, over and over. From somewhere in the distance, she could hear his voice and the rumble of the truck over speed bumps and the whoosh of cooling air vents. The turn signal clicked on, and she felt as if they were flying. She tried to breathe and open her eyes but was trapped in the unseeing world trusting that Ben would get her home before all breath and sight and feeling stopped.

Am I crying? she wondered. But she couldn't distinguish that pain from any other. It was all crowding in on her at once, overwhelming her senses.

Still, her brain tried to work through what had happened, trying to make sense of it. Had she caused this to happen to Briggs? Was it her fault? Was she being selfish to bring this pain to another family, simply because she was in her own hurting world? Was it really worth it? And how could a woman who was supposed to love her children be so cruel as to simply walk away? Again.

The flying finally stopped, and she felt Ben pull her to him, breaking through the pain. She could breathe at last, and the tears came in a torrent.

"Kate, breathe, just breathe. Look at me." She felt him wiping her cheeks with a calloused palm. She shuddered and opened her eyes. They weren't at the cottage, or anywhere near it.

"Where are we?" she mumbled.

"I pulled over. I was worried about you. Are you okay?"

Kate leaned into him and shook her head. "No," she said.

She felt him push the damp, flattened tendrils of hair out of her eyes, and he held her tightly as she slowed her breathing and began to relax into him.

How many times had he been the rock that she needed? How many more times would he have to be that rock? How many times would he want to? Kate pulled away.

"Can we go back to the cottage now?"

Ben reluctantly let go of her. "Sure, if that's what you want." He shifted back into his seat and started the engine.

At the cottage, Kate walked straight into the shower, leaving her dampened clothes on the floor. The water was as hot as she could stand it and she stood and let it flow over her, willing the film of guilt and anger to wash away down the drain.

Davis had said his main concern was for his family. Kate understood that and really wouldn't have expected anything less. But it was clear that he didn't include her within that familial group. She was still an outsider and needed to know her place.

Davis said they needed to put this all behind them, but Kate knew she couldn't do that. He should have understood that she couldn't walk away, not now.

And then there was Jenny. She shouldn't have been surprised that the woman simply walked away. This was exactly why she never wanted to find either one of her birth parents. She knew she would only be hurt by them a second time. Her worst nightmare had become a reality.

Kate finally stepped out of the shower and dried off. She put on clean jeans and a tee shirt and ran a brush through her tangled hair, twisting it into a loose bun. She went into the living room, expecting to see Ben there but the room was empty.

The sound of a bottle being opened on the deck drew her attention. She went to the screen door but stopped. Ben was slumped into one of the deck lounge chairs, his back to her. He ran his hand through his hair, then heaved the bottle top over the railing. He looked as defeated as she had ever seen him. His hand hung over the arm of the chair, the open bottle of beer held by his fingertips.

Kate had thought about what she had said to him, in anger, at the hospital. She knew he would never deliberately hurt her, and she had to trust him. And what had she done for Ben lately? How had she been there for him through all of this? She knew that everything that was happening to her was happening to him, too. Billy was like a brother to him, and he was just as worried about his health as she was. They were a family, one that Ben hadn't experienced in his lifetime, and she knew that the relationships meant everything to him. He had always been there for her. But how had she cared for him lately?

Kate stepped out onto the deck and sat down in a chair next to Ben. He didn't look at her. She took a deep breath.

"I'm sorry," she started quietly.

"No, Kate. You don't need to say you're sorry. You shouldn't apologize for being you."

His words came with finality as if he thought she couldn't or wouldn't change. As if he knew he would always need to be the one to pull her through these times. Kate realized suddenly that it had taken a toll on him. Her beautiful, strong, loving Ben gave everything he had just to be there for her and it had depleted him.

"No, I do need to apologize. I shouldn't have pushed you away. It wasn't fair. I know that now. You didn't hold back that information about Renee to hurt me. I can see what all this has done to you. I thought these episodes of panic were getting better, but it's happened twice since we've been here. The minute something goes wrong, I go off the deep end. I'm going to get help for it, Ben. I've never thought I needed it, but now I know I do. I have to learn how to cope with things better. This situation with Billy and the Wingates is not going to get better any time soon. I still have a lot to get through."

Ben set down his beer, reached for her hand, and entwined her fingers in his.

"What tears me up is seeing you in this kind of pain," he said. "I hate it. But, Kate, you're still thinking that it's just you who has to go through this. Don't you know by now that I'm in this with you? All the way? We're both going to feel pain and disappointment, and we'll worry and doubt what we're doing. But I love you and that's never going to change."

"I feel like all I do is take and take and give you nothing back," she said, tears welling up her eyes. She gathered the hem of her tee shirt and wiped the dampness from her face.

"Stop right there." He sat up and faced her. "You've given me everything I need. You rescued me, too, Kate. You and Billy are my family now. I thought you knew that. Come here," he said, pulling her into the lounge chair. She molded herself next to him as if she were created for just that purpose. "When I met you, I didn't think I could love anyone again. I'd been hurt too many times. I didn't think I could ever be a good father. I didn't have an example to follow. All I had was my mom, but I couldn't burden her with the things I was going through. You changed all of that. I found what I needed when I met you. And Billy is just as important to me as he is to you. So, we'll get through this together," he whispered. "I promise."

She nestled into his arms even closer. "I know."

"Do you still want to go home tomorrow?"

"I need time to absorb all that's happened. And I still need to make sure Briggs is okay." She looked up at him. "We have the cottage for two more days, so I'll call Mimi tonight and make sure everything's okay there; but what do you think if we stick around?"

"I think that's a good plan," he said, as he lifted her face to his and tenderly kissed the tears from her eyes.

25

"DELIA?" SUZY MCNEILL GENTLY LAID a hand on Delia's shoulder. Briggs had been moved to a room and Delia sat, head bent over her son's still form. "Delia, dear. I'm here to take you home."

Delia raised her head slowly. "No, I can't leave him. I have to be here when he wakes up."

Suzy pulled a chair up beside her friend. "You can come back. After you get something to eat and get refreshed. Davis and Marie are here. Abby, too. They'll let you know if anything happens."

Delia didn't move.

Suzy tried again. "Please, Delia. I'm worried about you. It's been hours since you moved from this spot."

"This shouldn't have happened, but I let it. I let him down with my own stubbornness," Delia said, clenching her fists. "This is all my fault."

"No, no." Suzy's voice was soothing. "Some things are just out of our control. You can't blame yourself."

"Well, I do." Delia straightened. Her eyes were bloodshot, her skin pale, her hands shaking. Suzy's eyes widened at Delia's appearance.

"Delia," Suzy said firmly, "if you don't come home right now, I am calling the doctor in here and have you taken to the Emergency Room. You don't look well, so those are your choices. I mean it."

Delia looked at her son, unmoving in the bed, with tubes for oxygen in his nose, bandages on his head that still showed tiny spots of blood, hooked up to monitors, and IVs in place pumping heaven knows what into his veins. She touched his cheek and stood slowly and stiffly from her chair.

"Suzy McNeill, you always were a pain in the butt." She reached for her cane. "I'll go on one condition."

"Oh, and what's that?"

"You will bring me back in no less than two hours. Is that understood?"

Suzy sighed. "Sure, Delia, whatever you say."

"And Davis will be with Briggs the entire time that I'm gone."

"Well, that's two conditions, but okay."

At the house, Delia showered and changed. She heard noises in the kitchen and found Suzy stirring a pot of soup on the stove. Suzy ladled out two bowls.

"Crackers?" Suzy asked as they sat at the breakfast table.

Delia waved her hand. "No, thank you. I don't know if I can even manage this."

They sat in silence. Delia tasted the soup and laid her spoon on the table.

"Do you remember the day we met?" Delia asked.

"Of course," Suzy answered. "You were holding interviews for an administrative assistant before you and Frank opened the winery. I was so nervous. I don't mind saying, I was a bit intimidated by you. Davis was easy to talk to but you?" She shook her head. "Not so much."

"Well, that is by design, you know. Helps me keep the upper hand."

"I thought as much at the time, and I respected it. I still do. But why do you ask?"

"That was over twenty years ago. It seems impossible. So much has happened. Davis married Marie. Abby was born. Frank passed." There was a hitch in her voice. "I've been thinking about him a lot lately. Though I don't know why." She took another spoonful of the soup and reached for the crackers, crumbling a few into the steaming liquid.

"You see," she continued, "you've grown in that time, Suzy. You overcame a nasty divorce. You reinvented yourself after that. I kept promoting you because you excel in everything you do. This place wouldn't work without you, you know."

"Thank you, Delia. You've never actually said that to me before now."

"Well, I should have. And I'm sorry about that. Now myself? I've learned a lot about the wine business, I've kept up with the technology and pushed this place into the future. I've made savvy business decisions."

"I sense there is a 'but' there?" Suzy urged.

"But have I grown? As a person? Have I poured everything into this business trying to look to the future and at the same time clung to the past so much that it has poisoned me?" She picked up a napkin and dabbed at her eyes. "Me and everyone around me? Tell me I haven't done that, Suzy? Please tell me I haven't destroyed everything and everyone I love!" The tears flowed and Suzy moved to put her arm around her friend to comfort her.

"No, no, Delia." She hitched her chair closer and sat down. "Delia, look at me." Delia slowly raised her head, reluctant to be as vulnerable as eye contact would make her, even with her close friend.

"You did what you felt you had to do at the time, all those years ago. Did that set into motion something you could control? No. It was completely out of your control after that. You've tried to protect Briggs because you love him so desperately. He's your son. And you blame yourself for things that happened afterward that you were not in control of. His time in the military could have gone differently, and we all hate that he has the effects of those deployments. But that was not your fault."

"But I forced him into it. I made him go to that military school. I made him do that."

"Yes, you did. You've told me the reason why. And you can't change that. You can't change Briggs either. He deals with his life the way he needs to now."

Delia looked out the window. The earlier storm had passed through leaving an unnatural stillness in the air. Delia briefly wondered how the vendors had fared through it all. But she pushed the thought from her mind. There were other, more important things to worry about right now. Someone else would need to deal with that.

"I need to tell you something," Delia said. "Maybe you'll understand the situation better after I tell you."

"What is it?"

"The young woman you agreed to have interview Davis, Kate Tyler."

"Yes, what about her?"

"It seems that she is looking for her father. At first she thought it was Davis, but now she believes it's Briggs."

"Oh, Delia, I had no idea. I would never have allowed it if I had known!"

Delia waved a hand to dismiss Suzy's concern. "You couldn't have known. None of us could. But there's something else." She seemed to steel herself to say her next words. "Our third judge for the competition, the woman I personally invited here as a coup for me, for the festival ...."

"Yes, Renee Scott. Go on."

"I met with her today, at the B&B where she was staying." Delia dabbed at her lips with a napkin, then crumpled it into a ball. "She confessed to me that she is actually Jenny Howard, the triplets' biological mother."

Suzy sat back in her chair, her mouth agape. "No, that can't be possible."

"Well, it is. I'm sure of it. And she said horrendous things to me when we met. Then I informed her that one of her daughters was there looking for her, too. I wanted to hurt her, Suzy. I'm not proud of that now. But I was so angry that she had the nerve to confront me like that, to manipulate me in that way."

"So, you've been dealing with this and now on top of everything Briggs is in the hospital. No wonder you've been so distressed." She clasped Delia's hand. "I'm so sorry. What can I do to help?"

"You're doing what I need and that is being a good friend. But I've thought a lot about that meeting. Yes, she said some horrible things but maybe I deserved them, Suzy. Maybe I deserved every word of it."

"I don't like the thought of anyone being that mean to you, Delia. And for her to show up in that way, now, just to get back at you? It wasn't right."

"No, perhaps not." Delia stood and took her unfinished bowl of soup to the sink. She walked to the bay window and looked out over the vineyards. The sun was setting, and remnants of the storm could still be seen strewn about the lawn. "But I'm tired, Suzy. I'm so tired of trying to be in control of everything and everyone. I haven't been able to let go and now it's that obsession that's controlling me. Maybe I see it now because of Briggs's accident. Maybe because the two people from my past that I thought I had banished, and never wanted to see again, just suddenly appeared. Or maybe I'm just getting older. But it's shown me how easily things can fall apart, how fragile everything in life really is."

Suzy stood next to her friend. "Do you know if Kate Tyler or Renee Scott is still here?"

"No, I don't know. They might have gone home but I'm not sure."

"I could find out for you if you want."

Delia nodded. "Yes, that might be a good idea. But if they're still here," she said, wagging a finger at Suzy, "just let me know and keep it between us."

"Of course."

"Thank you, Suzy." Delia got up from her chair. "I'd like to go back to be with Briggs now."

As the two women made their way back to the hospital, Delia gazed out at the passing scenery. For years, she had been surrounded by acres and acres of vineyards. She had moved from the city to the small tourist town of Pine Ridge in wine country to protect her family. But she admitted to herself now that she had done it to protect herself, too. Even after Briggs left, she had been on high alert for any hint of judgment or scandal, and was sure that it surfaced from time to time. Frank never saw it and couldn't understand what she was so afraid of. So she began searching for something that could take them away from Winston-Salem, something that would be good for the family, and a place for Briggs to come back to. The winery in New York State was the perfect solution. They had been going to the cottage on Deep Lake for years and when the opportunity to buy a nearby winery presented itself, she convinced Frank that it was the right thing to do. And even though she had never been fond of the cottage, the winery was something they could rebuild together. And it had been good for them. Except for Briggs. It had never drawn him home again. But just like the vineyards that kept renewing themselves, year after year, and her firm belief that the next year's wines would be better than the last, she embraced the hope that maybe next year, next season, when Briggs was healed, he would come back for good.

26

KATE AND BEN SPENT THE NEXT TWO DAYS exploring Deep Lake, mostly keeping close to the shoreline. They avoided using the motorboat and chose instead to paddle quietly in their canoe in and out of the coves and once out to Wingate Island. The soft waves near the island wanted to push them closer to the rocks, but they backpaddled against the swells, holding them steady until it was time to push on to explore the next inlet. They took picnic lunches and found empty beaches to land their canoe where they wouldn't be disturbed or bother anyone else.

Kate always felt Ben's presence behind her in the canoe's stern as they sliced through the water. It was his strong strokes that propelled them, determining their speed and the course they took. She was determined to hold her own, though, and the effort stretched her muscles to their limit. He didn't seem to tire at all, keeping the boat steady and always in forward motion.

It was good, she thought, that partnership in the canoe. They depended on each other, but it took Ben at the stern to do the hard work. Kate was new to canoeing but she quickly learned that one person can't paddle solo from the bow of a canoe. You may think you are in the lead, but you won't get anywhere fast. If you are alone, you must sit in the stern, but two in a canoe is always better.

Sometimes she laid the paddle across the gunwales in front of her and let her hand trail through the cool water, creating its own small wake, as Ben pushed on. The sun warmed them, the lake buoyed them, and they discovered that their strength together took them where they wanted to go. The effort made them a team again. Without conversation, except for what was needed to navigate the lake, beach the canoe, and eat their lunches, they let the strain of the last few days settle without words. And Kate felt herself falling in love all over again.

Their solitude was occasionally disrupted by visits from Abby, although she said that her parents and Delia had tried to discourage her from going to see them. It was only during her visits that Kate allowed herself time to think about Briggs. Otherwise, it was buried deep down with all the other hurts and guilt she felt in her life. But Abby was allowed in, and Kate was grateful for her support. She kept them informed of Briggs's condition, which had been slowly improving although he was still unconscious. He had not been wearing a helmet at the time of the accident, so the doctors said it likely caused a more severe head injury than he might have had otherwise.

Abby said that she had finally insisted that her father tell her what was going on. She had too many unanswered questions and was confused at everyone's antagonism to Kate. It had made no sense until her father explained everything. Abby's heart broke over the situation, and she told her parents and Delia that under no circumstances was she going to abandon Kate now. No matter what they said, she would be staying in contact with her and Ben. No one argued with her.

Kate was not allowed to go back to the hospital, and she respected that decision. Davis finally asked Abby to tell Kate that the best thing for her to do was to return to Howard's Walk and that he would keep her updated on Briggs's progress. While Kate doubted he would, once she left the area, she knew he was right. Their time at the cottage had ended, and she was ready to go home.

They left the next morning.

27

KATE FORCED HERSELF BACK INTO A ROUTINE at Howard's Walk, stumbling through her days, spending hours in the gardens to assuage a guilty conscience and her failures. She had lost control of everything except this place that had always been a place of beauty and growth and healing, even in her darkest days. She desperately needed that feeling again and with each passing day, she dug deeper and deeper into the soil, as if she could find it buried there.

She confided in Dr. Bartlett about the situation at Deep Lake. He was encouraged that she had most likely found her biological parents and was surprised that it had all transpired that quickly. But the disappointment and frustration were evident in Kate's voice when she explained that, yes, she had found Briggs, but she felt she had lost ground, too, and caused a life-threatening accident. As it was, he was still in the hospital, unconscious, being watched over by the family. *His real family,* she thought. And the situation with Jenny had been left with too many unanswered questions. The brief connection they made had been wrenched apart the second Jenny walked away. She had met her, but she still had no idea who the woman really was. She still didn't understand how Renee could have walked away from her like she did.

Kate told Dr. Bartlett that she didn't know if either relationship could ever be salvaged. She still felt distant and disconnected.

"You're asking too much of yourself, Kate," Dr. Bartlett had said. "You've made great progress. Billy is still doing as well as can be expected right now. His kidney function is still good."

"Yes, but can he be put on the transplant list?" She was grasping for some concrete steps that they could take. "I know it can take a long time to find donors. Just in case, I mean."

But he said it was too early for that with the strict criteria that must be followed.

"You continue as you have been. But keep in touch with Briggs's family. He still might be your best bet."

Kate left his office discouraged by the conversation. Her calls to Davis now went unanswered. Abby texted frequently but the news was the same and Kate wondered if she really knew what his status was, or if they weren't telling her the true story either, just to keep her optimistic. And would they show enough compassion to let Kate know if his condition worsened? Maybe she didn't deserve even that courtesy, but guilt drove that fear and it ate away at her.

Kate tried to call the hospital directly for information on his condition but was told that since she wasn't family, they couldn't release anything to her. *If they only knew,* she thought.

Doc was right. Billy was doing okay and was still with Mimi and her caretaker. At least she was well enough, with help, for Billy to stay there. But did that give Kate the space to heal or the freedom to wallow in self-recrimination? She wasn't thinking clearly enough to be able to answer that question.

At night, she lay awake for hours, and when sleep finally did come, troubling dreams came with it. The faces of her adoptive parents swam before her, slowly melting into images of Briggs and Renee. In a small lost voice from her childhood, she called out to them, searching those floating images for some recognition of her, but they drifted past, unseeing and deaf to her cries.

She spent her days digging, planting, and weeding, leaving few areas of the gardens untouched. Ben encouraged walks in the woods; sometimes alone and at other times he would join her. Their hikes were silent except for the crunch of fallen leaves underfoot and the sound of geese heading south and the whisper of a chill wind through the trees. She couldn't explain to him that there were words and feelings inside her that she couldn't let out, not the ones that conveyed the complete sense of abandonment she felt by anyone that could have ever been called family. The torture of losing her adoptive parents and her twin sister was bad enough. But the nightmare scenario of finding and losing her biological parents that had haunted her had come to pass. Kate was terrified that if she let out the pain she was feeling, it would break her. She hated that there was still that part of her that she couldn't share with him. But their passion for each other was as strong and honest as it had ever been, and they both took solace in that.

On a crisp afternoon in late September, Kate answered a knock at the front door. Abby stood there, her familiar smile beaming into the room, and into Kate's heart. Abby hugged her tightly and Kate clung to her, trying to hold back her tears. But it was hopeless. A dam broke inside her at the sight of Abby. Abby felt it too and for the first time ever, her cheerful face crumpled into sobs.

She clung to Ben as soon as Kate released her, dampening his tee shirt with her tears.

"I wasn't sure you'd be happy to see me," she said through her sniffles. "I haven't been in touch like I should have. I'm so sorry."

"No, no," Kate assured her. "Of course, we're happy to see you. But is everything all right? Is Briggs ... is he okay?" she asked, her brows knitted in worry.

"He's okay, Kate, even better than okay. He's conscious and talking now."

"Thank God," Kate said, relief washing over her.

"He's still in the hospital but improving every day. The doctor finally said there's no permanent damage."

Kate quickly remembered her manners. "Well, come in. Can I get you anything? Have you eaten?"

"I'm fine. I ate on the way."

"Did you drive all this way by yourself?" Kate suddenly had a thought. "Does your dad know you came?" Abby laughed. "I'm sorry, I'm asking a lot of questions. Come on in." They walked to the back patio. "We were just having some wine. Would you like some?"

Abby agreed and took a seat. Ben soon returned with a glass and poured a Pinot Gris from a local winery.

"Yes, I drove by myself. And yes, Mom and Dad know I came. Nana, too."

Kate's eyes widened. "And?"

She shook her head. "They didn't want me to come, especially Nana, of course. But I wasn't going to hide the fact that I wanted to see you both. I'm an adult and I can make my own decisions, despite what they think."

Kate knew this was a big step for Abby, not only making the trip but going against the wishes of her parents and her controlling grandmother.

Abby took the glass of wine from Ben. "And I figured, if I want to travel as a career, I'd better start somewhere! I've never been to North Carolina. But this is where my family is from, right? So I'm going to Winston-Salem, and then to Asheville, and then to the coast ... somewhere," she said, waving her hand. "Oh, and I've started my blog, Kate!"

"That's great, Abby, I can't wait to see it."

Abby swirled the wine in her glass. "And one other thing."

"What's that?"

"I'd like to meet Billy while I'm here. If it's okay with you, of course. You can introduce me as a friend ... at least I hope that we are?"

Kate didn't hesitate. "Of course, I would love for you to meet him. He's at home with his mother right now so we'll do that tomorrow. And, Abby, you've shown more compassion to us than I could have ever hoped for. Of course, we consider you a friend."

Abby was, unless proven otherwise, a biological cousin to Kate and Billy. They had the same interests and despite a few years' difference in age, Kate thought Abby also needed a friend. Abby grew up without siblings or close cousins and Kate knew without hesitation that if Abby needed that relationship with Kate, she would be more than happy to provide it.

"Thank you. That makes me feel better. Listen," she said, setting down her glass of wine. "I know I barged in on you guys so if you can let me know where there's a place to stay while I'm here?"

"You'll stay with us, of course. We have plenty of room."

Abby reluctantly agreed, but finally admitted that she had hoped they would ask her to stay. They toured Howard's Walk and talked late into the night, with Abby sharing misadventures on her trip. A flat tire in Pennsylvania where she met a handsome roadside assistant, then a long tortuous detour through the hills of Virginia. It made Kate wonder if the life of a travel journalist was really in the cards for Abby. But the evidence was that Abby had made it there in one piece and Kate knew that sometimes those little side trips not only made great content for her readers, but they were the things that would test Abby to her limits. Only then would she know for sure if this was the life for her.

Kate felt as if a weight had been lifted by Abby's arrival. The link she thought was broken was reconnected, and it grounded her to the reality of the situation. She realized that she had no control over what had happened at Deep Lake, and going forward she could only worry about the things that were in her control. She had been in this place of pain before, and she had to believe that she would get through it again.

28

NOTHING HAD BEEN RESOLVED by Abby's arrival, but simply hearing that Briggs was recovering calmed Kate's anxious thoughts and she slept worry-free for the first time in weeks.

After breakfast, Kate and Ben walked with Abby down a winding flagstone path leading to Rebecca's Rose Garden. It was the first garden to be replanted in memory of Kate's sister and soon became the most popular spot in the Gardens at Howard's Walk.

The walkway was edged with pink cosmos, red-tinted dahlias, and white alyssum and ended at a simple vine-covered archway with a brightly painted pink gate. Ben unlatched the gate, and they stepped into a romantic and dreamy place, just as Kate had imagined it to honor Rebecca. Abby stopped to breathe in the heady fragrances that surrounded her. The whisper of a waterfall drew her further into the garden to a charming pond, filled with brightly colored Koi fish.

"I think I want to live here," Abby whispered, a contented smile on her face. "This is so beautiful. I had no idea what you had made here."

Kate laughed. "We'll make you an honorary caretaker, how's that?"

"I'll do it!" Abby said excitedly. "But really, Kate," she said, running her hand through the waterfall. "You've done something wonderful here. It's amazing."

"Thank you. I certainly didn't do it all by myself. It wouldn't have happened without Ben and our friends Sam and Martin. And a lot of local help from people in Eden Springs."

Abby snapped pictures to send home and include on her website and asked about each type of rose until there wasn't a single flower left unmentioned.

They soon left the rose garden at its far end and circled back to the entrance. It was a sunny autumn morning that normally would have been used for outside work, but as their guest, Abby was given a choice: stay at Howard's Walk to garden or visit some of the local wineries. Abby answered by taking an extra pair of gardening gloves from Kate.

"Just point me in the right direction," she smiled. Even with Kate's obsessive toiling in the gardens over the past weeks, there were still plenty of chores to be done, and Ben laid out their usual plans for that time of year. Fallen leaves would be raked, which was Billy's job, or mowed over to be used as mulch. The perennial gardens always needed weeding and mulching. New quart and gallon containers of asters and hardy mums were lined up along the perennial garden perimeters, ready for planting.

Soon, they would prepare beds for the spring-blooming bulbs. But the chore of the day was to plant cool-weather annuals: pansies and snapdragons and ornamental cabbage.

"Is it always nice like this in the fall?" Abby asked, tilting her head to the cloudless sky to soak in the warmth of the sun.

"Not always," Ben said. "It's still hurricane season through the first of November, which can impact the coast. But you should be okay with a trip there if you decide to go now. It doesn't look like there's anything on the horizon you need to worry about."

"But before you leave, we'll take you to some of the new wineries," Kate promised.

After about an hour, they stopped working for a water break.

"Do you still want to meet Billy today?" Kate asked.

"Yes, if you think it's okay."

"I do. I talked to Mimi when we got back from Deep Lake just to explain the situation; so she knows who you are. But for Billy, we'll tell him you're a friend from up north. Warning though, he'll want to show you our 'Where In The World Are You From?' map in the visitor's center. One of his favorite things to do is to ask our guests where they're from and then put a marker on the map. I'll call Mimi and see if now is a good time for him to come over."

Kate called Mimi and explained that Abby had come to visit them and wanted to meet Billy. "If it's okay with you of course," she said.

"Well, if you think it's okay then so do I," Mimi said. "I would love to meet her too, but I can't right now. Sara is taking me to my doctor's appointment. So it would be fine for Billy to come over this morning, if that works for you?"

Kate said that would be fine and asked if her therapy was helping in her recovery.

"It's been slow, dear, too slow for my taste, but I'm always getting better. Doc Bartlett says I'm doing as well as can be expected. I'll tell Billy to be on his best behavior since you have a guest there."

About an hour later, as Kate and Ben were going over plans for the fall plantings in the greenhouse, Billy appeared at the door, holding Abby by the arm.

"Hey Kate, look who I found in the garden! This is Abby. She's a friend of yours from ... where are you from?" He turned to Abby, a perplexed look on his face.

"Up north, Billy."

"Up north, Kate. We're going to find her house on the map and put a pin in it, so we remember where she's from. Come on, Abby. Let's go see the map," and he hurried off to the visitor's center, with Abby in tow.

"Well, I guess she's met Billy." They put their work aside and followed the two down the path to the recently renovated visitor's center.

Billy had already put a blue pin into the lake configuration on the map. Abby was patiently telling him about the lake and the vineyards and their winery.

"Ben and Kate have wine sometimes," Billy said. "But I can't have any. But I like grapes and Ben is going to plant some and I'm going to help and then we can have grapes, right Ben?"

"That's right, Billy. And maybe some grape juice, grape pies, and jelly ... and maybe even some of our own wine."

Abby frowned at Ben. "Suzy told me you had started the wine classes during the festival. I hope you were able to finish them."

"I was. I've already teamed up with some vintners around here to get me started. It'll be at least three years after the first vines are planted, but with any luck we'll have our own Howard's Walk label someday."

"If there's anything I can do to help, just let me know. I mean, I do know a little bit about wine. I couldn't call myself a Wingate if I didn't."

Billy showed Abby around the Visitor's Center, explaining the history of Howard's Walk, at least as much as he understood it. He stopped at a group of photographs of Bessie and Enoch Howard and told Abby how Miss Bessie was a good friend of his and his mama's.

"But then she moved away, and I never saw her again." They walked around the displays in the room with Abby in rapt attention. When Billy started at the beginning again, she caught Kate's attention. "Kate, could I talk to you for a minute?"

Kate nodded and they walked to the greenhouse on the other side of the gardens, leaving Ben to get Billy occupied with some new chores.

"Is everything okay?" Kate asked as she opened the door to the greenhouse. A rush of warm air greeted them, and Kate propped the door open.

"I got a text from my mom this morning," Abby said. "She's not as upset with me as my dad and Nana are about this trip, so she's keeping me in the loop about Uncle Briggs."

"How's he doing?"

"Better. He was discharged from the hospital. He'll be staying at our old cottage, *Sunny Days*, at least for a while. Nana wanted him to stay at the big house, but he refused. I don't know if it's stubbornness or if he's so used to being on his own that he doesn't want a lot of people hovering over him. He says there was enough of that at the hospital."

"As long as he has someone checking on him, though."

"I think Mom will be in charge of that. She can do it without intruding."

"Is Evan still there?"

"No, he had to go back home to his mom's."

"Abby, speaking of your mom, I haven't asked you how she feels about all of this. I didn't get to know her at all while I was there."

"Mom is a very compassionate person. Her heart is breaking over this. She doesn't understand Nana and why she acted the way she did. But she won't interfere either unless she's pushed. She doesn't stand up to Nana often, but when she does, she makes her point very clear."

"Delia will watch out for her own family first," Kate acknowledged. "I wouldn't expect anything less than that. But I do hope I can meet your family on better terms someday."

Abby laid her gardening gloves on a nearby potting bench.

"Kate, I need to know something."

"What's that?"

"Is Uncle Briggs really your father and Billy's?"

Kate took a long moment to consider Abby's question. She didn't blame her for asking. Maybe no one in her family had been able to convince her that he was. Or maybe she just wanted to hear it from Kate.

"I guess I can't be positive unless he takes a paternity test," she began. "But from his reaction at the winery when I confronted him, and everyone else's reactions, I think he believes he is. And that's what I'm hanging on to right now."

"I know it means a lot to you and Billy to know that." An unusually serious look on her face told Kate she had more questions.

"Was there something else?"

"Well, you don't have to answer if you don't want to, but did you always know you were adopted?"

"Yes, our parents were very open about it."

"Did you ever look for your biological parents before now?" She raised her hand when Kate crossed her arms and winced as if physically hurt by the question. "You don't have to answer that. I'm sorry if that was insensitive."

Kate shook her head. "It's not insensitive. You've probably been on the outside of all of this until now. I'm happy to tell you the whole long story sometime." Kate wondered if the wiser course was to save Abby from the more painful truths of what she was feeling. But maybe there had been too much of that lately. She decided it was time to talk about it honestly.

"The more I learned after I started this journey, the more I realized that the truth about my birth had affected me more than I cared to admit. I told you the story of how I came to be here at Howard's Walk. So when I learned that I was a Howard and that this home was my birthright, I still buried any feelings I had about my origins. On the surface, I knew who I was. But underneath, emotionally, I had locked it all up inside. I vowed I would never risk the pain of finding my birth parents and then being rejected by them for what I felt would be a second time."

"And that's what happened, right?" Abby said softly.

Kate nodded sadly.

"So, you do know who your mother is, right? Have you met her?"

Kate took a deep breath and paced through the greenhouse, straightening pots that had tipped over, probably from Billy's overenthusiastic planting. She turned on the water spigot and swept the spray over the tops of the plants in a long arc.

"Kate?"

"Yes, we've met," she finally answered. "But your parents and Delia might not know that we have. Believe it or not, she was at the festival."

A look of surprise spread across Abby's face. "Really?"

"Really. She was one of the judges Delia invited and she must have confronted Delia about who she was at some point. Of course, your grandmother had no idea who she really was when she invited her. Then Delia told her that one of her daughters was looking for her, too. I get the feeling that it wasn't a good reunion for the two of them. I think there's more to their story than meets the eye."

Kate turned off the spigot and rewound the hose. "She was at the hospital, too, Abby. Ben and I ran into her outside the Emergency Room on the day of the accident. She had heard about it and thought maybe she could speak to someone in the family, I guess. Once she realized who I was, which is another whole story in itself, I showed her Billy's picture and told her what his problems were. She seemed upset but then she just got up, wished us all well, and walked away. Just like that."

Kate's voice trailed off. Abby wrapped her arms around her.

"I'm so sorry. I had no idea."

'Thanks," Kate said, disentangling herself.

"I'm glad you shared that with me. I've never had to even think about any of that, who my family was, or where I belonged."

"I had a good life, Abby. A really good life with Becky and my parents. I wouldn't have traded it for the world. But now I know there was a hole there, something I was missing. After I learned that my real father's name was not on the original birth certificate, and then when I had to start looking for him because of Billy's disease, it opened up a lot of buried hurts."

"Uncle Briggs and I have a saying. *'Eeease' into it,"* and she made the dipping hand motion as her uncle had taught her. "I know you didn't get a chance to do that; everything happened too fast when you got to Deep Lake. But maybe going forward, you can ease back into it. And maybe I can help?"

Kate smiled at Abby. She was the most genuine, caring, innocent person Kate had ever met. She gave her a quick hug. "I'm glad you came, Abby."

"I don't know anything about what happened between Uncle Briggs and your mom all those years ago," Abby said as they walked back to the gardens to find Ben and Billy. "They were really young when this happened. I don't know what made them decide to give you up, but I do know one thing. Uncle Briggs is a good person who's gone through a lot in his life and still struggles with what happened. Sometimes it's like he's walking a tightrope and none of us knows when he might slip off. He must have been shocked when he met you and realized who you were. But, deep down, I think he always wants the truth about things. At least that's what he tells me is most important in life. To always be honest. I think there's still a chance with him. I really do."

"Your grandmother would never allow it. And I can't risk making things worse than I already have."

"But you haven't. Everything just happened to collide all at once. I mean, who would have thought that the three of you would be there at the same time? So maybe it was meant to be this way, right?"

"I guess."

"Promise me you'll think about trying again, okay?"

"I promise." But Kate knew that the second time might be even harder than the first.

29

ABBY STAYED AT HOWARD'S WALK for the week, but then decided that the mountains, or maybe the beach, were calling her; she wasn't sure, but she said she would know which direction to go when she reached the interstate. The mountains won out when she made a right instead of a left, and Kate followed her travels by checking her social media posts and her website. She was more and more impressed as the days went by. Abby had a wonderful presence in her videos; she was relatable, fun, and interesting. Her best posts were of the wine scene from all across the state where she showed off her expertise, meeting and interviewing interesting people who were eager to share their love of wine with her and who seemed to genuinely like her. She was able to reach into their personal lives as well, asking all the right questions to have them open up and make them share things they might not have otherwise shared. She was gaining followers, and Kate encouraged all of her friends in Eden Springs to share Abby's posts on social media.

Abby finally went back to Deep Lake. But a week later a call came with unexpected news.

Kate was in the gardens cutting flowers for an arrangement in the house when her phone rang. Abby's name came up on the screen and she answered with a cheery greeting.

"Abby! How are you?"

"I'm fine, Kate. How's everyone there?"

"Good. Things have slowed down a bit for us, but it gives us time to gear up for Christmas." Kate sensed something was wrong. "You sound a little down, Abby. Is Briggs okay?"

"Yes, he is," she assured her. "He's been home from the hospital and has improved a lot. But I have some news."

Kate steeled herself. "All right. What is it?" she said. She pulled off her gardening gloves and sat on a nearby bench.

"You remember the information you sent to us? About how to contact Billy's doctor and take the tests to see if any of us are a match?"

"Yes, I remember. I knew it was a long shot. I guess it wasn't well-received?" Kate held her breath.

"No, that's not it. Dad took the test. He's not a match. I'm so sorry."

Kate slowly let out the breath she was holding.

"My mom will take it if you think she could still be a donor. But Dad told her to wait. I volunteered, too, but Dad said no. He said I was too young to even consider it. I hope that's okay."

"That's fine. I understand." So that left Briggs.

There was silence on the other end. Kate found her voice first.

"And Briggs?"

"Uncle Briggs said he took the test, Kate. But we don't know the results. He hasn't told anyone. I wish I had better news for you. But he did tell Dad that the doctor said he didn't have that disease that Billy has. So I guess that's something right?"

"Yes, and of course I'm glad he doesn't have it."

"And?"

There was silence. Kate was at a loss for words.

"Are you there, Kate?"

"Yes, yes, I'm here. I'm just in shock, I guess. But what made them decide to take the test?"

"Well, we've all been doing a lot of talking here. It's been hard for us because it was never anything the family talked about before. And of course, I never knew about it until after you left. But I hated to see everyone in so much pain, and for what? For hiding secrets for all these years? It didn't solve anything. So I guess I forced the issue and made everybody sit down and open up about it."

"Even Delia?" Kate asked.

"Yes, even her," she said with a brief laugh. "And Uncle Briggs, too. It wasn't easy for him. They still have a lot to work through. Nana was afraid Briggs wouldn't be in any kind of shape to go through giving up a kidney if he were a match and if Billy needed it. She worries about him so much. She's still trying to protect him even after all these years. But Uncle Briggs said the doctors wouldn't let him do it if he wasn't physically able to, so she shouldn't worry about that."

"That's true. I guess I never thought about it like that. And I would never expect him to put himself through something he wasn't perfectly able to. I guess there's a lot I never thought about. I'm just trying to help Billy." She sighed. "I wonder why he's keeping it to himself. If he's not a match, I would just as soon know that now."

"Of course. So, what's next for Billy?"

Kate explained that his condition still wasn't urgent enough for him to be considered for a transplant. But she would talk to the doctor again and see what he recommended.

"I hope this doesn't mean you won't come to see us or that we can't come to see you," Abby said. "I don't have any other cousins. And, well, you've become more like a sister to me. I hope that's okay."

Kate had been feeling the same way but had been afraid to say it out loud. She had lost her only sister. Abby was nothing like Becky, but they had an undeniable connection as cousins.

Kate had kept her distance to a degree, but she had a feeling Abby needed this relationship as much as she did.

"Of course, that would be okay. I'm grateful for all you have done for us. But I'm not sure Delia ...."

"Please don't let that stop you. I know now that she wasn't very nice to you when you were here. But we all want to invite you and Ben back. So I'm extending the invitation on behalf of all of us. And Billy, too, if you think it would be okay."

"I appreciate that. I'll talk to Ben about it. But bringing Billy would be out of the question right now. We've tried to take him on day trips, but he gets very anxious being away from home and his routines."

"I understand. Can you let me know? The fall colors are still beautiful here. I'm sure we could put you up at the Lake House."

"Thank you but I'll see if the cottage is available for a few days, that is if we decide to come."

"Okay, just let me know. And Kate, I am sorry I didn't have better news for you."

"I appreciate that, Abby. And I'll let you know if we can come."

They ended the call and Kate stayed in the garden for a while longer. Ben and Billy were in town. The last tour had left earlier in the day, and she sat in welcomed solitude.

Kate had been so worried about Billy over the last few weeks, focusing everything she did on what he needed. She had experienced an awakening at Deep Lake that still haunted her. But today, after talking to Abby, Kate realized that it wasn't just about Billy anymore. Now it was about finding the truth of what happened so many years ago. It was true that Billy needed healing. But maybe she needed it just as much as he did. Maybe, in the end, the search wasn't only for Billy but for her own inner peace.

30

FOUR DAYS LATER, Ben and Kate returned to Deep Lake, but this time they drove past the *Summer Winds* cottage, then several miles further along Lake Road, and pulled into the long driveway of the Wingate's massive Lake House. The last time they were here, they had arrived by boat with Abby at the helm. On that trip, Kate was worried about accidentally running into any of the other Wingates, but this time, they came at the family's invitation.

So much had happened since their first visit to Deep Lake. She never thought she would return there on good terms with the family. Abby seemed to be convinced that all was well. But until she knew otherwise, Kate would be cautious, especially where Delia Wingate was concerned. What was Abby's quote from Briggs? *"Eeease into it."* Maybe that was good advice.

They parked beside Abby's Volvo and Ben turned off the engine.

"She must be inside," Kate said when no one came out to greet them. "Maybe she didn't hear us drive up."

Ben agreed, then turned to Kate. "It's not too late to change your mind. We can take the week and go somewhere else if you want."

Kate shook her head. "No way. I'm not running away from this anymore. It sounds like attitudes might be changing here, so I'll give them the benefit of the doubt until I see otherwise. Besides, I wouldn't do that to Abby. I think she's tried to help us out and I don't want to disappoint her."

As they pulled their bags from the back of the truck, Abby burst out of the house, her arms outstretched.

"You're here!!" she squealed, running to them and launching into a torrent of words. "How was your trip? Did you see a lot of color on your way? The countryside through Virginia and Pennsylvania must be gorgeous this time of year. We're at our peak here almost. You'll have a great view from the front of the house." Abby rambled on as she led them through the kitchen and into the living room, where a fire burned brightly in the huge fireplace to take off the autumn chill.

She pulled Kate and Ben to the windows that overlooked the lake. "See? Isn't it beautiful?"

The scene in front of them was stunning. The brilliant reds and oranges of autumn spread across the far hills like a quilt. The setting sun cast a yellow glow up onto a sky of feathery clouds turning them golden. They stood, mesmerized, as the sky mutated from baby pink to russet red, and the lake mirrored the multi-hued transition from day to dusk. Kate wished that she and Ben were part of the lake's vibrant display, gliding through the colors in a canoe without a destination or care, just the sound of water splashing against the paddle, the two of them in perfect tempo with each other. She glanced at Ben and knew he was longing for the same.

"This is perfect, Abby," Kate said softly, breaking the silence. "I'm glad we came."

"I am, too."

They pulled themselves away from the window and sat in front of the fireplace while Abby poured a glass of rosé for each of them.

"Abby, is Briggs still around?" Kate asked. "You said he was going to be staying at the cottage."

"He is. He's doing pretty well. And we want you to come to dinner at the big house tonight," Abby said. "That is if you're not too tired."

"Is Briggs coming, too?" Kate asked. Even though this was what she was hoping for, she would need to prepare herself for anything that might happen when they met again. What would she say? How would he react to her? Would he blame her for his accident?

"He said he would," Abby replied, her voice sounding both hopeful and doubtful.

Kate took a deep breath. She pressed her hand to her stomach, but it did nothing to stop the jittery reaction she felt. "Okay. What time should we be there?"

"Around seven?"

When Kate didn't respond, Ben said they would be there and thanked her for the invitation.

Abby left after giving them a tour of the house. Ben carried their bags to the upstairs bedroom, leaving Kate in the living room taking in the beauty of Deep Lake.

"What are you thinking about?" he asked when he rejoined her. She wrapped her arms around his waist and leaned into him. "I was just thinking about the power that water has on us, how it influences our moods, our stress levels. Our bodies are so connected to water biologically that I guess we shouldn't be surprised that we're drawn to it. Maybe that's why Briggs likes to stay at their cottage. Maybe it brings him peace.

"I've always had an attraction to water. But before this, I never really thought much about the why of it. Look what it did for us the last time we were here. I was a mess and it brought me a sense of peace. It gives us a different perspective on life and the world around us, too. When we were out in the canoe, we saw things differently: the shore, the hills, the island. I felt small and fragile just thinking that there was only a thin bit of metal between us and two hundred feet of water. But I also felt strong and in control, too, because I could go wherever I wanted, and the lake would take me there."

Ben looked at his watch. "Come on," he said with a grin. "We've got time. Let's take the canoe out. I think we both need it."

Kate smiled in return, and they raced down through the fallen leaves on the lawn to the overturned canoe waiting for them.

At seven o'clock, Davis and Marie Wingate greeted Kate and Ben at the door of the Wingate's home, or as Abby called it, The Big House. They were cordial and polite, but Kate knew there was as much a wall around them as she had kept around herself. But then Abby appeared like a ray of sunshine and embraced them both. She kept a protective arm around Kate until they reached the living room where Delia was seated.

"Kate. Ben." Delia nodded at each of them without getting up.

Delia looked older, Kate thought. Not the formidable woman she had words with at the restaurant just six weeks earlier. At that time, her gaze was intense, and her voice firm. She was different now, revealing a sense of frailty that wasn't evident before. What happened to Briggs must have taken a toll on her, and it showed.

"Thank you for inviting us, Ms. Wingate," Kate managed.

Marie motioned their visitors to take a seat. Davis poured wine, and the conversation turned to Abby's adventurous trip to North Carolina and then moved on to what was happening at the winery.

The mood lifted as they navigated through the lighter topics, but Kate felt Briggs's absence. No one, not even Abby, mentioned him, and Kate steeled herself to ask, "Is Briggs coming tonight?"

She noticed a look dart between Delia and Davis.

Delia began to speak but Davis interrupted her. "He said he would be. He's just running a little late, I guess. He's not one to keep a schedule."

A few more minutes passed in conversation when a woman approached Delia and whispered something to her.

"We should go ahead and eat," Delia said, pushing herself out of her chair with Marie's help, even though Briggs had yet to appear.

"I'll give Briggs a call and see where he is," Davis said.

Everyone except Davis followed Delia into the dining room and found their seats. A few moments later, Davis joined them. "I just talked to Briggs. He said he couldn't make it after all. He said something came up."

From the look on everyone's face, Kate wondered if that was code for *'I'm not coming, I'm not doing well, I can't face this right now.'* But no one dared voice those thoughts.

Dinner was served, a delicious chicken caciatore and pasta with a Wingate Pinot Noir in keeping with the rustic tradition of the dish. The conversation was casual and surprisingly easy, but Kate noticed that it was mostly led by Marie and Abby, keeping things light to avoid the question that she was sure was on everyone's mind. Ben asked a lot of questions about growing grapes and winemaking, which they were happy to answer. Delia was mostly silent and did not once meet Kate's gaze.

When everyone had finished eating, Delia rose from the table and reached for her cane. "Kate, I won't rush you but perhaps we could meet in the living room?"

"Of course, Ms. Wingate," Kate managed to answer. She took two large swallows of wine and followed Delia.

In the living room, Delia stood at the windows looking out over the vineyards with her back to the door. She finally turned and seemed to be deciding how to start. Kate felt her eyes on her, but she held her gaze, hoping she had the strength to withstand anything this woman threw at her.

"Kate," she began thoughtfully, "since your visit here in September, we've had many family discussions about the situation in which we have found ourselves. It was difficult, as you can imagine, when you arrived here. And shocking, to say the least." She said her words slowly, almost unwillingly.

Kate interrupted. "And I hope you know that I had no intention of doing any harm here, and I still don't. I was doing this for my brother because he can't do it for himself. I don't want money. I don't want any part of the Wingate legacy. That's not mine to even consider. I have no claim on it."

Delia nodded. "I understand that now. And I hope you understand that I have, for many years, protected Briggs to the extent that I could. Perhaps it wasn't a wise choice, but it is the one I made."

"We all make choices and have to live with the results," Kate said. "I know that as well as anyone."

"That is true, isn't it?"

Delia joined Kate on the sofa. Kate saw a softening in the lines of her face, a glistening in her eyes.

"I behaved badly," Delia confessed. "I apologize for that. Can you forgive me?"

Kate didn't know what must have transpired for Delia to have this change of heart, but it touched her deeply. She felt a wave of emotion rising to the surface.

"Of course, Ms. Wingate," she said, a lump forming in her throat. "Of course, I will."

Delia wiped her eyes and nodded once as if the moment was over, and everything was as it should be again. Kate knew that the apology was hard for her. She suspected it wasn't in Delia's DNA to express regret or even consider that she had done something wrong. But if Delia could do it, then so could she. She drew in a shaky breath.

"I'm sorry, too, for any part I might have had in hurting Briggs. I've been in anguish over it." There, it was done.

Delia waved her hand, dismissing Kate's apology. "Briggs is responsible for his actions. It's in the past now and I think we should keep it there, hm?" There was a brief upturn of Delia's mouth. Kate's eyes widened in surprise. It was the first time she had seen such a show of emotion from the woman, and her nervousness disappeared with that fleeting smile. It made her believe that going forward she could work through any challenges with the Wingates that might relate to Billy and what he needed.

They heard a tentative tap at the door, which Delia had left open a bit, and she waved the family in. Kate wondered how much of the conversation they had heard but knew there was nothing to hide anymore. She smiled at Ben, who looked relieved that she was still in one piece. Delia moved to a wing chair next to Davis and Marie, and Ben joined Kate on the sofa.

Kate glanced at Abby, who had taken a seat on the edge of an ottoman. Her smile was encouraging as always.

The old Delia quickly resurfaced, and she was in charge again as she addressed her family. "We are concerned that Briggs did not come tonight. He said he would but we're quite sure that nothing came up to prevent him from being here. This has happened before."

"I hope that he's all right, though," Kate said. "How did he sound to you, Davis?"

Davis frowned. "He sounded sober at least. But talking fast as if he didn't want to stay on the phone long."

Davis's honesty took Kate by surprise. So, Briggs probably had a drinking problem on top of everything else, not unusual for sufferers of post-traumatic stress disorder.

After a moment, Kate said, "Abby told me you took the test, Davis. I want you to know that we appreciate that very much. And Briggs, too, of course."

"We talked about it as a family," Davis said. "And even without a paternity test, we felt quite sure that you and Billy are Briggs's children. Everything fell into place with what you were telling us. And I'm sorry that I'm not a match. Of course, you may know that Briggs hasn't shared his results with us. I wouldn't recommend pressuring him about it yet. Still, we hope that everything works out for Billy."

"Thank you."

Delia rose from her chair, her hand on the ever-present cane. "If you'll excuse me, I'll say good night. Thank you for coming," she said, addressing Kate and Ben. Kate wasn't sure what was appropriate to do next. Davis's announcement about Briggs and the results of their donor tests had shifted into an awkward silence. Ben made the first move and stood.

"Thanks for the meal. But I think we should be getting back to the house. It was a long trip today."

Abby jumped up. "But we'll see you tomorrow morning, right? You never got a tour of the winery last time you were here."

"Of course," Kate smiled and hugged her.

Kate left the Wingate house with a sense of relief from her conversation with Delia. She and Ben had been right to return to Deep Lake and face the family again. Even without knowing the results of Briggs's donor matching tests, he had cared enough to take that step. And she knew that small steps were all that she could expect from him. But his absence from the gathering worked on her mind, and she wondered what the next day would bring.

31

DEEP LAKE WAS IN A DIFFERENT MOOD the next morning. Large waves tumbled over each other like ocean surf, sending the frothy white caps onto the dark slate stones on the beach. Kate rose early and stepped onto the balcony of the bedroom to witness the sunrise. But instead of a golden orb rising gloriously over the hills, all she saw were angry brushstrokes of gray smeared across the horizon and up into the vault of the sky. She felt as if the rain was at a tipping point, and that at any minute there would be a deluge.

They decided to forego a morning canoe ride, and after breakfast made their way to Wingate Winery for the tour Abby had promised. The dreary weather hadn't dampened Abby's spirits at all and, as always, she greeted them with an enthusiastic hug.

As they began their tour, they learned that the grapes from this year's harvest had already been crushed. The juice was now in tanks for the first phase of fermentation, while the earlier harvest was now in oak barrels where it would stay for eighteen to twenty-four months.

Abby explained the filtering, or clarification, process that removed impurities which led them to the next step, which was bottling the wine. Kate made notes in her journal and took pictures as Ben asked questions about the processes.

As they finished the tour, Davis stepped in from outside and joined them. A light rain had started, and he shook the water off his work coat and hat. He seemed distracted by his cell phone.

"Have you heard from Uncle Briggs, Dad?" Abby said hesitantly.

Davis pulled out his phone a third time to check for messages. "Not yet, honey. I'm sure he'll be in touch."

"Maybe we should check the cottage. That's probably where he is, and he just isn't answering his phone."

Davis sighed. "I did that this morning. I'm afraid there's no sign of him there. His bag is gone, too."

"But where would he go?" Abby said, her voice filled with concern. "He's still got a cast on his arm and his motorcycle was toast after the accident. He never got it fixed. Dad, we have to find him."

"We will," he reassured her. "Maybe one of his friends came to pick him up. We'll check around town, too. I don't think he'd head out without at least letting me know. But right now, Mother wants to see us all in her study."

They followed him out of the bottling and packing area to Delia's study. She was seated at her desk. "I don't like this, Davis," she said abruptly, without any greetings. "He never said anything about leaving."

"He's done this before, Mother. He always gets in touch."

"No. This is different. You thought so when you talked to him. And he left me a message on my phone. It must have been sometime during the night, but I just saw it. He wasn't very coherent. I don't think he'd been drinking. It was something else."

"His head injury?"

"Maybe. At any rate, we must find him."

"Shall I call the sheriff?" Davis asked.

"No. Not yet. We'll handle this ourselves for now. Kate and Ben, are you willing to help?"

They quickly nodded. "Of course, whatever we can do."

"Good. Davis and Marie, start asking around town without raising any red flags. Keep it casual. Abby, ask the neighbors by *Sunny Days* if they've seen him."

"The Corcorans and Blanfields aren't around, Nana. They're gone for the summer."

"Well, then find neighbors who are there and ask them. Kate and Ben, we've got an outboard motorboat at the Lake House. Do you know how to run one of those?"

"Yes, ma'am," Ben replied.

"Good. The keys are on a hook in the kitchen. Take it on a slow run along the shore and let us know if you find anything that might be helpful. I'll check with the staff here. Maybe they've heard from him. I'll stay here in case he comes back."

They stood rooted to the floor, waiting for more instructions. She waved a thin arm at them. "Well, don't just stand there. Go find him!"

Kate and Ben quickly drove to the Lake House, grabbed the boat keys, and ran down to the dock. The boat had been raised on a lift for the fall season and Ben struggled to lower it. But finally, they jumped in and motored off into the lake.

They began their search along the shoreline as Delia had instructed, but they weren't entirely sure what they were looking for. Kate had picked up a pair of binoculars at the house to scan the beaches and homes, but they circled the entire lake with nothing to show for it. They stopped at a fueling dock to fill up and Ben chatted with the staff, discreetly asking about Briggs. They said that they knew him but hadn't seen him in months.

Ben pushed the boat hard through the rough waves to get back to the Lake House. He backed up alongside the dock where Kate quickly tied it off. Abby was waving from the front door of the house, and they ran to meet her. Davis and Marie were in the house and reported that someone saw Briggs early that morning with his backpack heading north on East Lake Road as if he might have been hitchhiking. But by the time they drove along that side of the lake, there was no sign of him. Abby had nothing to show for her canvass of the neighbors around *Sunny Days*. Kate and Ben had no news either.

"I've called Mother to let her know there's nothing so far. Marie and I need to go back to the winery; there's a problem with one of the tanks, and I need to check in with Mother. But I don't want to stop looking either."

"Can't we notify the police now?" Kate asked, impatient with the lack of progress they had made.

Davis shook his head. "The police in Pine Ridge know Briggs comes and goes like this. They're not likely to send anyone out to look for him. But I promise, if we don't get any results by tonight, I'll give them a call."

"Dad, I have some friends in Evergreen I can check with," Abby suggested. Evergreen was at the other end of the lake, about eight miles away, but they were desperate to try every avenue.

"Good idea. And keep trying his phone. Kate and Ben, I know the weather's nasty out there right now but if it lets up, can you take the boat out again and do another search?"

"Of course," they quickly agreed, glad to be able to contribute even in some small way.

"Don't worry about putting the boat back on the lift. Just tie it up securely at the dock for now." He looked around at the group. "Be safe, everybody." Davis and Marie left the house.

Abby started for Evergreen soon after her parents left. Kate and Ben made a quick lunch of sandwiches and then watched through the front windows of the house as the storm swung from mist to downpour and back again.

A late afternoon sun had broken through the clouds for a brief respite from the earlier rain, and they took another sweep of the lake. But they returned with nothing to show for their efforts.

An hour later, there was still no word from any of the Wingates. As Ben and Kate pondered what their next steps should be, there was a knock at the front door. Ben answered it, hoping it might be Briggs, but he quickly ushered an older man into the house and out of the drizzle. The man shook his coat and hat and then apologized for the puddle he had created. He reached out a wet hand to Ben who shook it.

"Can we help you?" Ben asked.

"I hope so. I'm Tom Barwell, we're two houses down from here," and he pointed in that direction. "I saw a light on here; not many people on the lake anymore, and we've got a problem. A branch came through our patio door in a gust of wind earlier. I've got plywood to board it up with, but I was hoping you could help me. I gave it a try but can't manage it by myself. My wife can't be out in this, and I don't have the strength I used to."

Ben glanced at Kate who nodded. "Sure," he said. "Just let me get my jacket."

"I sure appreciate it." He addressed Kate as Ben went into the mudroom off the kitchen where they had hung their wet coats. "I didn't get your name, though. Are you one of the Wingates?"

Not sure, Kate thought, but she wouldn't divulge any family secrets to a stranger. "We're just visiting. I'm Kate Tyler and this is my boyfriend, Ben Evans," she said as Ben returned to the room.

"Nice to meet you, Kate and Ben. And we sure do appreciate this. We don't usually stay this late in the season, but we wanted to have one last week here. I guess it wasn't the best time to come."

"I'm ready whenever you are, Tom," Ben said as he pulled his ballcap down tight on his head. He turned to Kate. "I shouldn't be long. Give me a call if you hear anything though, okay?"

She nodded and Ben stepped out into the storm with Tom.

32

BEN AND TOM DISAPPEARED into the mist. The lake grew surly again. Gone were the sun-glinted waves of late autumn. In their place was turbulence rising here and there at random, like sea monsters raising their humped backs to the surface, then disappearing into the depths. A new storm loomed in the distance, rumbling toward the lake. Kate stepped out onto the deck, her arms close around her against the bitterness of the wind, momentarily stunned by the horrible beauty of the sky's colors, shades of gray and purple whirling into black like a bruise.

The menacing storm gathered its strength and took aim at the valley that cradled Deep Lake, roaring down between the hills, whipping the waters into a frenzy.

Everything scattered. Anything still untethered, docks and boats, lawn chairs, and umbrellas, twisted and turned against the impending gale. Animals scurried across the lawn, burrowing low in the woods, and the birds grew silent.

Kate saw the Wingate's boat pitching crazily against the dock. As hard as she had tried, she knew it hadn't been tied up securely enough for these conditions. She grabbed her jacket and a pair of binoculars from inside and pressed her way against the storm to the dock. Water sloshed across the boards, soaking her sneakers and jeans. The ropes were slick, but she managed to retie them, even as the boat strained against the waves.

She looked through the binoculars for Mr. Barwell's cottage from the dock. If she could find Ben, she would be safer with him than by herself. But there were no lights visible in any of the nearby cottages.

Kate raised her arm to shield her face against the licks of the wind and rain. Something white out on the lake caught her eye. She put the binoculars up to her face again and saw what appeared to be a small sailboat in the distance. The waves were tossing it like a toy, and the only person she could see on the boat was struggling to get the single sail under control.

Kate wondered who would be crazy enough to take a sailboat, or any boat for that matter, out in this weather. The wind and rain slashed against her and smeared the lenses of the binoculars, but when at last she got the boat in her sights again, she gasped.

It was Briggs; but with one arm still in a cast, managing the boat was going to be a losing battle.

What are you doing, Briggs? She desperately dug into her jacket pockets for the keys to the motorboat, but Ben had left them in the house. She raced back up across the lawn, grabbed the keys, and ran back to the dock, twice losing her footing on the wet grass. She struggled once again with the ropes but finally managed to free the boat from its moorings. Finally, she started the engine and roared out across the lake, fighting with the wheel as she bounced over the churning waves, barely able to stay in control. The wind drove sheets of rain at her from above, and the lake water jetted up at her across the bow.

As Kate drew closer, she recognized the boat as a single mast Cat boat; she and Ben had seen many of them on the lake, but she had never seen one manned by just one person. The thought crossed her mind that there may have been two people on the boat, but .... She shook off the thought that there might be two people to rescue and focused on getting to Briggs.

The sailboat tipped precariously, buffeted by the wind, and as Kate drew closer, she saw that it had taken on water and was about to capsize. Suddenly, the boom swung wildly. Kate screamed as she saw Briggs flying over the side, landing with a heavy splash in the water.

Kate cried out to him as she slowly made her approach, trying to keep a safe distance from the sailboat and yet close enough that he could hear her. He was struggling to stay afloat with his one arm in a cast and the other tangled in the lines. The life jacket he was wearing was loose around him and she doubted if it would do the job of keeping him above the surface. Kate pulled up as close as she dared, hoping he could reach her boat. But she could see that he would not be able to help himself.

She shut the motor off and looked in the boat for the life jackets. She quickly put one on and grabbed the other, but she still wasn't close enough to reach him. Without an attached ladder, he wouldn't be able to pull himself in anyway. Her only option was to untangle the ropes herself and get him to shore. They were still quite a distance from the rocks ringing the island, but they were drifting dangerously closer.

Going into the water in these conditions had to be her last option, but there was no other choice. With the extra life jacket, she made a decision and jumped into the water, the shock of the cold taking her breath away. She surfaced and tackled the waves, leaving the boat behind to go where the wind would take it. After a few strong strokes, she finally reached Briggs. He was alert, and she shouted over the waves for him to hang onto the life jacket. He was shaking with the cold, but he grabbed it, giving her enough time to untangle the ropes. Twice, she felt him go limp, but she managed to hold on even as the waves battered them. Finally, he was freed, and Kate tossed the ropes as far away from them as she could.

Her next movements were instinctive. Muscle memory from her lifeguard training kicked in. She got behind him and hooked an arm underneath his good arm. Her muscles were burning, but she began to kick towards the shore. The boat had already drifted away, so she knew it was useless to try to get him to it. It took whatever strength she had left, thrusting with her long legs, just to keep moving through the relentless churning waves. They finally hit the shallows of the shale beach and she hauled herself and Briggs onto the shore. But Kate only allowed them a moment's rest before dragging him, inch by inch, completely out of the water.

They were drenched and exhausted, but alive.

"Briggs! Briggs! Can you hear me?" He was breathing heavily and seemed to be in a daze. She shook him until he looked at her. "It's me, Kate. We have to move, Briggs. We can't stay here on the beach."

He kept pushing her away, but she persisted. "Come on. We just need to get to those rocks." Finally, he nodded, and she helped him to his feet. Clinging to each other, they stumbled to a cluster of large boulders a few yards from the shoreline and huddled together behind them, shivering from the drop in the temperature and their exertions in the frigid lake water.

Kate finally caught her breath and turned to check on Briggs. His face was ashen, and his whole body was shaking. She had nothing to dry him off or warm him with, but she started rubbing his arms and back to get his circulation going. She said a desperate prayer that help would come soon. But as concerned as she was, the idea that Briggs had been out there alone in the storm infuriated her.

"You shouldn't have been out there by yourself," she said, now that she didn't have to shout over the wind anymore in this sheltered spot. "Not with your arm in a cast. And not in this weather."

"I would have been fine," he finally managed to say without coughing. His color was improving slightly, and he was more alert.

"It didn't look like it."

He finally shifted himself to a sitting position and studied her. "How did you see me? And why are you even here?"

"I was at the Lake House. Your family invited me. But that's not important. We've been looking for you all day."

He shook his finger at her. "It's nobody's business where I go, dammit. Everybody needs to leave me alone!"

He began to cough again. Kate ignored his words and urged him to come even closer to the shelter of the rocks. She checked for her phone which was still in her zippered pocket, but it was wet and unusable. She knew she should have called Ben before she left the house, but it was too late to worry about that now. Her only hope was that when Ben got back, he would realize she had taken the boat out and know something drastic must have happened for her to take that chance.

Through the downpour, she could see the outline of the motorboat drifting farther down the lake, pushed by the wind and waves. The sailboat had flipped over and was now a tangled wreck, smashed against the rocks of the island. She hoped the Wingate's boat wouldn't meet the same fate.

"Why'd you drag me out of the water? You shouldn't have done that. You could've drowned. You shouldn't have risked your life for me," he said, pushing his hair out of his eyes and dragging his hand across his face. Then he looked at her with puzzlement. "How did you manage that anyway? I was dead weight." He shivered again and began rubbing his legs with his good hand.

"Lucky for you I had some training as a lifeguard. But in this weather, I don't know how I did it. But don't you dare say I shouldn't have tried," she quipped.

He made a noise of disagreement.

"Are you okay?" she asked, truly concerned that his condition could worsen at any time.

He grunted. "I'll be fine."

"Your sailboat is pretty much totaled," Kate informed him, trying to keep him talking and alert.

He grimaced. "Well, I kind of borrowed it, so ...."

Her eyes widened. "You borrowed it? Whose is it?" When he didn't answer, Kate looked at him with dismay. "You borrowed a sailboat and took it out in this weather? We're in the middle of a terrible storm, in case you haven't noticed," she said as a gust of wind slapped rain over the rocks at them. "And who in their right mind—?"

"Yeah, yeah, yeah," he said, waving his hand at her.

"They don't know you borrowed it then, is that it?"

Briggs wobbled his head. "I guess you could say that."

Kate let out a deep sigh.

"I'll make good on it, don't worry," he said. "Not that it should matter to you."

"Oh, I am definitely going to put that on my list of things that I don't have to worry about." Kate scooted away from the stream of water flowing down the rocks behind her.

"So does anybody know you're out here?"

"Not exactly. Ben went to help a neighbor and I didn't call him before I came out to rescue you."

"For the last time, I didn't need rescuing! But now, thanks to you, we both need it, so maybe you just made things worse."

Kate looked at him and shook her head. *You're a stubborn man, Briggs Wingate,* she thought.

"You got a phone? Or did you lose that in the lake?" he asked.

"No, I didn't lose it in the lake, but it's pretty useless since it's wet from when I jumped in the water to save you." Briggs shook his head again. Kate realized she was having a perverse bit of fun at his expense, even in their dire situation. But he needed the truth, and the truth was that he probably wouldn't have made it without her help.

Kate squeezed the water out of her hair and weaved it into a loose braid. Constant rubbing of her arms and legs was the only thing that kept her circulation moving and she wondered how long they would have to wait for Ben, or anyone, to find them.

"How is your arm?" Kate asked. "When was the cast supposed to come off?"

"Next week," he answered reluctantly.

"And your back? That boom hit you pretty hard."

"It's fine. I've had worse things happen to me. But if you must know, a friend of mine asked me to get his boat out of the water since he's out of town and I was staying at his place."

"So you decided to take it out even with the storm coming?"

"I've sailed these boats all my life and it wasn't storming when I went out."

"Still ...."

He exhaled loudly, "Yes, I've been known to make bad decisions. So can we drop it now?"

The wind finally began to calm as the storm moved on down the lake valley. The rain tapered off and the clouds broke open enough to let some late afternoon sun peek through. Kate knew she should go down to the beach to look for help, but she couldn't manage to move. Her legs were too shaky to try to stand. She decided a few more minutes of rest wouldn't hurt.

The silence grew between them. Kate could never have dreamed that she would be sitting here with Briggs, who was still a stranger to her. And yet somehow she felt she knew him. Maybe it was the forced intimacy of the rescue that connected them now. Or maybe there was a genetic bond that existed which, until this moment, had nothing physically to connect to. Time and space and decisions had separated them for thirty years, but maybe some invisible thread remained.

"Abby said you took the donor match test for Billy," she started, knowing that it was important for him to understand that she was grateful for it. "I want you to know I appreciate it. And I apologize for the way I acted when we first met. It wasn't a good moment and I know it upset you. And then you had the accident ...."

He raised his hand to stop her. "The accident didn't have anything to do with you or what you said. I was going too fast on a wet road without a helmet and should have known better. That's all there is to it."

"Thanks. But part of me will always feel responsible."

After a moment, Briggs turned to her. "Aren't you going to ask me what the results were?"

"Of the test? No. I figure you'll tell me if and when you want to."

"Well, the truth is, I didn't take the test."

"You didn't?" she said, incredulous that he would be dishonest about something like that. "Why did you lie to everyone then?"

"I didn't take it because I knew that I wouldn't be able to donate a kidney, not to Billy, not to anyone."

"But why?" she persisted.

"Because I only have one. They took the other one out after an injury when I was deployed. I'm doing fine with only one but I'm not exactly in the position to hand it off to anybody else."

Kate took a moment to absorb this news. "Does anyone in the family know about this?"

He shook his head. "And give Mother something more to worry about? Nope. And they don't need to hear it from you, either, got it?"

"You should tell them."

"Well, I don't think I should."

"Okay," she said, raising her hands in defeat. "I hear you."

"Listen, I know you had a good life, Katie. And I'm glad about that. You don't even know me. Maybe you don't need to. Now that we know I can't donate a kidney to Billy if he needs it, we can go our separate ways and that'll be okay if that's what you want."

And that is what Kate always thought she wanted. A clean break, no attachment, no ties, everyone goes their separate ways. He was setting her free from any future connection. Wasn't that what she had wanted all along?

Now she wasn't sure.

"I did have a good life," she said. "But I've had my share of tragedies, too. I lost Mom and Dad, and that was devastating but I still had my sister Becky. But then," she said, hesitating, knowing this might be hard for him to hear. But she had no reason to hide it. "Becky died in a car accident about three years ago. At the time, I thought I had nothing to live for. The only thing that saved me was finding a home at Howard's Walk and having Ben and Billy in my life. And I know now that people are depending on me. I have to be there for them. Billy, especially. If, or when, something happens to his mother, he'll be coming to live with me. I've made that clear."

"I'm sorry about Becky and your parents," he said, more subdued after taking in the news of their passing. "Do you live at Howard's Walk now?"

She nodded. "It's a long story."

"Is he a good boy? Billy, I mean." She felt Briggs's eyes on her, and she could tell he sincerely wanted to know. Briggs knew Billy's age. But she couldn't blame him for thinking of him as a boy. She found herself viewing Billy the same way sometimes. But there was more to him than that, and maybe Briggs needed to know.

"He is. And he's becoming a good man, too; well, as good as he can ever be. Ben is making sure of that."

"This guy Ben. I'm guessing he's your boyfriend. If you two are getting married, that's a lot for him to take on."

At first, Kate wanted to tell him that her relationships were none of his business. And he didn't have any say in how Billy was being cared for. But she was too tired to argue.

"I hope we will someday. And don't worry about Ben and Billy. They're like brothers and Ben knows exactly what he would be getting into."

Kate shrugged out of her life jacket and laid it aside. She realized that all the worry she had put herself through about finding her father in order to help Billy had been pointless. But then maybe the whole point was to find out what she didn't know, good or bad. Otherwise, she would have always wondered. Now, that burden had been lifted. And she could make a new plan to help Billy.

"I suppose you know where Jenny is."

Kate considered her next words carefully. What would be the benefit of telling Briggs that she had met her mother? It was an awful experience she wanted to erase from her memory. She told a half-truth instead.

"No, I don't know where she is. Do you?" she asked suddenly curious about how much he might know.

"No. I don't."

There was silence as if he was considering what he might say next. He cleared his throat, staring out over the lake. "It took something from her to carry the three of you and then give you all up."

Kate felt a lump in her throat. This is something she never expected to talk to Briggs about. The distance between them was being narrowed, and she felt unexpectedly grateful. But she had nothing to say to his words.

"It was hard on her physically and emotionally. She told me, once it was all over, that she didn't want to be that person anymore."

"That person?" Kate's anger flared. "What, she didn't want to be our mother? I guess that was pretty obvious."

"No, no, not like that," he protested. "I meant that she didn't want to be the person that was so angry. She was mad at me. She was mad at her parents, at my parents. She was mad at the world like most seventeen-year-olds, and now she had this to carry, too. She didn't want to be dragging the whole experience behind her for the rest of her life."

His words hit her like a punch to the stomach. Tears welled up in her eyes and she turned her head.

"I'm sorry," he apologized. "I'm not saying any of this right. It wasn't like that. You see, she had to prepare herself for the fact that she wasn't going to be your mom. It took a toll on her body. She was on bed rest for two or three months at the end. But she did it. She cared for you three little ones the best she could through the whole pregnancy and did everything she was told, did everything you needed. But then, after it was over and after she had you and you were put up for adoption, she knew she needed to move on. And she couldn't do that in Eden Springs for sure."

"So you were in touch after we were born?" she managed to ask.

"Not really. I only talked to her once after she had you. It was a good talk, but we knew we had to go our separate ways. That much was clear."

Kate pulled her knees up and buried her head in her hands. She couldn't look at Briggs. It was all too raw, too unexpected. A lifetime of questions, some buried, some not, had just been answered. All out there in the open. Laid bare like broken glass; razor-sharp when you touched them, piercing if you examined them too closely.

Is this how Briggs felt, too? Was his past, his life, too brittle to probe without risking a complete collapse? It was as if they both had lived two lives. The one they lived in their daily routines and the other filled with secrets that were suddenly exposed, needing to be faced head-on.

Kate wiped her face with her sleeve and struggled to her feet. She needed to walk away, put some distance between her and the uncomfortable closeness with Briggs. "I'm going to see if there's anyone out there on the lake. Maybe I can flag them down."

Kate made her way through the boulders to the beach, praying for a miracle but all she could see were flickering lights from houses across the lake. The wind had died down, but it still chilled her to the bone. She rubbed her arms and checked her phone again. It was dead. She walked back to where Briggs was sitting.

"Anything?"

"Nothing. But they'll find us. Ben will be looking for me once he gets back to the house. He was helping a neighbor. I should have waited for him, I guess."

"What you did was brave." He hitched himself further up against the rock. "Davis says you're a travel journalist."

Kate sensed he felt the same awkwardness she did and was glad for the change in the conversation. "Yes. I've traveled all over the world."

"You know, maybe we're not so different, Katie."

That was the second time he had used a nickname that felt too personal. "My name's Kate, not Katie," she said, cutting him off.

"Okay, I'm sorry." He held his hands up as if in surrender. "Anyway, I wanted to see the world, too, but I guess maybe I saw too much of it, how people really are, how they can hate. I was in places where most everybody hated me. When I lost my men, I lost everything."

Kate softened. He had suffered great losses, too. "But you saw the wrong side of it, Briggs. You went to those places so the rest of us wouldn't have to. I'm sorry you lost your men. I can't imagine what that's like."

"I went where I was told to go. That's all. Mother thinks she pushed me into the military. And she did, at first. But after I joined, it was all my decision. And I don't regret it. I hated some of it, what we had to do and what we saw. But it was my choice. And I have to own up to that."

In the distance, Kate heard the thrum of a motor out on the lake. She ran to the beach and saw a rescue boat in the distance.

"Help! We're over here!" she called, waving her arms.

The boat slowed and she heard voices calling back to her. One of the voices was Ben's, and she cried in relief. The boat quickly turned towards them, and they pulled as close as they could. Ben jumped into the water and waded up to Kate, hugging her tightly.

"Kate, what happened? You weren't at the house, and I saw the boat was gone ...." Ben stopped as he saw Briggs limping over the rocks toward them. "You found him?"

"We'll tell you all about it. Right now, we need to get warmed up."

"Of course." He helped them into the boat, where they were quickly wrapped in blankets. Ben called Davis and told him the good news.

With Ben's arms encircling her, Kate buried herself into the blanket as the rescue boat skimmed over the water, leaving Wingate Island behind. She felt Briggs watching her and wondered if they would ever have another moment like this. The experience opened up new vulnerabilities for both of them. Two hours ago, they were strangers. Now they both had to redefine what they would be to each other. She made a vow to herself that whatever happened, it would be what they both agreed on, not something that was forced on them by anyone else. With that thought, she closed her eyes.

Epilogue

IT WAS SIX O'CLOCK IN THE EVENING on Thanksgiving Day at Howard's Walk. A turkey-induced stupor was threatening to settle in, and the guests found quiet places throughout the house, on the patio, and in the garden to relax and contemplate the blessings the past year had brought them.

Everyone that came for dinner said it was the best they ever had. Mimi was just happy that she didn't have to cook a turkey, and provided homemade biscuits and sweet potato pie instead. Billy ate too much of Ben's deep-fried turkey and all of his favorite side dishes specially prepared for him by Sam and Martin. He was snoring on the couch by the warmth of the fireplace in the newly decorated living room where Kate had first started the search for her parents.

Sam and Martin had been there from the crack of dawn cooking a gourmet meal that somehow managed to complement Ben's deep-fried turkey, after all. Even so, Sam insisted on roasting a small turkey breast just because he was adamantly opposed to deep-fried anything, especially on Thanksgiving.

A case of wine had arrived earlier in the week from Wingate Winery, including a bottle of champagne. None of the guests understood why Ben and Kate were holding it aside; it was obvious they intended to open it since it was chilling in an ice bucket in the living room. But everyone was too polite to say anything, so they waited.

Soon, Ben and Kate gathered everyone for dessert in the living room, and the reason for holding back on the champagne became clear. Ben stood and made a toast to Kate, the love of his life, and to their engagement. A cheer went up, even from Billy, even though he didn't quite understand what all the hollering was about. But he joined in anyway; if everyone else was happy, then he was happy, too.

Ben had proposed to Kate not long after they returned from Deep Lake. He took her to their favorite beach town for a weekend getaway and said he had waited long enough and couldn't bear to think of another day without knowing if she would be his wife, and before he finished all of the reasons why he needed her to marry him, she had said, "Yes, yes, yes!!!" and he slipped the diamond he had been saving for her onto her finger.

Abby called later on Thanksgiving Day and told Kate that Briggs was still staying at the cottage. But winter was quickly approaching, and he said he thought he might move into the Lake House for a while, maybe through Christmas, since the cottage was not meant for the weather that was already nipping at the windows and doors of the old building. After that, though, he said he'd have to be on the road again. But for now, he seemed content to be working with Davis at the winery. Abby said that having the family together again would make it the best holiday season ever. She begged Kate and Ben to come for Christmas, but they told her they simply couldn't leave Billy, and it would be their first holiday as an engaged couple. Their place was at Howard's Walk.

The next day, Kate and Ben grazed on the Thanksgiving leftovers and put the finishing touches on their Christmas decorations, beginning their own family traditions. The outside had been finished in mid-November so that guests visiting the gardens could enjoy the light displays. By late afternoon, several trees had been decorated in the house, and fresh garland was placed on the stair rail and the mantels, spreading the scent of fresh pine into every room. Candles lit the quiet with a soft glow, making the house a cozy respite from the outside world.

After supper, Kate retrieved a stack of mail that had been accumulating on the kitchen counter over the last few days and went to the Koi pond to sort through it.

There was the usual assortment of bills and advertisements, but a few Christmas cards had already started slipping into the mix. The last one in the stack was a yellow envelope with a handwritten address; a very un-Christmasy color, Kate thought, but maybe it was a thank you note from one of the tourists at Howard's Walk. She turned it over and took in a sharp breath when she saw the address label on the back. It was from Scott Hill Vineyards, California. "She wrote me a letter?" Kate whispered. "Renee Scott actually wrote me a letter?"

She slipped a shaking finger under the flap to open it, then slowly unfolded the pale-yellow stationery inside.

Kate took a deep breath and began to read.

November 10, 2022

Dear Kate,

I have struggled with writing this letter to you. Perhaps it is the coward's way out, but I knew it needed to be the first step if there are to be any steps for us after this.

I shouldn't have walked away from you at the hospital. It was wrong of me to leave you in such pain, and I hope you will forgive me for that. None of this is your fault. You are Billy's champion in so many ways and he is so lucky to have you in his life now; you have the true meaning of family in your heart and soul, and I admire you tremendously for that.

I want you to know that it was impossible for Briggs and me to keep the three of you together and make a family. You have probably understood by now that age and family circumstances conspired to put us on the path we took, and that was to put you up for adoption. But I knew that you all went to good homes where you would be loved and cared for. My parents made the right decisions in that regard. But I also know now that you have suffered losses, too many and too tragic in your young life, and to have me walk away from you as I did must have been devastating for you. I am so sorry if I caused you any additional pain.

So I am reaching out to you by letter as an olive branch of sorts. If you want to meet again, I will welcome that. We have so many years to catch up on.

Please know, too, that I will do whatever I can to help Billy. <u>Anything</u>. Financially, donor testing, health care, caretakers ... whatever he needs. I am in a position in my life now that I can do this for him if you will let me. And this extends to you as well.

If you feel you are not ready to meet with me again, I will understand. I wish you and Ben all the best in your life together. You deserve all the good things that a loving relationship can provide. Your journey is just beginning.

Sincerely,

Jennifer Renee Howard Scott

Kate refolded the letter and held it to her heart. Briggs was right. Jenny did all that she could for her babies in the short time they were with her, and that was to nourish them, protect them, and give them life. Briggs had never really wanted to be removed from the situation, but his choices were made for him. It was then that he first learned to follow orders.

Kate knew that there might be hard times ahead for Billy. She had always known it in her heart, but his recent health issues made it crystal clear that while life was precious and unpredictable, it was still wonderful. She and Ben together would find the right path to follow in any challenge. They had each other, and that made everything possible.

The early winter sun was setting behind the tree line and as if on cue, the Christmas lights in the gardens lit up, illuminating the pine trees and sparkling along the edges of the flagstone walkways, the picket fences, and the greenhouse. The roofline of Howard's Walk was trimmed in white lights and each window reflected the soft glow of a candle. Ben and Billy had decorated a potted Christmas tree on the patio *'so the animals and the birds can have Christmas, too,'* Billy had declared. Everywhere Kate looked, she felt the beauty of a shimmering winter wonderland.

She heard the kitchen door open, letting out a fragment of Christmas music from inside the house. Ben stepped out onto the patio. He waved and leaned on the stone railing, never taking his eyes off her. He smiled and Kate's heart was filled with joy. She adored him and knew they were going to build a beautiful life together.

The last few months had shown Kate that the deep places inside everyone where hurts and fears lie can be unlocked and brought into the light. Allowing herself to examine those painful beliefs and anxieties was one of the hardest roads she had ever traveled. But that was the only way to understand those emotions and be healed from the pain they had caused, not just for her but for everyone around her. She was stronger now for facing what she had feared the most. She regretted nothing about the search for her birth parents.

She waved at Ben, tucked Jenny's letter inside her pocket, and began to think about everything she wanted, and needed, to say to her mother in return.

Acknowledgments

EVERY SUCCESSFUL AUTHOR DEPENDS on the advice of others when putting a story together and this book is no different. I am very grateful for those who have helped me navigate the unfamiliar territories of adoption law and winemaking and, for each of the Kate Tyler novels, horticulture.

I am indebted to John P. Paschal, Attorney at Law, for his advice on North Carolina adoption law. His patience with my questions is deeply appreciated.

Fred and Jennifer Johnson, of Johnson Estate Winery, in Westfield, New York, provided valuable insight into grape growing and winemaking and generously took the time to give me a tour of their beautiful vineyards.

My husband Dan has always been there for me as a sounding board for all things horticultural and for this book, he has also been an expert resource in grape growing and vineyard management. And I couldn't write a word without the support of my entire family who always encourage and support this zany idea that I can write stories!

My daughter, Michelle Crocker and award-winning author Nancy Panko generously gave of their time as beta readers with helpful insights to make this book the best it could be. And I must mention my appreciation for the ongoing advice during the writing of this book of my talented writing group friends, NC Scribes, whose guidance I treasure.

For everyone who has purchased my books or borrowed them from a library and has written reviews; for the book clubs that have read them, loved them, and discussed them, thank you! It is a great privilege to go on that journey with you and gain insights from you, the readers.

Thank you to my fantastic editor, Jori Hanna, and the entire talented team at Torchflame Books who always make my books better than I could ever imagine.

To my loyal readers of *Heirloom* and *The Legend* who begged me for a third book, my heart is full of appreciation for you. You are the engine that keeps me putting words down on paper!

ABOUT THE AUTHOR

AWARD-WINNING AUTHOR NANCY WAKELEY grew up in the New York State Finger Lakes region and now resides in Apex, North Carolina, with her husband. She completed her degree in health information management from Stephens College, Columbia, Missouri, and spent her career in the health information management and clinical research fields until the writing muse lured her into retirement.

Nancy belongs to the North Carolina Writer's Network, NC Scribes, is an editor with the Military Writers Society of America and gives back to her community through volunteerism. She embraces all things fashioned out of words and musical notes as a reflection of life's beautiful journey.

Secrets at Deep Lake is the third in the *Kate Tyler* series following award-winning novels *Heirloom* and *The Legend*. Connect with Nancy:

Facebook @authornancywakeley
Twitter @nancywakeley
Instagram @nancywakeley2
www.nancywakeley.com

OTHER KATE TYLER NOVELS

HEIRLOOM. Kate Tyler is already in a life crisis when she inherits Howard's Walk in Eden Springs, North Carolina, after the sudden death of her twin sister, Rebecca. When she learns that a powerful and vengeful man who was denied ownership of Howard's Walk in the past is determined to finally own it at any cost, Kate must decide what Howard's Walk means to her and if she has the strength to battle for its survival as well as her own.

THE LEGEND. Desperate for a change of pace, Kate Tyler packs her bags and heads to the ancient town of Rye, England where she hopes she'll find inspiration for her new travel blog.

But when she arrives, mysteries follow her everywhere she goes. Strangers seem to know her, a book of ancient legends contains her mirror image, and Virginia Calloway is insistent that Kate come over to discuss the Legend of Arabella Courbain. Hoping to solve one of the many mysteries of this spontaneous trip, Kate agrees.

But the deeper Kate digs into the truth of what happened to Arabella back in 1766, the more she learns that the present may not hold the answers she needs. When legends cross with reality, Kate must find the truth before history repeats itself.